P9-BZG-433

THE CRITICS LOVE WILLIAM MURRAY

"William Murray is some kind of great storyteller.
. . . You'll like this book. Lay odds on it. (Some say
Murray writes better racetrack mysteries than Dick
Francis; I give Murray the nod by a nose.)"

—*San Diego Tribune*

"Murray has a magic touch."

—*The Houston Post*

AND *I'M GETTING KILLED RIGHT HERE*

"A fast-moving story . . . Murray is on the pace in
this absorbing comic caper."

—*Playboy*

Murray's plot, characters, and dialogue establish
racetrack mystique as a vibrant bit of backstretch
Americana . . . *Getting Killed* runs a heck of a race."

—*Chicago Tribune*

"Murray gallops in a winner."

—*Kirkus Reviews*

William Murray's Shifty Lou Anderson Novels:

TIP ON A DEAD CRAB
THE HARD KNOCKER'S LUCK
WHEN THE FAT MAN SINGS
THE KING OF THE NIGHTCAP
THE GETAWAY BLUES
I'M GETTING KILLED RIGHT HERE

Other Books by William Murray:

THE AMERICANO
BEST SELLER
THE DREAM GIRLS
THE FUGITIVE ROMANS
HORSE FEVER
ITALY: THE FATAL GIFT
THE KILLING TOUCH
THE LAST ITALIAN
MALIBU
THE MOUTH OF THE WOLF
PREVIEWS OF COMING ATTRACTIONS
THE SELF-STARTING WHEEL
THE SWEET RIDE

I'M
GETTING
KILLED
RIGHT HERE

William Murray

BANTAM BOOKS

NEW YORK · TORONTO · LONDON · SYDNEY · AUCKLAND

All of the characters in this book are fictitious,
and any resemblance to actual persons, living or
dead, is purely coincidental.

I'M GETTING KILLED RIGHT HERE
A Bantam Crime Line Book

PUBLISHING HISTORY
Doubleday edition published November 1991
Bantam edition / July 1992

CRIME LINE and the portrayal of a boxed "cl" are trademarks of
Bantam Books,
a division of Bantam Doubleday Dell Publishing Group, Inc.

All rights reserved.
Copyright © 1991 by William Murray.
Cover art copyright © 1992 by William Schmidt.
Library of Congress Catalog Card Number: 91-18633.
No part of this book may be reproduced or transmitted in any form or by
any means, electronic or mechanical, including photocopying, recording,
or by any information storage and retrieval system, without permission
in writing from the publisher.
For information address: Bantam Books.

If you purchased this book without a cover you should be aware that
this book is stolen property. It was reported as "unsold and
destroyed" to the publisher and neither the author nor the publisher
has received any payment for this "stripped book."

ISBN 0-553-29638-8

Published simultaneously in the United States and Canada

Bantam Books are published by Bantam Books, a division of Bantam
Doubleday Dell Publishing Group, Inc. Its trademark, consisting of the
words "Bantam Books" and the portrayal of a rooster, is Registered in U.S.
Patent and Trademark Office and in other countries. Marca Registrada.
Bantam Books, 666 Fifth Avenue, New York, New York 10103.

PRINTED IN THE UNITED STATES OF AMERICA

OPM   0 9 8 7 6 5 4 3 2 1

This one is for Fred and Diane Papert,
who know about horses
and the pursuit of dreams.

Botas (2) $20 —
necklaces 4   40 —
Knifes   4-5   50 —
Knives   110

Posters/
Prints $150

Book   40 —
ceramic tile $ 2 —
  small

"There are people who don't like cats, there are people who don't like dogs, but I've never heard anybody knock horses."

—Brian Mayberry, horse trainer

chapter 1

EASED

"She's the most beautiful thing I've ever seen," I said, as I watched Eddie Jones lead Mad Margaret out of her stall. "She's an Elgin Marble."

"A what?" Charlie asked.

"The horses' heads that used to be on the Parthenon frieze in Athens," I explained. "They were spirited off to the British Museum in London in the early eighteen-hundreds by a guy named Lord Elgin and they've been there ever since. You've never seen them?"

"Frozen horses' heads? What are you, some kind of weirdo?" Charlie said, outraged.

"No, Charlie, you don't understand. These are sculptures—"

"Eddie, give her to May," Charlie called out to his

groom. "Just walk her today. I still don't like the feel of those shins, okay?"

Eddie nodded, his pale, wrinkled face set in its usual expressionless mask, then led the filly out toward the area between the stables where several other hands were leading horses around in a tight little oval between the long shedrows. I watched them go, my eyes still fixed on the filly. Her chestnut coat gleamed in the early-morning sunlight and the muscles of her shoulders and thighs rippled as she moved, her head raised, her eyes alert, her ears cocked. She was a miracle of nature and I hoped there was nothing seriously wrong with her. I looked at Charlie. "A little heat, that's all," he said. "These young horses get sore shins from the hard surfaces out here, Shifty. Usually they get 'em when they're two and they first go out on the track, but this filly had no problems. Until now."

"What's it mean?"

"We ease up on her for a month or two," Charlie said. "It's gonna be a long season of racing and we want her ready for Del Mar." He winked. "You got yourself a nice horse here, Shifty. I guess old Lucius really appreciated what you done for him, the crazy old coot."

I lingered at the corner of the barn for another twenty minutes, watching May lead the filly around with the other horses, while the haze began to burn off Old Baldy in the background and the sky above the Santa Anita grandstand turned a pale blue. The filly seemed to be moving well, her front legs enclosed in thick protective bandages. All I had to go on, really, was Charlie's expert estimate of her condition; to me she looked eager and ready to run again, just the way she had when she'd broken her maiden nearly three weeks earlier and enriched me by about thirty-five hundred dollars. "You bet a grand on her?" Charlie had said to me down in the winner's circle, as we were getting our picture taken. "Didn't I tell you there's ten thousand ways to lose a race?"

He was right, of course, but every now and then in life, as well as in racing, you have to step out and go for the gold. I had seen the filly's first effort, when she had broken poorly, then rushed up on the inside and tired in the final stages to be well beaten, and I had known then that she would win her second time out, especially because Charlie had put a couple of more works into her and elected to stretch her out to a mile and a sixteenth. At that distance, I had figured, and with her first race behind her, she would be really unbeatable; her speed would enable her to get out of trouble early in the going and I was certain she had the intrinsic class and desire to be a winner. And it had all happened exactly as I had foreseen it. She had romped in, winning by ten, only a second off the track record. For the first time in a couple of years I now had a little financial cushion to fall back on, thanks to her. So I could have fallen in love with her just off that one race, but the incredible part of it all was that I now owned her. Miracles do sometimes happen, which is something that all true horseplayers know.

Charlie's disquieting news about her sore shins hadn't really cast a pall over my day. I knew enough about the game by now, after all the years of betting on these animals, to understand how chancy it was. Racehorses, in all their great strength and beauty, are among the most fragile creatures on earth, since everything they do depends upon the ability of slender ankles and delicate joints to support a thousand pounds of bone and muscle in action. They are always breaking down or getting sick and even the most minor ailments can lay them up for weeks at a time. Sore shins are caused by an inflammation of the cannon bone and the best cure for the ailment, if you're a real trainer and not some butcher with a firing needle in one hand

and a hypodermic syringe in the other, is rest. I trusted
Charlie and I had to accept his verdict, no doubt about
it, but I had no idea how long it would take before
she'd be racing again. I had a cushion now, but it costs
a lot of money to keep a Thoroughbred in training at a
major racetrack these days, at least two thousand dollars a month, not including vet bills, and it wouldn't be
long before I'd find myself broke again. I'd have to
hear it from Charlie, because somehow I had to make
it work for me. Sleight-of-hand artists don't make big
bucks and this filly was my chance, maybe my only
chance ever, to waft me, at least temporarily, out of the
genteel poverty that is endemic to my profession.

Meanwhile, it was nice to stand there and watch *my*
filly being led around as if for my private entertain-
ment. It was also nice to watch May doing it. She was a
tall, lanky brunette who was wearing a man's plaid
shirt, open at the neck, shorts, and sneakers. She had
lovely legs and an attractive face with a strong jawline,
high cheekbones, and large dark green eyes. She
seemed not to know what to make of her looks, however, because she wore no makeup and her hair was
badly cut, falling in uneven, straight strands toward her
shoulders. I had only seen her a couple of times, but
she had yet to smile at me and Charlie hadn't introduced us. Something about her seemed fragile,
wounded, an impression reinforced by the thin line of
a scar that ran from just under her temple down to her
neck. I had a feeling that something unpleasant must
have happened to her somewhere and that maybe she
had no use at all for men or for mankind in general,
but I still liked to watch her. Not only did she have
those fine legs to look at, but she clearly had a way with
animals. She handled the filly with grace and confidence and it was easy to tell that the horse trusted her.
From time to time as she walked her, May would pat
Maggie on the neck and talk to her. I couldn't over-

hear what she was saying, but the filly would nod or bob her head up and down, as if agreeing with her. The sight made me want to laugh, but then, in regard to racehorses, I'm easily entertained.

"Come on, let's get over to the track," Charlie said, suddenly emerging from his tack room. "I got a horse going out, just for a gallop, but I want to see how he's moving. He come up a little sore on me."

"Yeah. Then I suppose I'd better go over and do something about getting my owner's license," I said.

"No rush, Shifty. She ain't gonna run for a while."

"Still, Charlie—"

"Yeah, well, go do it. You know where the office is?"

"Around behind the grandstand," I said. "There shouldn't be much of a wait this time of year."

"Not this late in the meet," the trainer said. "If you wait till we all move over to Hollywood Park next week, it'll be a zoo. Always is at the start of every meet." We turned the corner of his shedrow and headed briskly toward the gap, where the horses move out onto the racing surface from the stable area. "By the way, is it official now?"

"Yeah. It was a fast probate, Charlie," I said. "Lucius didn't have any other heirs but you and me. Everything he had he left to the L.A. Public Library, except for the horses."

"Ain't any of 'em much good but yours, Shifty. I'm sellin' the others."

"A couple of them are okay, aren't they? There's that colt that runs pretty well on the turf—"

"Nah," the trainer said, cutting me off with a quick, impatient wave of the hand. "He's real common, if you want to know the truth. Anyway, I've got him sold, along with the whole string."

"To whom?"

"Oh, different guys. Some crazy people who think they know horses, but then who don't in this business?"

"Only you and I, Charlie. We're the only sane ones."

"I know about me, but I'm not so sure about you. I mean, you're a grown man who does card tricks. That's normal?"

"We're in the same racket, Charlie," I said.

"Yeah? How do you figure that?"

"We're both doing a high-wire dance in the reality-illusion game," I said. "We can both make people see and believe what we want them to see and believe. You know what that's called?"

"You sure can spin a line of bullshit, Shifty."

"It's called magic, Charlie," I said. "I do it with cards and coins and bits of this and that, you do it with horses. You think it's easy?"

"Nothin's easy," Charlie said. "Here he comes."

We stood at the rail between the gap and Clockers' Corner and watched Charlie's sore horse gallop past, the exercise boy standing up in the stirrups as the animal, whose head was bowed against his rider's tight hold, moved heavily under him. I could tell that Charlie didn't much like what he was seeing, but I kept quiet. Now that he had apparently decided to sell off the animals he had inherited from our joint benefactor, he would have only six or seven horses left on the grounds and none of them, except Maggie, seemed likely to do much for him.

Charlie Pickard was one of the best, most honest horsemen I'd ever met, but he didn't know how to be charming and lie to owners. The result was that he had spent most of his professional life surviving as a trainer of cheap and unsound horses mostly either bought privately or at the local sales, and, though he had always managed to win his share of races, he had never finished among the top ten in the trainer standings at any meet. Now, after his one rich owner's death and the selling off of his inherited stock, he was facing a fairly bleak year. I gathered that none of the prospective buyers of the horses would leave them with Charlie to train, which meant that he would have to start pretty much at the bottom again—not too good a spot to be in any profession, if you're over sixty and have nothing to offer in this world but talent and integrity. Still, nothing bothered Charlie very much. He was short and a little too fat and smoked too much and drank enough to keep his big, stubby nose an unflattering shade of pink and he looked about as formidable, under his ever-present brown cap, as an overweight shoe salesman. He was a survivor and I'd have trusted him with my life.

"Not too good, Charlie," the rider said, when he came back along the outside rail on the sore colt. "He didn't really warm up out of it too good."

Charlie nodded. "Thanks, Polo." He watched the horse walk past him back toward the barn, then turned to me. "Want some breakfast?"

"Had some, Charlie," I said. "I've got to get back to town. I have a meeting with my agent."

"Comin' back this afternoon?"

"No, but I'll be here tomorrow for getaway day. I never miss that." A couple of Charlie's cronies hailed him from a table above the small crowd of onlookers at the morning workouts and he waved to them, then moved toward the coffee counter under the stands. "Meanwhile, though, I've got a problem," I called after him. "I mean, if Maggie isn't going to run soon . . ."

"You can't afford her, right?" Charlie said, turning back to me. "Even if I cut my training bills down?"

"That's about it. Unless my agent tells me I've lucked into a television series or something."

"You want to sell her?"

"No."

"I can maybe get a quick eighty thousand for her," the trainer said. "Her breeding ain't much, but she's proved she can run and she's already a winner. That's worth something, Shifty."

I hesitated. I mean, eighty thousand dollars, even minus a five percent sales commission, represented a terrific temptation. I could move up in class a little, get a better place to live, a new car, pay off all my credit cards, join the cheery money dance that keeps America spinning. "No, Charlie," I heard myself say, "no, I want to stay in the game. Whatever happens to Maggie, I want to be a part of it. I'll never get another chance. And, in a way, it would be like selling old Lucius out. I think he'd have wanted me to keep her."

Charlie looked thoughtfully at me from under the brim of his cap, his shrewd brown eyes sizing me up. "Lucius is dead, Shifty," he said. "He won't know what you decide to do or don't do."

"Why don't you throw in with me, Charlie," I suggested. "You can have half of her, but you carry all the expenses."

The trainer shook his head, slowly but firmly. "Can't do that, Shifty. I can't operate that way. I'm a horse trainer, not an owner. It would make me do things different and I don't want to do things different. No, it wouldn't work. Tell you what, though, how about I find you a partner?"

"Okay, as long as you go on training her. That's the only condition I'll accept. We don't want to lose control of her."

"I'll see what I can do."

"You got somebody in mind?"

He nodded. "Yeah. Gantry told me he's got a client—"

"Gantry? That fraud?"

"It's one of his owners. The guy's new in town and lookin' for horses in training. Don't worry, Shifty, Gantry ain't gonna get his hands on this filly. This owner of his is building a racing stable. He plans to use two or three trainers. He might even take me on, if Gantry throws him my way."

"Who is it?"

"Some guy named Cameron. He's some dude who builds these shopping malls all over. Anyway, he's got money comin' out of his ears."

"Has he ever been in the game before?"

"Not so far as I know. Gantry tells me he's gettin' into it to keep his wife busy."

"Oh-oh."

"Wait till you see her, Shifty. She's a looker and she's a lot younger than he is. You ain't gonna mind at all if you get her for a partner."

"Well, okay, but we have to keep control of Maggie and you've got to train her. Otherwise, no deal. We'll find someone else."

I waited until he picked up a container of coffee and a roll, then walked him back to his barn. I said good-bye to him at the gap and headed for the parking lot. "Hey, Shifty," he called out after me, "you know you just broke the golden rule of racing, don't you?"

"What is it, Charlie?" I asked, glancing back at him.

"You went and fell in love with your horse. You ought to know better."

"I want you to give it to me again," Happy Hal Mancuso said, slumping back into his seat and regarding me with the weary resignation of a beleaguered parent.

"But I told you—" I began.

"No, you didn't," he said. "All you told me is that some crazed old man went and killed himself and that

9

you inherited a horse. This guy sure must have hated you to do that to you. It's like giving a junkie a free forty-pound sack of crack.''

I laughed, mainly because Happy Hal can always make me laugh; his view of life is so relentlessly bleak that he could be set down in the Garden of Eden and see nothing but a wasteland. He'd been my agent now for five or six years and I was probably the only client he had for whom he had no hope whatever. Close-up magicians, even the best ones, can't hope to make the kind of money commanded by the big acts that can make elephants disappear, saw ladies in half or change them into tigers, the sort of show-biz extravaganzas, all construction and mirrors, that we call pots-and-pans acts. The only reason Hal stuck with me, I knew, was because he liked me and admired what I could do with a deck of cards. But he'd have cut his own throat before admitting as much. Now, as I grinned at him, he scowled back, looking exactly like an angry bullfrog on a lilypad, and waited for me to enlighten him. It was after three and we were alone in the Hamburger Hamlet on the Strip, only a couple of blocks from his office.

I related for him, in some detail, the curious saga of my relationship to Lucius J. Bedlington, the seventy-eight-year-old multimillionaire horse owner whom I'd met through Charlie only a few months earlier and for whom I'd become a part-time driver and confidant. I had to admit to Hal that I'd never in my whole life met anyone quite that eccentric before, but that I had also become fond of the old aristocrat, with his nostalgia for the graciousness of a long-vanished way of life and his passion for the operettas of Gilbert and Sullivan. When Charlie had introduced me to him, mainly because I was down on my luck and needed a job, the old man had been happily planning to commit suicide, quite oblivious of the havoc it was causing around him. How could he have imagined that he would stir up such a mess, including a couple of murders and an attempt to kill me as well? Anyway, old Lucius had eventually gone and done it, leaving behind him all he had left to give away—his Pasadena mansion, the remains of his art collection, his books, a few bottles of fine wine, and his Gilbert and Sullivan records. "Oh, and the horses," I told Hal. "I guess he gave me Mad Margaret because he knew I liked her and he must have grown fond of me."

"I guess he would, seeing as you pinpointed the villain in the piece," Hal said glumly. "But he sure showed poor judgment. So how come she's got such a dopey name? She nuts?"

"No, Hal, he named all of his horses after characters in the various G and S operas. This filly is actually a very nice, calm animal, like a big dog, except when she's running. Then she's all business."

"Shit," Hal said, "horses are about the dumbest animals there are, except for the suckers who bet on them. So now what? You're going to sell her, I presume, if she's worth anything."

"Well, I'm going to sell a piece of her or try to," I said. "I don't want to sell her at all, but I can't afford to keep her all by myself."

Hal snorted contemptuously. "You're a poor, sick, sad sonofabitch. I don't know why I waste my time on you. You've got a chance to bank a little money, but no, you're going to blow it all on some horse."

"Hal, I know why you keep me around," I said. "I'm integrity relief."

"What?"

"If I was like all those club singers and lounge comics and rap freaks and TV personalities you have to deal with every day, you'd have dropped me like a hot penny years ago," I told him. "I'm the only real artist in your stable."

"You're beginning to sound like the rest of my

clients," he said. "What, you've got a big ego, too, now? You're a bust-out, that's all, a bum."

"Hal, I'm the best at what I do," I said. "Maybe not as good as Vince Michaels in Vegas, but with cards, the best. Give me my due, you bastard. Tell me how wonderful I am just once, in your dismal, dark, soul-destroying way."

"Shut up and listen," he said. "You're okay. What do you want, a statuette or something?"

"Maybe just the time of day, Hal, or a big kiss."

"That you don't get. Listen, I've got a gig for you. Two weeks in San Diego at the Laugh Hour."

"What's that?"

"A new comedy club downtown there. I know you can wow the people, but can you make them laugh?"

"I've got a patter. You've heard some of it."

"It isn't that funny."

"The only thing that would make you laugh, Hal, is a plague. What's the setup? A stage?"

"Yeah, but it's a small room, maybe seats a hundred and twenty. I got you two weeks, three-fifty a week."

"How many shows a night?"

"Two."

"I'll think about it."

"I have to know by tomorrow noon, Shifty," he said. "Look, I know it isn't terrific money, but it's a job."

"Good point."

"And if you take it, maybe I can get you on a TV show down there, I don't know."

"Okay, I'll probably take it, but I'll let you know. It's a good time for me, because I don't much like Hollywood Park anyway. This will be like a vacation."

"So can this horse of yours really run?" Hal asked me, as we left the restaurant ten minutes later and I headed for my car.

"Yes, she can, Hal. We have to back off her for a few weeks because she has sore shins, but she's a good one," I said. "My problem is finding a way to hang on to her financially until we can get her back to the races."

"You know, it's like you're a monk or something," Hal said.

"What do you mean?"

"You took vows of poverty and abstinence."

"Not abstinence, Hal," I said. "Hey, look around you. The sun is shining, it's a beautiful day. Let the sun shine, Hal."

"When the sun's out, you get the smog. Anyway, we need some rain."

"Hal, wherever you are it's raining all the time."

I was lying on my bed, watching the six o'clock news, when Charlie called me. He had arranged a meeting in the Turf Club at Santa Anita on Monday with the people he thought might buy a share of Mad Margaret. "Michael and Linda Cameron," he said. "You'll really like *her.*" I thanked him and was about to hang up when he added, "What do you think about the killing? Isn't that guy a friend of yours?"

"Who? What killing? What are you talking about?"

"Tony something or other, that big Italian guy who's always around, bets real big."

"Tony Huge?"

"Is that what they call him?"

"Yeah. It's because of the size of his bets. What he means by passing a race is betting only two or three hundred on it."

"He's going to be passing a lot of them now," Charlie said. "Somebody blew his head off last night, if it's the same guy. I thought you might know him. He's a degenerate, just like you."

"Thanks, Charlie. If it wasn't for degenerates like us, what would you be doing for a living?"

"Good point, Shifty—"

I didn't hear the rest of Charlie's reply, because at that moment an account of the killing suddenly showed up on my television screen. I quickly said good-bye to Charlie and hung up, just as Tony's body was shown being wheeled out of his Beverly Hills mansion toward an ambulance backed up into his driveway. In the foreground, the TV reporter was delivering, in an apparently solemn tone, a fairly detailed account of what was known about the event so far.

Tony Huge's real name, I found out, was Gaetano Fazzini. He and his twin brother, Giorgio, whom the police had not yet been able to locate, had a construction business called Rhineland Sand and Stone, which had main offices in downtown L.A. and reportedly did a lot of business with the city. Somebody had apparently broken into Tony's house sometime during the night, walked upstairs to his bedroom, and blown his brains out as he lay sleeping. He had been alone at the time, as his wife had reportedly moved out on him several weeks earlier, and his teenage children, a son and a daughter, were away at boarding schools in the East. The police doubted that the motive had been robbery, because nothing in the house, a pillared Grecian mansion on Beverly Drive below Sunset, had been touched, including the victim's wallet, which was stuffed full of hundred-dollar bills. Tony must have had a good day, I figured. He had been a popular fellow, according to this reporter's account—a *bon vivant* who liked to frequent the racetrack and was generous with his money to many charitable causes. The police were investigating.

Gaetano Fazzini. Funny how you can know people at the track for years, talk to them every day, have drinks with them even, and never know their real names. I had seen Tony around for at least a decade, talked horses with him, shared information on handicapping, swapped jokes and stories, and yet hadn't even known his real name. He'd been just another presence, a member in good standing of that great, secret, international confraternity of horseplayers, among whom I felt comfortable and of whom I was certainly a charter member. What could Tony have done to merit such a death? But then what did I really know about him? Nothing.

George Bush's dreary face, speaking to us mendaciously about some new fiscal crisis afflicting the nation, now filled my screen. I quickly popped him off into oblivion. I'd miss Tony Huge, as I'd miss any part of my racing scene, but I could do without politicians.

chapter 2

BREEZING

Linda Cameron was sitting alone in the Turf Club at a table over the finish line when Charlie brought me around that afternoon, about an hour before post time for the first race. I was practically struck dumb by her, because she was one of the most beautiful women I had ever seen. She had finely honed, soft features with large light blue eyes, honey-colored hair that cascaded nearly to her shoulders, a seemingly flawless lightly tanned complexion, and a full-lipped, sensual mouth. When she smiled, her perfectly aligned teeth sparkled, framed by a sudden set of dimples. I must have stood there in something of a daze, because I can't recall what Charlie said or even when I sat down. All I know is that I was in place opposite her, agog with admiration and lust, when I heard her say, "It's so sweet of you to consider allowing Michael and me to become part-owners of your horse, Mr. Anderson. Mr. Gantry has told us what a nice filly she is."

"Well, you know, I guess she is," I babbled, feeling suddenly as if somebody had stuffed pebbles under my tongue. "I'm . . . I'm . . . that is, I need—well, I guess Charlie here explained it to you."

"Yes, he did," she said. "I suppose it's difficult in your profession, having to do so much traveling and all. I mean, being able to do as well as you've been doing and still be able to manage your racing interests. I quite understand. As for Michael and me, well, I just love horses. I grew up around them and now that we've moved out here Michael wants to get involved." She paused, as if not certain that she had explained it quite correctly. "I guess what I mean is, Michael wants me to become involved. He's . . . he's pretty busy and he's away a lot." She smiled briefly, then tossed her head slightly and gazed out over the infield, where part of the arriving crowd for the last day of the meet was milling about the refreshment stands, studying programs, tout sheets, and racing forms, spreading blankets and unpacking coolers and picnic baskets in the warm April sunlight. It was a pleasant enough scene, but I didn't think it had really caught her interest all that much. I had the feeling that something had been left unsaid or still needed to be explained and that it hung in the air around her like a small, faintly toxic haze. When she turned back to me, she flashed that wonderful smile again, but it didn't seem quite as genuine as before. I had the odd feeling that there was music playing somewhere that was audible only to her and that I might not have enjoyed the sound of it. "I guess maybe we should wait until Michael gets here," she said. "I don't know where he could be. He said he'd be right back."

"I have to see another fella about some horses," Charlie said. "I'll be inside, Shifty, probably around the bar, in case you need me. But I guess you and Mrs. Cameron can get along without me."

"Did Charlie tell you what the conditions are?" I asked, as soon as the trainer had left.

"Conditions?"

"I mean, about buying a share of Mad Margaret."

"Oh, yes, he did say something about it."

"Whatever happens, the filly has to stay in Charlie's shedrow," I explained. "I don't want anybody else to train her."

"That's fine with me, Mr. Anderson. Michael was against it, not because he doesn't like Mr. Pickard, but simply on business principles, that's all."

"He doesn't want anybody telling him what to do with his property."

She smiled. "Something like that."

"Why are you so interested in this particular horse, Mrs. Cameron?" I asked. "I gather that Gantry's your main man. He has a lot of horses and then there are sales all over."

"Because we were told that Mad Margaret has real potential." She smiled again, then blushed and looked away from me. "And Michael's so impatient."

I had the feeling she was a frightened bird or maybe this was a studied technique she had adopted to draw men to her. Whatever it was, it made her vulnerable and even more attractive to me. I found myself wanting to enfold her in my arms, to reassure her that everything would be perfectly wonderful between us and that she was not to worry about anything. Perhaps, to make her happy, I should just give her the filly. "Impatient?" I asked instead. "You mean your husband wants to build a good stable right away."

"Yes, I guess that's what I mean."

"Gantry's a specialist at doing that kind of thing. If you've got the money to spend, he'll spend it."

"Yes, Michael knew all about him. I suppose he's famous."

"Well, he's bought himself with other people's

money right to the top of the business in just a few years. He's a great salesman."

"There's something you're not telling me, isn't there?"

"I don't think he's the greatest horseman in the world," I admitted. "That's one reason I want Charlie to have Maggie."

"Maggie? That's what you call her? How darling! She does look like a Maggie. I'll call her that, too." She turned those incredibly blue eyes pleadingly on me. "Oh, Mr. Anderson, I do hope you'll let us become partners with you. I'm sure we can work something out. I'd be delighted to let Mr. Pickard train her. I know he's a very good horseman and I appreciate that. We do so want to have only good horses and we want them well taken care of. I know how fragile they are and I couldn't bear it if I felt our horses were being mistreated, you know. Please believe me."

"I do, I do," I said, grinning at her. Who wouldn't have believed her? If she had told me at that moment that she was the Virgin Mary, come back to earth to right all the wrongs of mankind, I'd have immediately rejoined the church and taken vows of abstinence and chastity. "But please do me a favor."

"What?"

"My name is Lou, Shifty Lou Anderson," I said. "Either Shifty or Lou will do. Did Charlie tell you I'm a magician?"

"Yes, he did."

"Shifty is because a shift is a way of dealing cards and it's one of the moves I'm good at," I continued, babbling on about myself like a high-school freshman trying desperately to impress his first date, "while Lou is my real name. Either one is okay. Actually, my real first name is Louis and . . ."

"Oh, that's fine with me," she said, her smile trembling on the edge of laughter. "I'll call you Lou.

Shifty sounds—I don't know—strange. My name's Linda.''

I held out both hands to her, palms up. "See? Nothing there."

Then I quickly turned them over, making two fists. "Which hand?"

"Which hand what?" she asked, puzzled.

"Which hand has the small token of my esteem?"

She hesitated, then tentatively reached out and touched the back of my right fist. I turned it over and produced a little bouquet of violets, which I now solemnly held out to her. "Oh, how lovely," she said, taking it from me.

"You haven't tried the other hand."

"No, really?" Her mouth was parted in wonder, her gaze now shifting to my left fist. "Oh, this is such fun." And she touched the back of my knuckles. I snapped my hand open and produced a tiny Japanese fan. "Oh," she exclaimed again, "this is incredible!"

"In case it gets too hot," I said. "And the violets are to bring you luck."

"They're real," she said, raising them to her nose. "Oh, Lou, this is so nice!" She looked up and I watched her expression of pure pleasure change to one of palpable unease, as if a light were being dimmed inside her. "Oh, Michael," she said, "we were wondering where you were. This is Mr. Anderson."

"I was taking a crap, sweetheart," a dark, heavy male voice replied. "I figured you could keep the man entertained for a while."

I stood up, turned around, and felt my right hand disappear into a huge paw, as I found myself confronted by a large, grizzled bear of a man. He was in his mid-fifties, well over six feet tall and heavily built. He was wearing expensive handmade black boots, black jeans, a wide leather belt with an ornate silver buckle, a pink silk shirt, and a gray cashmere jacket.

His face was round and craggy, with a small, thin-lipped mouth all but hidden by a gray beard, and his eyes were deeply set and dark, mere specks of light under a heavy brow. His hair was thick, flecked with gray, and looked as if it might be growing straight down his back and all over his body. I wondered if he howled at the full moon.

"I see you've been entertaining my wife," he said, as he dropped himself into a chair beside her. "Pickard said you were real hot at what you do."

"I'm pretty good," I admitted. "Want to see something?"

"Oh, sweetheart, he's wonderful," Linda said. "Show him, Lou, how you—"

"No, that's all right," Cameron said. "I'll take it on your say-so. Actually, I could care less about magic."

"Oh, so you like it."

"I just told you I didn't."

"No, you said you could care less," I said, smiling. "I take it that means you do care, at least some."

Cameron stared at me. "You being funny?"

"Funny? No, Mr. Cameron. Maybe I just misunderstood you. If you had said you *couldn't* have cared less, then—"

"Hey, forget it," he said. "I didn't know I was dealing with a college professor."

"No offense," I said. "I'm sorry you don't enjoy magic."

"I make my own kind of magic," he said. "I'll give you a hundred thousand for the filly. Write you a check right now."

"I only want to sell a share of her," I said. "Up to fifty percent, no more. I thought Charlie explained that."

"He did, but I figured I needed to talk to you about it. In my business, Anderson, I only deal with the principals, you hear me?"

"Sure, I hear you. But Charlie told you right," I said. "And the horse stays with him and he calls the shots."

Cameron leaned back in his chair as if to get a better focus on me. I assumed that he had expected me to be bowled over by his offer. "Okay, tell you what," he said, his big hands resting lightly on the tabletop, as if to emphasize the finality of his offer, "a hundred and twenty thousand and that's it."

"Mr. Cameron," I said, standing up, "I don't think we have anything more to talk about."

"Anderson, sit down, goddamn it, I'm not through."

"Michael, you promised," Linda Cameron said, turning a flushed countenance toward him. "You said—"

"I know what I said," Cameron snapped. "Sit down, Anderson. I'd have been a fool not to try you. How much of her are you willing to sell and what do you want for her? I won't take less than half."

"That's what you can have, then," I said. "Fifty thousand for your half, we become general partners in her with equal votes and, if we don't agree, Charlie gets to cast the deciding vote, okay?"

"No. I'll give you forty for her."

"You offered me a hundred and twenty, Mr. Cameron."

"That was for all of her. I'm not going to pay you that kind of money for a piece of property I don't control," he said. "You want to keep your trainer and you fix it so the two of you can outvote me all the way down the line. I don't do business that way. You want control, you got to pay for it."

"Fair enough," I said. "We'll split the difference. Forty-five."

Cameron laughed. "No. Forty it is or nothing."

By this time I had had enough of Michael Cameron, so I started to get up, but then I caught sight of his wife's face and stayed put. She looked devastated, as if something alive in her were in the process of being snuffed out. The strength of her emotion kept me in the game. "For that amount you get forty-five percent, take it or leave it."

Cameron laughed again; he was clearly enjoying himself hugely. "Sure," he said, "what the hell. Being outvoted two to one is about the same as not owning half anyway. You got a deal." He did not offer to shake hands. "Send me a partnership agreement and I'll look at it. If it looks okay, I'll sign it and give you your money."

This time I did stand up, because the arrogance in the man made me want to kiss him off and I had decided not to. I was going to get less money than I'd hoped for, but it would do and I'd keep control of the horse. And then, too, I'd be seeing Linda again. "Fine. I have to run," I said. "I guess Charlie knows how to get in touch with you. I'll get a standard partnership agreement from the racing office. It's a simple little document, I'm told, but this is a simple little deal."

Cameron thrust a business card into my hand. "Call my office," he said, then turned to his wife. "I'm only agreeing to this shitty deal because of you. Order me some lunch. You know what I want. I'll be right back." And he got up and left as abruptly as he had come, without so much as a parting nod.

I looked at Linda Cameron. Her face was pale and her eyes were wet, but she was smiling. "Don't mind him, Lou," she said. "It's just his way. You won't be seeing much of each other. It was I who insisted on your filly. I just have a feeling about her. Michael simply wants to be on top of everyone and everything. Please try to understand. Is it all right if I go see Maggie?"

"Sure, of course." I shook her hand. "I'm not

good at business, I guess," I explained. "It's not my line of work."

"It's not you. He's like that with everyone."

I had a few observations I could have made right on the tip of my tongue, but uncharacteristically I let them wither there. Linda Cameron couldn't be held accountable for her husband's boorishness, so I simply said good-bye to her and left. What I couldn't figure out was why such a beautiful, obviously sensitive woman had married this slob in the first place, but then I didn't know anything about either of them. Some people like to suffer.

Pinhead was standing in the aisle outside Jay's box, looking glumly down at the small change in his hand. The horses entered in the first race had just appeared on the track below us and the six or seven people, including Pinhead, who relied on Jay's selections to enrich them were engaged in last-minute consultations regarding their betting action. "What's the matter, Pinhead?" I asked, as I joined them. "The first race hasn't even gone off. You can't be tapped already."

"No, but my wife's got me on a new regime," he said. "She only lets me bring two hundred a day to the track now. But after you put in your doubles, the Pick Nine, the Pick Six, and the first triple, a man hasn't got any money to bet."

"I can see that would be a hardship," I said.

Angles Beltrami leaned out of the box. "It don't make no difference to him," he said, cocking a thumb toward Pinhead. "He don't know what he's doin' anyway. He don't deserve to win."

"I heard the six is a mortal lock in here," Pinhead said. "The horse is six to one. I have to have something on him straight."

"The last mortal lock was in the Panama Canal,"

Arnie Wolfenden observed calmly from his seat behind Jay. "Perhaps you should just go with what you've got."

"No," Pinhead said, "Marty Joyce says the horse can't miss. I got to get something on him straight." He glanced hurriedly around, hoping to spot someone he could borrow money from, then bolted down the aisle toward the Turf Club. He knew better than to ask Jay or any of our group for a loan to finance his action, but in the Turf Club he'd probably be able to find the money by trading his information for it. Pinhead was very tall and thin and his view of life was a distorted one in which nothing was as it seemed and the universe was in the hands of people who knew the outcome of events before they took place. It was a paranoid's view, typical of many racetrackers. No one, not even Jay, could make a winner out of Pinhead, because Pinhead trusted no one and took information from everyone. Luckily, he owned an accounting firm in Pasadena that evidently kept him supplied with enough income to fund his action, but I wouldn't have let him try to balance my checkbook.

"Ah, Shifty," Jay said, as I sat down next to him to watch the first race, "who but the Dummy God could protect dummies like Pinhead? Did you make a bet in here?"

"No. I couldn't isolate a real contender out of this bunch of cheap claimers."

"That's what I told all of them," Jay answered, indicating with a wave of his hand the group of departing acolytes fanning out toward the betting windows, "but it's like Cassandra crying in the wilderness."

"Cassandra cried on the walls of Troy," Arnie, the only other remaining occupant of the box, declared. "You are mixing your prophets."

"Well, not even I know everything," Jay said, raising his binoculars toward the starting gate. "Let's watch the race, friends. We might learn something."

I spent most of the afternoon watching the races with Jay and Arnie, a pleasant way to pass time. Jay Fox was my closest friend at the track, a professional handicapper who had become a point of reference for me in the tough racket of picking enough winners to show a profit. He believed in the sanctity of numbers and the irrefutability of facts, a faith which, combined with self-discipline and patience, had made it possible for him to survive, even occasionally flourish, at his chosen profession. "It's hard work," I had once said to him. "Work?" he had replied. "No, hard work is being an ant. It's getting into a car every day and battling a freeway to go to a job you hate for less money than you deserve and having to battle the freeway again to come home to a wife and kids and endless bills and television. That's work. What I do is what I love, what I can't imagine *not* doing. That's living."

"Aesop would have loved Jay," Arnie said.

"Who's he?" the handicapper asked.

"And you a UCLA graduate. Shame on you. He was an old Greek who wrote these fables that all end in a nice elevating moral. Your versions would turn the morals upside down and inside out."

"Well, lumbering along with the herd has never been my thing," Jay said. "You get eaten that way."

This kind of racetrack banter fills me with contentment, partly, I suppose, because I agree with it. Almost everyone I knew at the track, even the Pinheads, seemed happy to be there, which could not be said about your average factory or bank. Look at Jay—about forty now, an ex-athlete (he'd been a top tennis player), with thinning dark curly hair and the beginnings of a paunch, but still in good shape and gazing out on life through sharp blue eyes with the zest of a teenager. And consider Arnie Wolfenden, a cynical old campaigner and survivor, still battling the vigorish and the pari-mutuel machines with the élan of a World War

II Polish cavalry officer leading a charge against a Panzer division. I didn't know anybody wiser than Arnie, a fairly recent fugitive from the grimmer climes of the New York racing scene, who had settled among us like an established sage in a gathering of scholars. No campus in the world provides a better education for life and its hard times than the racetrack, while simultaneously entertaining the denizens with high drama, adventure, and lots of low comedy. "The track is a metaphor for the human condition," Arnie had once informed us, after a winner we had all backed had been disqualified by the stewards and placed last for what had seemed to us the most minor of infractions. "There is no justice in it, only the law."

I bet on only two horses during the course of the afternoon, both of them losers, but I wound up making a small profit because both of my animals ran second and I had been prudent enough to back up my action with money in the place hole. I kept quiet about it because Jay disapproved of such betting tactics, having long ago taken a firm stance against any sort of straight wager except on the nose, and he himself had failed to cash a ticket. It is not considered good form in these wars to flaunt your successes in the face of adversities afflicting your friends and colleagues. When a radiant Pinhead stopped by our box again after the fifth to remind us that his six-to-one shot had indeed romped home first, enriching him to the tune of over seven hundred dollars, the announcement met with the frosty silence it deserved. And after Pinhead had again departed, leaving in his wake another tip from one of the Turf Club touts he frequented, an ice age of disapproval settled grimly over our little company. It took Arnie to dispell it. "What's the definition of a dead heat?" he asked, looking up from his *Form*.

"What do you mean, Arnie?"

"Two touts trying to borrow money off one another at the same time," he said.

We laughed and the sun came out again. After all, as Jay never failed to remind us, there's always another race and there's always fresh. And there's always good gossip to ease time along. It was Angles Beltrami who had the latest on Tony Huge. He came back to the box just before the San Jacinto Handicap, Santa Anita's traditional closing-day feature, to inform us that the police wanted to question Tony's brother, George. "I wonder what the angle on that one is," he said. "I mean, do they think he killed him or what?"

"Probably just want to question him," Jay said. "They're twins."

"So what? Maybe they hated each other. I never saw them together."

"The only times we ever saw Tony was at the track," Jay said. "I remember him telling me once that his brother—what's his name?"

"George."

"No, Giorgio. Anyway, Tony said his brother didn't like the track," Jay continued. "But they were close. They were also partners."

"Yeah, that don't mean nothin'," Angles said. "They could have hated each other, you know? Hey, like when it's brothers, it's always worse than when just friends have a fight. Maybe Tony blew too much money at the track."

"And his brother had him shot? Come on, be serious."

"I am serious," Angles said. "Giorgio's disappeared, nobody's seen him. I hear the cops want to talk to him, but nobody knows where he is. I heard they called his office downtown, but nobody knows a thing."

"Who named him Tony Huge?" Arnie asked.

"Who knows?" Jay answered. "When I first met

him ten years ago, they called him Tony Tiny, because he used to bet two dollars a race. Then all of a sudden, a few years ago, he started to bet real big money."

"He was a loser," Angles said, "a big loser, I'm tellin' you."

"He and Giorgio started to make a lot of money in the construction business about then," Jay said. "They underbid for a lot of big city contracts and then last year they finished some huge private jobs, including one for Jed Hunter."

"Who's he?" Arnie asked.

"He owns Sovereign Acres, down near Ramona," Jay said. "I heard they built a great racing and breeding facility down there, including all the housing and also the main house, which is like a showplace. I've seen pictures. There was a story about it in the Sunday *L.A. Times Magazine* last spring."

"Yeah, well, I was told there was some kind of trouble over that, too," Angles said. "They were way over budget and the Judge—that's Hunter—was gonna sue."

"I still don't believe Giorgio had Tony killed. It doesn't make any sense."

"Well, somebody blew him away and it wasn't just some armed robber either," Angles concluded, raising his binoculars to focus on the entries for the San Jacinto as they moved toward the starting gate. "Who'd you bet on in here?"

"Nobody," Jay said. "Any one of four or five of these horses could win it."

"Root for the six horse. He's the only one who can bail me out."

The six horse ran sixth, which left Angles in a state of shock, and I said good-bye to my friends. I wanted to beat the crowd out before the last race, so I headed for the parking lots. On the down escalator I found myself standing a few feet behind Charlie Pickard, who turned around and winked. "I hear you made a deal for the filly," he said, smiling. "Cameron told me."

"I couldn't resist his wife."

"Yeah, she's a looker, ain't she?"

"When are you turning Maggie out?"

"In a couple of days. I'm shipping her down south to Sovereign for a month or two, like I told you."

"It's quite a place, I hear."

"State of the art, Shifty. There ain't a better one in the country and I got a guy there who takes good care of my horses. The filly'll do fine there."

"I'll be down in that area for a couple of weeks," I said. "I'll go and see her."

"Good," Charlie said. "The Camerons just bought a place in Rancho Santa Fe. You can drop in on them, too."

"Not if he's around," I said.

"He ain't around much, Shifty. That's what I hear."

I didn't know exactly what to make of that piece of information, but I thought it might be nice to give Linda Cameron a friendly phone call, just from one partner to another.

chapter 3
TURNED OUT

I couldn't see the Cameron house from the road because it was hidden by acres of well-tended fruit trees through which the driveway meandered in a series of gentle ascending curves until it topped a small rise, then descended into a hollow ringed by tall cypresses. I could tell that the ranch-style building was larger than it seemed, because it hugged the ground, lying flat under the weight of sun and sky, and spread out around a central courtyard that also contained a swimming pool and a tennis court. Beyond the trees, from the height of a flagstoned terrace above the pool, I could see an open meadow leading to a riding ring and stables. "How many rooms do you have here?" I asked, as Linda Cameron emerged from the kitchen area with two tall glasses of iced tea.

"I haven't even begun to count them," she said,

smiling. "We just moved in and we haven't unpacked half our stuff. We have boxes all over. I've barely managed to make a dent."

"It's a beautiful place."

"Yes, but there's so much of it. We had a big house in Houston, too, but nothing like this. Do you realize we have four hundred orange trees?"

"Good ones?"

"So they tell me. I wouldn't know."

"You didn't ask, when you bought the property?"

"I never saw it," she said. "Michael bought it. He was out here on business and Judge Hunter told him about this place, that it was up for sale and was a real bargain and all, so he bought it."

"Without you looking at it?"

"He sent me pictures. We were planning to move out here anyway."

"Who's Judge Hunter? Is that the guy who owns Sovereign?"

"Yes. Michael's done a lot of business with him."

"Seems pretty cavalier of Michael."

"Well, that's the way he does things. Want to see the rest of it?"

"Sure, why not?"

It wasn't much of a tour, since mainly it led through empty rooms piled high with unpacked cartons, crates, and furnishings, but I didn't mind. Linda Cameron was wearing sandals, white tennis shorts, and a man's blue shirt tied up above her waist and open at the neck. She had been working, presumably unpacking her boxes or organizing the kitchen, and every atom of her seemed to be throbbing with life. I felt like a starving man being teased by a succulent, forbidden feast; it was all I could do not to devour her. Instead I made polite conversation, nodding my head as she outlined her decorative schemes for each area, explained where pictures and books would go, occasionally asked for my advice. "I thought this room would be good for Michael's gun collection," she said at one point, as she opened a door into a large room at the extreme end of a long corridor. "What do you think?"

"His gun collection?"

"Oh, yes, Michael has a very fine collection."

"What sort of guns?"

"All kinds," she said, "everything from antiques to the most modern stuff. I don't go near them. They frighten me. But I thought in here, away from the rest of the house . . ."

"The farther the better," I said. "I'm not crazy about guns." I looked around the empty room. "Where are they?"

"Oh, Michael won't have them shipped until the security system is in," she explained. "They're in crates, back in Houston, along with all the special cases and display racks." She put a hand lightly on my shoulder as she ushered me out again. "I so agree with you."

The iced tea was delicious and cold, but it wasn't helping much. I sipped it occasionally as I trailed her through the house, but I remained on fire. I was annoyed at myself, but I couldn't help it. I told myself I'd been alone for too long, several months now since the death of a woman I'd cared for, but even so I couldn't account for the lust this other man's wife aroused in me. Was I turning into some kind of sex maniac? I didn't know, I didn't care. I wanted Linda Cameron.

We went into the kitchen, a spacious room between the two main wings of the house, for more iced tea. Then Linda Cameron showed me the bedrooms. Hers was at one end of a corridor, his at another, at least a hundred feet away. Hers was all frills and lace and contained a queen-sized bed under a cream-colored spread, with lots of cushions and a couple of antique dolls on a rocking chair and pastoral landscapes on the walls; his was fur and leather and heavy furniture of dark oak, a bed large enough to scrimmage on, with hunting prints on the walls, a grizzly-bear rug, mounted photographs of Cameron himself standing dourly beside various animals and large fish he had slaughtered. Her quarters smelled of life, his reeked of death.

"It's going to be quite a while before we're settled," she said, as we emerged again into the sunlight of the terrace. "Would you like more iced tea?"

"No, thanks, Linda, really," I said. "It's delicious, but no thanks."

"Want to see the stables?" she asked.

"Sure."

"Come on then." We put our glasses down and walked around the pool toward the gap leading to the open meadow beyond the row of cypresses. "You know, I don't like this house very much," she said. "We haven't been here even a week and I know I'm not going to like it, ever. It's dark and ugly, with no view at all. If it hadn't been for the stables and the riding ring, I wouldn't have moved in."

"You'd have made your husband sell it?"

"I don't know," she said. "Michael's very stubborn. He's a hard man, Lou, very hard. But I couldn't have lived here, not without the animals."

"How many animals have you got?"

"Two show horses, six dogs, and I don't know how many cats. Eight, I guess, if you include the two neighbors' cats that hung around our place most of the time."

"Where are they all?"

"The horses are on their way. The dogs and the cats will come on in a couple of weeks, when I can get organized here. My housekeeper Nellie's back there taking care of everything. And I'm trying to hire people to help me with this place. Right now all we have is a landscaping service.''

She gave me a tour of the empty stable area and the riding ring, striding ahead of me on those golden-brown legs, her long blond hair shining in the sunlight. ''At least I'll finally have room here for all the animals,'' she said. ''Back home, in Houston, I had to board the horses and Michael kept saying he was going to get rid of the dogs and cats. Of course I'd have killed him.'' She smiled, but her eyes were serious. We were leaning side by side against the fence and looking into the ring by that time and the tone of her voice had caused me to turn my head to look at her. ''There are some things Michael doesn't understand about me,'' she added.

I couldn't begin to imagine how she could have married him, but I didn't know her well enough yet to ask her. ''What made you and Michael decide to leave Texas?'' I asked instead, hoping for a clue.

''Michael's business,'' she answered. ''It was great down there during the boom years, which is when I met Michael. We were all up there on this big wave of money and I guess most people thought it would never end. For a long time, after the bottom fell out of the oil business and so many people lost everything, Michael did all right. He was building shopping malls and office complexes all over the country, not just in Texas, you know, so he didn't ever have a real bad time. He never got into the oil business, no way, and he didn't do much speculating in real estate either. I mean, Lou, Michael can be kind of crude and all, but he isn't dumb. What you see and hear is what you get with Michael. But he's very smart in business.''

''I believe you.''

''Anyway, it just got too depressing the last few years,'' she continued. ''Things have started to come back some since the crisis in the Middle East and all, but we'd decided to move a couple of years ago. Michael had some big projects to finish, one up near Louisville, Kentucky, and I guess that's how I got him interested in Thoroughbreds, after all these years.''

"How? By being around the horse people?''

"Yes, I suppose so,'' she said, laughing. "I'd always wanted some Thoroughbreds, but Michael couldn't see it. Then, when we were up in Louisville around Kentucky Derby time and he got to meet a whole lot of horse folks, he began to change his mind.''

"He got to like the game?''

"No, not Michael,'' she explained. "Michael doesn't like any animal he can't shoot. No, he got to meet the horse people around there and over in Lexington and he discovered they were as big a bunch of rednecks as he is. So he decided they were all right and he said that when we came out here he'd have a racing stable, too. I think it's just so he can be one of the boys. You know how a lot of the horse people are, I guess.''

I did know. Horse-racing people, the ones who dominate and run the game, tend to be conservative, chauvinistic, a little racist, insular, locked into attitudes and habits derived from generations of entrenched blood and money. From what I'd seen of Michael Cameron, he would fit right in. "How'd you get to Gantry?'' I asked.

"Oh, he was there, he was everywhere,'' she said. "The minute Michael said he might be interested in creating a racing stable, Mr. Gantry seemed to spring up out of the ground in full bloom.'' She giggled. "He's such a talker I thought even Michael wouldn't be able to cope with him and I was right.''

"It wasn't like Gantry to send you to anyone else,'' I observed.

"Well, I knew about your filly,'' she said. "When we started to ask around, her name kept coming up—a good young horse ready to run that we could maybe buy into."

"And it wouldn't have been too smart of Gantry to try and tout you off her. He's no fool."

"No, he isn't. Anyway, he's going to handle the rest of our stable. I just had my heart set on Maggie."

On the way back up to the house I kept wondering about her and Michael. She was so different when he wasn't around, so self-assured and cheerful, positive about life and herself. I tried to imagine that beautiful tanned body of hers in the meaty grip of the bear and I couldn't. And he had to be twenty years older than her at least. It was obscene, that's what it was.

Ten minutes later, out in the driveway in front of her new house, Linda Cameron kissed me. Not on the cheek, but on the mouth. Very lightly, like a brush of feathery wings in the moonlight, but it was a kiss. "So nice of you to stop by, Lou," she said. "You're going to be in the area for a couple of weeks? Wonderful! I want to come and see your show. And then we have to go out to Sovereign Acres just as soon as Maggie gets here. Oh, it's so exciting! You're a dear to take all this trouble."

When I drove away in my brand new blue Toyota convertible, she lingered long enough out on the front lawn to wave good-bye to me. She looked unreal in the hard California sunlight, like a naiad out of mythology, poised for instant flight on those long golden legs. I could see myself happily chasing after her, gamboling in pursuit through forest glades like a rutting centaur. And then I remembered Michael Cameron and his gun collection. I was obviously nursing a death wish.

The Laugh Hour, which was located in downtown San Diego, in the middle of the so-called Gaslamp Quarter, turned out to be a strange room to work in. It was long and narrow, decorated mainly by blowups of famous old jazz musicians, and with a small stage at one end, only a couple of feet above the floor. The audience sat at tables and, at the rear of the room, in booths too far back for my platform magic to make an impact. I told the owner, a large and affable retired black saxophonist named Joe Devane, that I'd open my act with some patter and a couple of platform effects, then move out into the audience, going from table to table with close-up, so as not to lose half my public. "Hey, baby, you make any moves you want in here," Joe Devane told me. "Long as you can entertain the folks it don't matter a damn to me how or where you do it. Go get 'em, baby." It turned out that the reason I'd gotten this job was that Joe had once caught my act in Las Vegas and, as he put it, "flipped, man, just flipped." He'd only been open about six months and, after an initial flurry, his business had begun to tail off. "The trouble is these damn comedians, man," he explained. "They just come on in here with their tired old jokes and shit or they're so goddamn dirty they scare the people away, you know what I'm sayin'? We got to bring a little class back to this place, get the real folks back in here."

I liked Joe Devane. He was a big man in his sixties with a large paunch who had let himself go physically and nursed few illusions about his chances of making it into his seventies. He had smoked so much, his lungs, he informed me, looked like Cajun cheese. "I can't blow no more," he informed me. "Shit, it's about all I can do to breathe." He wheezed if he had to move too fast, even for a few feet, but his mind was clear and he looked out on what was left of his life with no regrets. "Man, I had a party, baby. Now all I got left is this place," he said. "If we don't make it, I'm gonna be out there with the other homeless, sleepin' under some damn bush in Balboa Park. You better do good, baby, and bring some people in here. No more of these damn comedians, unless I can find one that don't make you want to throw up on your damn shoes. I'll bring music back in here, get some damn girl singer that can sing the blues and turn this place on, baby. You go get 'em now.''

He let me set my show up exactly the way I wanted to. I'd open onstage with either the Slow Motion Coin Vanish or my own variation of the Cut and Restored Rope, all the while keeping up a nice flow of under-stated patter about the idiocy of world events, in which I'd compare or equate my effects with the public behavior of the various rascals in the news. Then I'd move out into the audience. I'd usually open with Golden Thimbles or the Bewildering Ball Vase, then get into my various effects with cards, my true forte. I'd work one or two stunts for the people in the rear booths, then get back to the stage to close with perhaps my strongest comedy effect, a sucker coin trick in which I begin by pretending not to see the long black elastic to which my fifty-cent piece is obviously attached. I can now do this trick nearly as well as my pal Vince Michaels, who taught it to me in Las Vegas, and it never fails to delight. After my first two shows in the club, I knew I had the room figured out. "All we need now is the people," Joe Devane told me on opening night. "We had half of 'em tonight and this was Friday, man. Word of mouth will be good and maybe the papers will come and cover it. You got to keep me from goin' broke, Shifty."

"You serve dinner," I said. "So how's the food?"

"Good, good, man," Joe Devane assured me. "Ain't nobody I know don't like chittlins." And he laughed until he coughed himself purple.

I liked working for Joe Devane and I also enjoyed my first few days in San Diego. I hadn't been in the area since the end of the Del Mar meet in early September and I was glad to be back. I rented a room in an old motel right on the beach and took long morning walks, wading cheerfully through the morning tide. The ocean was still too cold to swim in and only the surfers braved it this early, riding the swells on their long boards or bobbing in place, waiting for the right wave. In their multicolored rubber wet suits they looked like large aquatic insects. Mainly, I was happy to be out of L.A., away from crowded freeways and polluted air. I even stayed away from the betting satellite on the Del Mar fairgrounds, on the sensible premise that I ought to give the newly opened Hollywood Park race meeting at least a couple of weeks to establish some form. I only dropped in once, to bet on a tough old claimer trained by Charlie Pickard, and went away fifty dollars poorer when the horse got fanned on the turn and ran fourth. I didn't mind. I was marking time, my life suspended in a pleasant void, with enough to do every night at the Laugh Hour to keep me engaged. I tried not to think too much about Linda Cameron, because I was basking in my new financial circumstances and didn't need distractions.

"So, Shifty, you are a rich man now," my landlord, Max Silverman, had said to me the morning I'd left L.A. He was standing on the sidewalk outside my apartment building in West Hollywood, leaning on his broom and watching me load suitcases into the trunk of my new car.

"Rich? Not exactly, Max," I said. "I had a small windfall, enough to buy a new car."

"You got yourself something fancy, I see."

"I've always wanted a convertible, Max," I admitted. "This isn't a new one. It belonged to one of my agent's clients, a rock singer—"

"One of those deaf people."

"She has a hit single and moved up to a Mercedes. I got a real buy on this car, Max."

He looked at it disapprovingly. "Can you afford it, Shifty? You, with your gambling habits."

"Oh, come on, Max," I said, smiling at him. "Give me a break. I could have told you I won the money to pay for the car with a giant exacta."

"That I would not believe. So?"

"So I had a little windfall. An uncle died and left me some money," I lied. "It was either move out into a bigger apartment or buy a new car. You don't want me to move out, do you, Max? What would you have to complain about, if I left?"

"Well, I have to admit that a new car you definitely need," the old man said. "That other thing you drove around in, that is a death trap." He was referring, of course, to my old, battered Datsun 310, a survivor of a hundred and forty thousand miles of freeway, a machine built for the ages.

"Never had a major breakdown, Max," I said. "You, of all people, ought to know better than to judge an instrument by its age and outward appearance. That was a Stradivarius on wheels."

"Ah, Shifty, you dare to compare a piece of Oriental junk to a handcrafted masterpiece?" he said indignantly. "You have the effrontery of youth, incorrigible." And he began furiously to sweep clouds of dust in my direction.

I loved Max. I probably would have moved out of the building years ago, if it hadn't been for him. He managed the place for the retired movie actor who owned it and by his very presence lent an air of civilized old-world charm to the basically shabby premises, a two-story structure of small apartments and studios built around a swimming pool and a barbecue area. Max occupied two rooms on the ground floor, where he lived surrounded by the memorabilia of his active career as a violinist with several of the world's best orchestras. He was a vigorous ancient whose attitude toward the world was one of bemused cynicism, but his commitment to life was wholehearted. He could no longer play, or at least he said he couldn't, but he compensated by looking at fine art, listening to good music, reading the great Russian writers, and worrying about his tenants, especially me. He had convinced himself that I would one day tumble into the abyss on the backs of too many beaten horses and end up like his favorite author, Fyodor Dostoyevski, a ruined gambler. I did nothing to put his mind at ease in this regard. Max was tall and thin and he looked under his omnipresent black beret like a benevolent Charon, the boatman who would one day whisk us all across the River Styx. I considered it my duty to exasperate him.

"So long, Max," I said, as I pulled away from the curb, "see you in a couple of weeks. I'll call you if I get any hot tips."

"Ah," he exclaimed, gesturing at me in disgust, then resumed his furious sweeping.

I had paid twelve thousand dollars in cash for the car. I had thirty thousand dollars in a C.D. at my local Wells Fargo branch and seven thousand in my checking account. Thanks to Bedlington and Mad Margaret, I felt financially secure for the first time in my life. I drove south with the top down all the way and feeling as if I could fly.

Halfway into my run at the Laugh Hour, on a Saturday night, Linda Cameron showed up. She was with a party of seven or eight people, all of them expensively dressed, and seated at a large table toward the rear. It was no accident that she had appeared, because Joe Devane came backstage with a message from her. "A real pretty lady says she's been trying to get hold of you, Shifty," he said, thrusting his large, sweaty face into my dressing room. "You know her?" He gave me a note sealed in a small, scented envelope.

"Lou, why haven't you called?" it read. "If I hadn't picked up the Weekend section in the *Union,* I'd never have known how to find you. I'm with some friends out front. We're all excited to see you perform. Please come say hello, whenever you can."

I finished dressing into my best set of black tails and went out to see her. I spotted her right away, as if her golden head had been isolated by a pin spot, and as I approached she rose up out of her seat, her face radiant with pleasure. "Lou, I'm so pleased," she said, giving me a quick hug. "Why haven't you called or let me know where you are?"

"I've been breaking in a new act, Linda," I said. "I was going to call you, of course."

"You know the filly's at Sovereign," she said. "I called the stable and Mr. Pickard told me he'd shipped her out last Tuesday."

"Yes, I heard from Charlie. I'm sorry, I should have let you know."

"Oh, I understand," she said. "Here, let me introduce you."

I was relieved to see that her husband was not a member of her party, which consisted of three couples in their thirties and Linda's escort, a trim-looking man of about fifty named Alden Berry. "Michael's out of town again on business," Linda explained, "so I invited Alden."

"Hello," he said, not getting up but merely holding out his hand for me to shake. It was small and bony, with manicured nails, and his eyes were cold, even though he was smiling. He reminded me of a swift, secretive forest predator, a small but efficient killing machine. "I understand you can make things appear and disappear. How about the check?"

The other couples laughed. The men had the glossy, ruddy look of entrenched WASP money and their women all seemed to be called Buffie, with speaking voices blocked by the small potatoes they nurtured at the backs of their throats. "Oh, Alden, how amusing," one of them said, flashing thirty-two brilliant teeth in my direction. "Can you really make things disappear, Mr. Anderson? How about my husband?"

"Only small inanimate objects, I'm afraid," I said. "As for the check, I can't make it disappear, but I can double it."

That got a small laugh, but I sized them up as a tough audience. They obviously thought they were slumming, since the Rancho Santa Fe crowd, all denizens of multimillion-dollar estates in the most fashionable area of North County, doesn't frequent downtown San Diego, unless it's to make an obligatory appearance at the opera, the symphony, or some splashy charitable event. Linda had obviously organized this party and her friends were prepared to tolerate it, even to be mildly amused, but they were going to have to be dazzled.

"What was this place?" Alden Berry asked, looking around the premises with mild distaste. "I don't think I've been down here, you know, since they began renovating this part of town. The Gaslamp Quarter they call it now. It used to be a slum, nothing but flophouses and tattoo parlors and porn stores."

"It used to be worse than that, Alden," one of the other men said. "I'm old San Diego and I know. It used to be called the Stingaree and it was all opium dens and whorehouses."

"Sounds like fun," one of the Buffies said. "When did it become so respectable?"

"Oh, I'm talking about way back," the man said, "turn of the century. Then after that it got seedy, especially with the military in here, until they began to redevelop the whole downtown area. Didn't Jed get involved in that? I know he was approached at the time the Horton Plaza project was in the works."

"I advised him against it," Alden Berry said. "I remember driving down to this part of town one day to have a look at it and all I can remember is sailors hanging out all over and bums pissing against the walls. Jed had enough going up in North County and Ramona without having to sink any money down here. The inner cities are not my idea of a good investment, anyway."

"Colorfully put, Alden," another of the men said, with a laugh.

"Oh, I think it's quaint," one of the Buffies commented. "Now it's all so like Disneyland, all these funny old buildings—"

"They're still pissing against the walls," Alden Berry said.

"Not in here," I assured him. "If you'll excuse me, I'm going on in a few minutes."

"Oh, Lou, I'm so excited," Linda said, smiling and waving as I left. "This is such fun. Will you join us afterwards for a drink?"

"I'll try, Linda," I said, not wanting to commit myself. I wasn't sure I could tolerate her party for any length of time and I was leaving myself an out.

My act went very well, but certainly not because of Linda's party. The Buffies talked through much of it, until Linda herself had to hiss at them to stop, and Alden Berry was so clearly uninterested that his indifference cast a pall over his end of the table. I coped mainly by ignoring the whole group and concentrating on the rest of the audience, which luckily turned out to be unusually receptive and attentive. I closed with the Quadruple Torn Cigarette Paper, a routine in which I tear a single sheet of cigarette paper into four pieces, roll it into a ball, and restore it under basically impossible conditions. It's one of the toughest effects I've mastered and I don't always close with it, mainly because I prefer cards and coins, but I knew I needed something special to wow Linda and her table. And it worked. When I ended the move by once again tearing up and restoring one of the two sheets I'd created from the original halves, two young couples at a table next to Linda's jumped to their feet, laughing and applauding. Linda herself was radiant with pleasure and everyone at her table clapped, except for Alden Berry, who merely sat in place, a slight smile on his face, his cold eyes regarding me as indifferently as if I were a side-walk buffoon. I decided as I walked off that I'd pass on Linda's invitation.

She came back to see me in the dressing room. "Oh, Lou, you were just wonderful," she said, as she came through the door and threw her arms around me. "I can't believe some of the things you did. You were terrific!"

"Thanks, Linda, I appreciate it."

"I'm so sorry about what happened," she said, looking genuinely distressed. "I thought it would be such a fun evening and everyone was so anxious to come. I can't believe they could be so rude."

"Don't worry about it," I assured her. "I've had lots tougher audiences, believe me. There are some people who just don't appreciate magic."

"Oh, they're such goops," she said. "I hardly know them. They're all friends of Alden's. I hardly know anyone here. And after tonight, I'm not sure I want to."

"Then you'll understand if I don't come out for a drink with you. Tell them I've got a cold or something."

"Oh, of course."

"What does your man Alden Berry do?"

"He's a lawyer. I'm so disappointed in him," she said. "He can be so charming and funny. I don't know what's the matter with him tonight."

"He probably lost a case or something."

"He has been working hard, I know, because he told me."

"Don't worry about it, Linda," I said. "It's sweet of you to care."

"Will you call me tomorrow? I want to go out and see Maggie."

"Me, too. I'll call, I promise."

She kissed me again, quickly, lightly, but with her mouth open, then let herself out. Either she was the world's most naive beauty, I decided, or a subtle enchantress. Whichever the case, I was clearly in some trouble, because, as I sat there alone, staring dumbly into my dressing-room mirror, I knew I was going to have an affair with her. I also had a very strong feeling that I was dangerously out of my depth.

chapter 4

RESTLESS

IN THE GATE

"I have a few basic rules about surviving at the track," Arnie Wolfenden said. "I think a couple of them apply to this race."

"Yeah?" Jay asked. "And what might they be?"

"Never trust anyone under five feet tall who speaks Spanish," Arnie said. "And never trust a trainer whose last name ends in a vowel."

I laughed, but Jay only smiled. "Mel Ducato is a New York sidewalk dude, but he's also a good trainer and he wins a lot of these cheap claiming races," he said. "And when he does win, he often uses Palestrina."

"I don't like the smell of it," Arnie said. "The faint but distinct aroma of a stiff job permeates the nostrils. I am passing."

"That's your prerogative, Arnie," Jay said. "But the numbers are good and four to one is my kind of price." He rose out of his seat to head for a pari-mutuel window and I went with him. "Arnie's been going so bad these first two weeks at Hollywood that he can hardly bring himself to make a bet anymore," he continued. "It has been tough so far, but you have to break eggs to make omelets. Arnie's just going to sit there until the luck changes, but how do you know it's changing unless you make a bet?"

"Is that why you came down here?" I asked, as we fell into a betting line. "To change your luck?"

"It was Arnie's idea, actually," Jay said. "Hollywood Park is such a dreary place even when you're winning, he thought it might help us to be in nice surroundings again."

"You call this nice?" I answered. "Compared to this scene, Hollywood Park is Versailles."

We were standing in line in the upper level of the satellite wagering facility at Del Mar. It was located in the grandstand of the fairgrounds, which for seven weeks of every summer happens also to be the scene of the annual Del Mar race meet. Then the stands and the infield and the stable area are full of people and the horses are out on the track and the old, familiar setting throbs with life, full of the color and excitement of a live race meet. During the rest of the year, however, the grandstand functions mainly as a huge legal bookie joint, a place for horseplayers to come and bet while watching the races from Santa Anita or Hollywood Park piped in on television monitors scattered strategically throughout the premises. In the Turf Club, which has a dress code requiring jackets for the men and a minimum of respectability from the women, a halfhearted attempt at decorum is maintained, with the bettors sitting at small tables, at the bar, or on sofas and armchairs. In the main betting areas, however, the horseplayers are treated with the casual contempt respectable society always reserves for the people it considers not quite acceptable in its midst. An atmosphere of lugubrious seediness dominates the proceedings, as the bettors squat on plastic chairs at long tables facing the TV screens or huddle against the walls in order to follow the fortunes of their favorites. "Attending a betting satellite bears the same relation to racing as masturbation does to sex," is the way Arnie had put it earlier.

"We are only here for a few hours," Jay now said, as we headed back toward our seats. "The rest of the time we are in Del Mar, which is a lot nicer than finding yourself in Inglewood or some other smog-ridden, trash-strewn area of the great L.A. basin. We needed the change of scenery, Shifty. With you being down here, it seemed a good reason to come."

We settled back into our seats toward the rear as the nearest large screen, about sixty feet away, showed us the horses being loaded into the starting gate for the seventh at Hollywood, a meaningless sprint of seven furlongs for mediocre animals. Mel Ducato's entry, a lightly raced four-year-old wearing front bandages, went into the gate last in one of the outside post positions and promptly broke last when the starter sent the race off. He was eight lengths behind when the leaders reached the turn, but had begun to move up and was showing signs of life. Halfway around the curve, just as I was becoming interested and had stood up to get a better view, the screen went black. A groan of frustration went up from the small crowd around us, but apparently it was such a usual occurrence that no one seemed surprised. By the time the technical difficulty had been overcome and the picture reappeared, the field had crossed the finish line and the horses were being pulled up or were coming back toward the winner's circle. It was another twenty or thirty seconds before we learned that Ducato's champion had finished first, getting up in the last jump to win by a head over the longest shot in the race. He paid $10.80 to win and $6.40 to place, which enchanted me, as I had bet fifty dollars on him. Jay had wagered far more than I had, but mainly in various exotic combinations—exactas and triples—and so had barely broken even, since he hadn't used the long shot. "Never mind," he said. "We are clearly unsalted and can now wager with gusto."

We did, indeed, hit the next two races, with Arnie coming out of his shell to strike for a couple of hundred dollars in the ninth, and we left the fairgrounds feeling better about our lives in general. Even Arnie went out with a smile on his face and humming Cole Porter, his favorite composer. The miracle of a winner can heal even the most broken soul.

Jay and I went jogging along the beach later that afternoon, as the sun began to dip toward the horizon. The tide was all the way out and it was fun to run along the water's edge on the hard, packed sand, with small wading birds scurrying away before us on a blur of bony legs and gulls swooping past us overhead. Out beyond the breakers a flight of brown pelicans skimmed the surface and a fresh, cold breeze off the water hustled us along. I thought I was in reasonably good shape, but after about a mile and a half, on our way back toward the motel, Jay began gradually to pull away from me and then sprinted the last hundred yards or so, while I slowed to a walk. When I finally caught up with him again, he and Arnie were sitting on a blanket in the sand, with open beer cans in their hands. "Whew," I gasped, sinking down beside them, "I am out of shape."

"You ought to get on a program," Jay advised me. "Once you hit forty, Shifty, you have to work to stay in condition."

"I don't know, Fox, it's never been my thing," I confessed. "I do work out with that women's defense class one or twice a month and then every day on my moves for two or three hours. But that's it."

"If God had wanted us to run," Arnie observed, "He would have given us four legs and smaller brains and put saddles on our backs. Anyway, look at me. I'm sixty-four years old and I get all the exercise I need walking back and forth to the betting windows. A women's defense class, Shifty? What the hell is that?"

"It's great," I said. "It relies on speed, indirection, hitting vulnerable points, all talents I use in magic."

"Your heart needs to work, Arnie," Jay warned him.

"My heart gets plenty of work just from watching jockeys and trainers butchering my horses," Arnie said. "Any more work and I'll have a stroke. A pox on exercise, I need peace of mind. A man could die just from watching what they do to me every week."

Arnie went on to recount all the misdemeanors and crimes that had been perpetrated against him during the course of the past two weeks until Jay finally cut him off. "Jesus, Arnie, give me a break," he said. "You're beginning to sound like Angles and the Weasel and Pinhead and all the other turf paranoids. Besides, we just had a nice winning day, we're in Del Mar on one of the most beautiful beaches in the world, Shifty is going to wow us later with his magic, what else do you want from life?"

Arnie smiled. Hunched into his brown duffel coat and sitting cross-legged on the sand, he looked like a fat old hermit crab, his small, shrewd eyes peering out at the world for passing tidbits. "Ah, well," he said, with a sigh, "you're right, of course. But it isn't exercise that will decide our fate, it's genes and luck. My mother used to tell me that the secret to a long life was good digestion, and to have good digestion, she insisted, you had to masticate really well."

"You mean chew," Jay said.

"She always said masticate," Arnie said. "The woman was a fount of erudition. She never used one syllable where two or three would do the job. So masticate it was. When I went off to Catholic boarding school, with a vocabulary awash in euphemisms, I told all my grubby classmates how to run their lives. I thought that's what my parent would expect of me. So one day this priest calls me in and asks me if I've been telling everybody to masticate and I said sure, so he washes out my mouth with soap and tells me that if I masticate every day, as I had conscientiously claimed to be doing, I would go blind and spend all eternity in hell. That's how I learned two important things in life. One, never give unsolicited advice, and two, you will never go broke underestimating the intelligence of the ruling classes."

We sat on the beach drinking beer until the sun went down in a sudden flash of blue and orange and dusk began to fall. Two long-legged California beauties ran past our observation post, ponytails flapping in the breeze as a light fog began to drift in off the water. The sight reminded me of Linda Cameron, but then I hadn't been able to get her out of my mind since our last meeting at the club two nights earlier. I stood up. "Time to go to work," I said. "Why don't you guys come down for the second show? I'll hold a table for you."

"By the way, how's your filly doing?" Jay asked, as he gathered up the blanket and we headed back toward the motel.

"Fine, I think," I said. "I'm going out there tomorrow to see her. She's at Sovereign, which is only about an hour from here. I'm leaving pretty early. Want to come?"

"No, I have to handicap," Jay said. "I think I'm getting a handle on this meet now."

"A portent of untold wealth to come," Arnie said.

"You will not regret my decision, believe me," the handicapper assured us. "Unless the Dummy God is on his throne again, the outcome will be in the hands of the informed and the skilled."

"We're all beginning to sound like Arnie," I said.

"Will we see you at the races?" Jay asked.

"I don't know. Depends what time we get back."

"We?"

"I'm taking Linda Cameron with me, maybe her husband, too," I said, annoyed at myself for having revealed my plan. The less my friends knew about Linda Cameron and my feelings about her, I thought, the better. "They own a piece of her, you know. That's how I'm in the chips these days."

"Oh, yeah, I meant to ask you about that," Jay said, as we reached the stairway leading to our rooms. "What do you make of Cameron?"

"He's a boor, but I've only met him once. Why?"

"You haven't heard about him being connected to the Fazzini brothers and Rhineland?"

"Tony Huge? No."

"The *Times* had an interesting story a couple of days ago," Arnie said. "Seems they've been involved in rigging prices on jobs all over, but especially around L.A. and San Diego. The Fazzinis would overbid on a job, get the contract, and kick back. Cameron was apparently in on a number of these deals. Nothing too unusual, Shifty—just the time-honored American pursuit of the inside fix."

"There was some big land deal north of San Diego, around Ramona. In fact, I think it involves Sovereign Acres."

"Anything concrete?"

"Lots of concrete," Arnie said. "That's what Rhineland Sand and Stone deals in."

"What exactly are they supposed to have done?"

"The story had no specific numbers," Jay said, "but essentially it's something along the lines of bidding on a job, corrupting the officials in charge of awarding the contracts, kicking back under the table, greasing politicians and bureaucrats, socking the city for cost overruns, padding payrolls, working sweetheart deals with building unions, buying off inspectors, that kind of thing."

"Nothing major," Arnie added, "just the healthy American pursuit of a buck. I love free enterprise, don't you? I wonder when somebody's going to try it."

"About the same time we give Christianity a whirl," I said. "So where does Sovereign come in?"

"I don't know," Jay said. "That was different, apparently. Something about water rights."

"And Cameron's involved in all this?"

"I wouldn't say that," Jay answered. "He's in maybe ankle-deep at the moment. His name keeps cropping up in connection with a couple of ventures."

"And they haven't located Giorgio Fazzini yet," Arnie added.

"Rhineland is in receivership and there's an ongoing investigation," Jay continued, "but nobody's come up with anything. A lot of people think Giorgio's at the bottom of it or that he may have bought it, too. The theory is that whoever hit Tony also took out Giorgio."

"Nice people you're involved with, Shifty," Arnie said, as we parted company on the second-floor landing. "Watch yourself."

"Listen, I've got the guy's money in the bank and I still have control of the filly," I said. "That's all I care about."

Jay smiled at me. "Yeah, and I hear Mrs. Cameron is a blond goddess."

"Her husband collects guns," I said. "He probably knows how to shoot some of them."

"Be careful, Shifty," Jay said, as he opened his door and let himself in. "Your partner doesn't sound like your average horse owner. You don't want to find yourself standing in cement at the bottom of a pool somewhere."

"A heartwarming thought, Jay. You go handicap, I'll make magic."

"And I will bask in the wisdom of my years," Arnie said, "which informs me that all is rarely for the best in this best of all possible worlds."

Voltaire would have loved Arnie.

Linda Cameron was waiting for me in front of her house when I showed up there early the following morning, just before seven. She was dressed in tennis sneakers, scuffed blue jeans, and a dark green cowboy shirt, open at the neck and with the sleeves rolled up above the elbows. She was wearing no makeup and her hair was loosely tied back with a big rubber band. As I pulled into the driveway in front of the house, a sleek black Doberman swooped toward the car from around the corner like a torpedo. "Thor! Heel!" Linda called out sharply. The dog stopped in his tracks, then reluctantly backed up toward her. "Sit!" Linda said and the animal sank back on its haunches, its gaze still focused on the car. Luckily, I had the top up and felt reasonably safe. "It's okay," Linda said. "He won't do anything unless I tell him to."

"I'm glad you're here," I said, as I opened the door and emerged. "This doesn't look like your average friendly neighborhood pooch."

"He isn't," she said. "That's why I thought I'd wait for you. We were down at the stables with the horses and then Thor took off on his own. I knew he'd hear the car and come running, so I decided to greet you personally. He's a guard dog, but I guess you knew that.''

I looked at Thor. The dog was sitting quietly in place, but his mouth was open, revealing a formidable set of choppers, and his black eyes remained intently focused on me. "Are you sure he's safe?"

"Oh, yes, he's a great dog, actually," Linda said. "Just a big puppy with people he knows."

"Uh-huh, sure," I agreed. "But maybe you'd better put a sign up. You know, 'Beware of the dog' or something. You don't want your friendly delivery people torn to pieces right in front of your eyes. It tends to discourage service."

"Oh, I know," she said, patting the dog affectionately on the head and scratching behind his ears. "He only got here last night, poor baby. We had him flown out ahead of the others because Michael said we needed some protection right away. The security system won't be in for another week or so, so now we have Thor in the house. Eventually, he'll be out in the back in a special pen we're having built for him. Once the outside fencing is in, he'll be out only when we're away and there'll be signs up and everything. He's better than any security system all by himself. Of course we have to keep him away from the other dogs, too. He intimidates them so."

"Yeah, he's a sweetheart, I can tell," I said, smiling but keeping my distance from him.

"You can pet him, if you want."

"That's swell of you, Linda, but I think I'll pass."

"He's a wonderful dog, really. He's just trained to obey whatever Michael and I tell him to do."

"What happens if you and Michael have an argument?"

"I don't know," she said, looking as if the idea had never crossed her mind. "He obeys both of us, but I think he's more my dog than Michael's. Michael hardly ever sees him and he doesn't spend any time with him. I take him along to the stables and out for rides and stuff."

"So your horses have arrived?"

Her face lit up and became positively radiant. "Oh, yes, two of them. They came in yesterday morning. Want to see them? Do we have time?"

"Sure. Maggie's not going anywhere."

With Thor at our heels, we walked around the house down to the stables, where a young Mexican in sandals and floppy work pants was stacking bales of hay at one end of the barn. He smiled and nodded to Linda, but I noticed that he kept a wary eye on the dog. "That's Pablo," Linda said, as we went inside. "I hired him yesterday and Thor already knows he belongs here. He's such a sweet boy, aren't you, baby?" And she leaned down to pat the dog on the head again. The animal licked her hand in gratitude.

"Ah, but does Pablo know Thor?" I said. "He didn't look all that enchanted to see him again. Knowing Thor is sort of like being friendly to your neighborhood psychopath."

"Oh, Lou, you don't know anything about animals, do you?"

"Not much," I confessed. "I like them mainly from a distance, with saddles and little men on their backs and my money riding with them."

I don't think she heard my flip answer, because by that time we had reached the first of the stalls containing her show horses. She leaned in and clucked softly to the animal, which now turned slowly and lumbered toward her. He was a huge bay gelding with a long, powerful-looking neck and the serene, self-satisfied expression of an established virtuoso. He thrust his head into her arms and she reached up to pet him vigorously. "My God, he's huge," I said.

"Well over seventeen hands and he's fourteen years old now," she said. "You don't recognize him?"

"The face is familiar, but then every horse looks like every other horse to me. Why should I know him?"

"This is Whata Dude," she explained. "He was a pretty good racehorse in his day."

"Hey, I do know him. I even bet on him a few times. He won a couple of stakes races at four and five. He was a miler with one big explosive move who had to come always on the outside or he'd hang. I was at the track the day he broke down. I think he was nine then. I wondered what had happened to him. I kind of figured maybe the killer got him."

"Who's that?" she asked, alarmed.

"It's racing terminology for the people who come around the tracks to buy the old hard knockers and the cheap mares who can't compete anymore and have no value in the breeding shed," I explained. "They show up with their vans and take the old horses away. Nobody talks about it in the backstretch. It's one of racing's dirty little secrets."

"How awful! What happens to them?"

"They get carted off to a slaughterhouse, Linda."

"And they allow that? These horses that have run their hearts out and earned hundreds of thousands of dollars for people? That's horrible!"

"Well, you do own dogs and cats, don't you?"

"What's that got to do with it?"

"Pet food."

"Oh."

She looked stricken, so I decided to change the subject. "How did you acquire Whata Dude?"

"We bought him at a sale back East, in Maryland, when Michael was back there on business," she answered. "I was looking for a good jumper and Michael asked around for me. The owner was the guy who had bred him, a wonderful old Irishman named Conway.

59

He told us he had this old Thoroughbred he'd been weaning back from the track and teaching him how to jump. We paid twelve thousand dollars for him."

"I think in his last race he ran for ten thousand, but he was at the end of his career then. How's he doing?"

"He's won eleven blue ribbons for me," Linda said, smiling and again patting her champion on his long neck as he now bobbed his head up and down in approval. "Isn't he a darling? He's worth probably a quarter of a million now, but I'd never sell him. When he's through in the show ring, he'll always have a home with me. I think that's terrible about the killer. I wish you hadn't told me."

"I wish I didn't know about it, Linda. Arnie would call it mankind in action."

"Who's Arnie?"

"The only true philosopher I know," I said. "He's a retired pool shark from New York who plays the horses." I strolled toward the adjacent stall. "And who's this?" I asked, peering into the gloom at a large gray rump. "Looks like your pal Alden Berry."

Linda laughed as she came up beside me. "It does a little," she said. "Oh, Lou, you are funny. This is Escort, my other jumper. He's nowhere near as good as Dude, but he's improving and he's only five. Watch out for him, though—he bites."

As if to confirm her warning, the horse now turned and came quickly toward us, his head thrust forward and his ears pinned back. I retreated, but Linda immediately began to scold him. "Don't you try any of that funny stuff with me, you big phony. You just behave yourself." She kept her voice at a light, even pitch and in a matter of seconds had the animal calmed down. "He's just nervous and doesn't like to be surprised," she said. "Aren't you, you big phony?" She grabbed his upper lip and pulled affectionately on it, while also patting him on the neck. By the time she let him go, he had calmed down and was gazing at her with the soft, liquid stare of a trusting child.

"You certainly have a way with animals," I said.

"That's because I love them," she answered, "and they can sense that. They always know if you're afraid or hostile and they react accordingly. This one was a basket case when we got him, almost a rogue. He must have been mistreated when he was small. He's calmed down a lot. He can't do much in the ring yet, but I'm bringing him along slowly and he's learning. By the time Dude retires, he'll be all right, maybe better than all right. I'm anxious to start working with him again, but we haven't got our ring ready, the fences and jumps in and all that. I hope to get going on a program again in a few more days."

"So now I know how you pass your time."

"Yes, it's a full-time job running a big house and taking care of all these animals and working with them. I'd do it professionally, if I could."

"Why can't you?"

"Well, I'm married, obviously."

"I gather Michael's away a lot."

"Yes, he travels a good deal, mostly on business."

"You never go with him?"

"No, only every now and then. If there are animals, especially horses . . ." She never finished the sentence, as if it should have been clear to me by now that she had nothing to add; Michael was Michael and she had her clearly defined role in his life and that was that. She gave Escort one last affectionate pat, leaned down once more to scratch Thor behind the ears, then headed briskly back up toward the house, with the dog trotting along beside her. "Come on, would you like a cup of coffee before we go?"

"I wouldn't mind."

"I'm sorry, I should have thought of it earlier. I was so excited about the horses."

As we walked up the meadow toward the house, one of the French doors onto the patio opened and Michael Cameron stepped out into the early-morning haze. He was dressed in a dark gray business suit, but was in the process of tugging off his necktie. "Oh, Michael, you're home," Linda said, obviously surprised, as the dog sprinted toward his master. "I thought you were coming tomorrow. You were going to call me."

"Yeah, well, we got through last night, so I just decided to get on a plane," he said, leaning down to greet Thor, as the animal suddenly slowed down and then cringingly crept up to him. "The fucking lawyers, I couldn't take one more day of it." Thor dissolved into a parody of servile delight, his tongue slobbering over the big man's hand.

"Lou and I were just going out to Sovereign to see the filly," Linda said. "Dude and Escort came in yesterday and—"

"Is there any coffee?"

"I just made some, in the kitchen."

"Get me a cup."

Linda glanced hesitantly my way, smiled briefly, then hurried past him into the house. Thor stayed behind, groveling at his master's feet.

"Nice place you've got here," I said. "Linda was showing me around."

"It's all right," he said. "I bought it for her." He gazed at me as if not quite convinced that I had legitimate business on the premises. "Is the horse all right?"

"Oh, sure, as far as I know," I said. "She just needs a little time. These young animals—"

"More fucking vet bills, I know that," he said. "This guy Gantry must get kickbacks from his vets. They cost more than doctors, for Christ's sake."

"I wouldn't know about Gantry," I said. "Pickard's honest. He doesn't pad his bills."

"How do you know he doesn't?"

"He just doesn't. He's a friend of mine and I trust him."

"You trust him? You trust a lot of people, do you?"

"Not many, a few. He's one of them."

"Yeah, well, we'll see. I'm beginning to think I was a fool to get into this business, as if I haven't got enough problems."

"It's about twenty to one against making any money," I told him. "It's like buying an over-the-counter stock in a highly speculative enterprise."

"So far I've put in over three hundred thousand," he said, "and I haven't see a dime back."

"It takes a while, especially with young horses, because you can't rush them. But we'll do fine with Mad Margaret."

"You think so, huh?"

"Yes."

"Well, I think you're full of shit."

"Oh, Michael, why are you so rude?" Linda asked, appearing in the doorway with a coffee tray. "I don't understand you sometimes."

"You don't understand me at all," Cameron said, picking up the mug nearest to him and taking a swallow from it. "But then why the hell should you?" He glanced my way again. "Okay, magician, do your stuff. Make me a winner and I'll kiss your ass. Fucking horses. I might as well have sunk my money into a Brazilian gold mine." He took another swallow, then headed for the house. "I need a shower." And he disappeared inside.

"I'm sorry," Linda said, setting the tray down on the patio table. "He must have had a very bad time. He isn't always like this."

"It's okay," I assured her. "I know it's nothing personal."

"I don't know how you take your coffee," Linda said, hovering over the tray like a nervous humming bird. "Sugar? Cream?"

"A little of both."

She handed me the other mug. "I hope it's all right."

I took a sip. "It's fine," I said, "really. Listen, maybe we should do this another day. I can come back tomorrow."

"No, please, Lou. Just give me a few minutes. He probably hasn't slept and he hates lawyers. I'll just go see how he's doing and then we'll go, all right?"

"If you say so, Linda."

"Please. Thanks."

She went into the house and I sat down to wait for her. As I lingered there, sipping my coffee and watching the haze over the meadow below begin to dissipate under the force of the sun, I again tried to put the two of them together. I couldn't make the connection, but then, I reasoned, perhaps I didn't want to. Who was Linda Cameron, anyway? All I saw was an extraordinarily attractive woman whom I wanted desperately to take to bed, nothing, in essence, but a sex object. And, for all I knew, she had nothing going for her but her looks. Then I thought about her and her animals and the way she related to them, with love and kindness, and I couldn't put that aspect of her together with Michael Cameron either. What could he offer her but money? I laughed, shut my eyes, and leaned back in my chair, the coffee resting in my lap. Money, the money that makes the world go around, for in the beginning there was money and only money and on the seventh day He rested on His money and . . .

I must have dozed off, because when I opened my eyes the sun had burned away the remaining mist and

Linda was bending over me, smiling. "Lou," she said softly, "we can go now. Michael's asleep. He was just exhausted."

"Oh. I must have dozed off. What time is it?"

"About eight-thirty. Shall we go?"

"Sure." I put my mug down and heaved myself to my feet. Then I heard a warning growl and I turned around. Thor was sitting a few feet away from me, poised to attack. "Has he been here all this time?"

"I think so."

"Good thing I stayed put, isn't it?"

"Oh, Lou, I told you he wouldn't hurt you. You have to trust—"

"You know what this old Italian horseplayer used to say?"

"I can't imagine."

"It is good to trust—"

"Yes, it is."

"—but it is better not to trust."

chapter 5
RANK EARLY

I found her presence next to me in the car so unsettling that, to cover my confusion, I talked steadily. I had put the top down and cruised along at about forty-five, as the narrow, two-lane road spun itself out through the low hills toward Ramona. She sat and listened, her hair blowing loosely in the wind, her eyes alive with pleasure. "Oh, it's so beautiful," she said, as we took a rise and then descended into a still unspoiled valley of orange and lemon groves. In the distance a ridge of dark mountains seemed to be propping up the sky, now a deep cloudless blue above the long rows of dark green citrus trees heavy with fruit. "If only they would leave it alone."

"Who? The developers?" I asked.

"Yes."

"Isn't that what Michael does?"

"Yes. I try not to think about it." She glanced at

me before continuing. "Oh, Lou, I'm sorry—I interrupted you."

"I don't even remember what I was saying. It couldn't have been important."

"You—you were telling me about your magic."

"Maybe I'll just shut up for a while," I said. "I've been babbling away like some idiot TV personality the whole trip instead of letting you enjoy it."

"No, please, I love to listen to you. Really. You know, I feel as if I've known you such a long time."

"What do you mean?"

"As if we met in some other life or something. Is that crazy?"

"No. I feel the same way about you."

"Is that why you think you're talking too much?"

"Yes. I like you far too well, Linda, for my peace of mind."

"So that's why you didn't call me right away when you came down here."

"Yes."

She didn't answer and I tried not to look at her, but kept my eyes firmly fixed on the road. We topped another small crest, then began a long, gently curving descent into a narrow valley with a triangular plowed field to one side and a vineyard to the left, the even lines of tiny green grapes laid out with mathematical precision up a slow rise to the white bulk of the winery itself. After about another quarter mile, the highway veered sharply to the left toward a crossroad with two gas stations and a few small stores. Behind them, about a hundred yards or so up the hill, a small motel nestled in a grove of eucalyptus and sycamores. "Don't you need gas?" Linda asked, as we slowed down for the stop sign.

I looked at the gauge. "We have about a quarter of a tank. These little cars don't use much—"

"Stop here, Lou," she said. "Let's get some gas. And I need to stretch my legs anyway."

I slowed down, intending to pull into the first of the stations, a Texaco on the corner before the stop sign. "No," Linda said, "not here."

"Where? The other one's on the other side—"

"Oh, Lou—up there." And she pointed to the motel.

"They don't sell gas—"

"Honestly, you are so dense. And you're supposed to be a magician."

My face flushed, but I didn't answer. I passed the Texaco station, stopped, then turned left after the stop sign and drove up the narrow road to the motel. It consisted of a strip of shabby-looking little white cabins with an office at the near end under a row of trees. I parked under the shade of one of them and turned to look at her. "Are you sure you want to do this?" I asked.

"Don't you?"

"Yes."

She leaned forward and kissed me, no longer lightly but with passion. I got out of the car and walked into the office, where a fat woman of about sixty sat knitting steadily behind the counter while watching a soap opera on a TV screen in one corner of the room. She had arms as big as my thighs and a flat, round face all but invisible beneath a layer of fat and thick rimless eyeglasses. I registered under the name of Harold Houdini and paid her twenty-six dollars in cash, after which she handed me the key to the cabin at the very end of the row. "There ain't no phone in the room," she said, without even glancing away from the screen. "In case you need to make a call you can do it from in here or there's a pay phone across the street. My name's Pearl, by the way."

"Must be a good show," I couldn't resist observing.

"Bunch of damn fools can't make up their minds whether they're comin' or goin' or nothin', but it passes the time. Checkout is noon."

"We won't be here that long."

"Drop the key in the mail slot if there ain't nobody here. My husband's sick."

"Sure thing. Thanks."

I let myself out, got back in the car, and drove to the end of the row of cabins, where I parked around the corner, out of sight from the rest of the lot. "Do you think anyone could see us here?" Linda asked, as I fiddled with the key in the front door.

"No, but I keep thinking about Michael and his gun collection."

"Oh, Lou, you are funny."

The cabin was hot inside and smelled musty, as if no one had used it for a long time. The wallpaper was dark and flowery and the room contained a couple of green armchairs upholstered in Naugahyde, a battered-looking dark brown wooden dresser, two floor lamps, a small desk covered with brochures about the area and the nearby winery, and an old-fashioned double bed with a brass frame that sagged slightly in the middle. An open closet door revealed a row of lopsided wire hangers and the bathroom consisted of a stall shower, a toilet, and a tiny metal sink. The single decoration, mounted on the far wall, was a framed tinted photograph of a wilderness scene, complete with brook, tall pines, and snow-topped mountains in the background.

"This is pretty depressing," I said. "Are you sure you want to do this?"

"I do, if you do."

"Well, I guess I do."

"Then shut the door."

"Wait, let's open a window."

She did so, but it didn't help; a hot breeze blew in through the curtains. I turned on the air-conditioning, but it made such a clanging noise that I immediately turned it off, then I closed the door and the room was plunged into darkness. I saw her outlined against the light filtering through the curtains and then she came into my arms.

We broke out of the starting gate together and went head to head in the early stages. She was just breezing, well within herself, but I had a tight hold and I was fighting it all the way. I mean, I was rank, I didn't know what to do with myself. I'd have lost it all early, if she hadn't been going so easy and been so gentle all down the backside, coming on with that fluid, graceful motion that I'd found so thrilling from the first time I clocked her, that day in the Turf Club. A couple of times I felt I might be lugging out, making moves too soon I wasn't sure I could make at all with her, but she always adjusted and got me back on the right lead, though it wasn't easy. I wanted her too much and so I couldn't find a rhythm, couldn't stay on the right lead and into stride. For what seemed like an eternity I was all over the track, ready to bolt at any second.

She waited for me to settle down and I discovered she had great hands, gentle and strong and ultimately soothing. As we began the long, sweeping turn for home, she came up alongside again, matching me stride for stride, the two of us locked as one, insepara-ble to the casual eye, the ground seeming to float away beneath us as we moved. Twice I accidentally pulled away from her, but always she would bring me back, neither of us wanting to end too soon, each of us in-tent on bringing out the best in the other, no whipping or flailing about or awkward, brutal movements to mar the needed effect, spoil the image of the event I had nurtured in my thoughts for all the time I'd known her.

At the head of the lane, with the end in sight down the long straightaway, I almost rushed it, but, as before, she was there and I found myself temporarily blocked, forced to check and steady until, on the right lead once again, I'd resume the run for home, picking up the tempo slowly, reaching out and feeling as if my whole life were flowing beneath me, all of me off the ground in one tremendous surge. No one could separate us, I felt sure, as I flattened out, feeling myself completely at one with her, blending into, over, and around her as we drove together for the wire. Past the eighth pole, with a roaring in my ears, blinded by the thrill of the race itself, I rose up out of the saddle just long enough to make absolutely sure of her before reaching up along her neck, my hands high up on her, every muscle in my body committed to the experience, and then I flattened out again, pumping like a man possessed. I never knew exactly when I hit the wire, because the roaring in my ears was so loud that it drowned out all rational calculations, but I do know that she was right there with me, that we hit it almost exactly together in the kind of photo finish, nose to nose, lip to lip, that no one could have predicted when it began and that can only happen rarely, so rarely that the event is invariably immortalized, cherished forever in memory for all time to come.

And then, after it was over, with both of us eased up and galloping out, drained and exhausted, but exultant from the event, we came back together toward reality, feeling, at least in my case, like champions. No trophies, no flowery wreaths, no photographs, no ecstatic friends and relatives, no tangible payoff of any sort and no post-race interviews—only the long dreamy cooling out in each other's arms, before the necessary but unwelcome return to mere reality . . .

*   *   *

"Where did you learn to make love like that?"

"Me? What about you?"

"It's never been like that with Michael, never."

"You're incredible, Linda, absolutely incredible."

"Don't say that."

"You are. Really. Who with, then?"

"Who with what?"

"I mean, if not with Michael, who?"

"No one," she said, "there's never been anyone."

"It doesn't matter, but I want to believe you."

"Please do believe me. Only you, Lou."

"You seemed to know—I don't know—everything."

"Everything?"

"About me. I could have . . . I mean, several times . . ."

"Oh, don't say it. It doesn't matter. It was wonderful."

"Yes, it was."

"And you were wonderful."

"We were both wonderful. Can I kiss you again?"

"Please do . . ."

"Oh, that was nice."

"Again . . ."

"Again?"

"Yes, yes."

"I don't think we should do this again so soon . . ."

"No?"

"No, Linda. I'm not sure—"

"It's all right," she said. "It's just fine. I think I want you all the time."

"Oh. That's marvelous."

"You know, it was when I saw your hands."

"My hands?"

"Yes, that first day in the Turf Club, when you did your magic."

"Oh."

"You have the most beautiful hands, Lou," she said, "like a surgeon's or a concert pianist's. I watched them. You were doing your magic for me and all I could see was your hands."

"They're all I've got, really."

"You ought to insure them."

"Too expensive, much too expensive."

"But what if something happened to them?"

"That wouldn't be good. Something did once."

"What?"

"A few years ago," I said. "I was cleaning my apartment and a screen fell and broke the little finger on my left hand." I held it out to her in the dim light. "Feel the little knob on the side of the knuckle? Right there?"

"Yes."

"I can't quite straighten it out anymore, but it's okay now. I had a cast on it and I couldn't do any magic for weeks and then it was months until I could do everything I can do. It was a bad time."

"And the scar? There, on your palm?" she asked. "Was that also from the screen?"

"No, that was something else," I said. "That was from a guy who wanted to kill me. He had a knife."

"Oh, what happened?"

"It's a long story. I'll tell you sometime. I fought him off, mainly because I practice self-defense. Anyway, the scar will fade after a while and it doesn't bother me now."

"I never saw it until I began to really look at your hands," she said. "They look, well, like hands, but when you do your magic they acquire a life of their own. I mean, you sit there and you talk and all that, but all the time your hands are doing these incredibly

73

beautiful things. Do all magicians have hands like yours?"

"I don't know. I never thought about it."

"I'll bet they don't," she said. "Nobody could have hands like yours. What time is it?"

"I don't know."

She sat up and leaned over me. "I feel like I've been here all my life."

"Don't exaggerate, Linda."

"The best part of my life." She came in closer and kissed me, her hair tumbling down over us like a feathery veil. Her mouth was warm and open. She moved a long leg over me, the flesh of her thigh gleaming in the darkness. "Lou."

"Yes?"

"Is it too soon?"

"No."

"Then . . ."

The time was short and sweet, not quite a track record, but quick. It was a short burst out of the gate, all out from the start, with little finesse and no tactics, just hard and fast and furious, riding right down to the bone, no breather anywhere, just a digging in and a booting and a scooting and a final whoop-de-do, a cry of triumph as the end came in one last frantic lunge, every fiber of me braced against her as her knees bent and her ankles locked on me, her arms flung out as if to grasp the sky, then her fingers tight on the frame of the bed as she rose to the effort, a tremendous upward drive that was not a counter measure but was on the bit all the way, a yielding intended only to achieve a victory, which it did. I pulled her to me and she lay beside me, so moved that, to my amazement, she began to cry and I held her until she stopped and then she lay in my arms until at last she began to talk . . .

* * *

She was an orphan, she told me, and had never known her real parents. She had memories of a green land, with a brook running through it, and of mountains, and days filled with the silence of the wilderness. Sometimes she dreamed of this place, which also contained a presence that had been warm and comforting. "I was lying in this bed, it must have been a crib because it had high wooden slats," she recalled, "and he was there, sort of looming over me. And I felt this terrific sense of being—I don't know—treasured. I was safe as long as he was there. It's the strongest memory I have of anyone, but I can never make out what he looks like. I only knew I was safe as long as he was there."

"And your mother?"

"Nothing, absolutely nothing. I suppose she must have died when I was very young or maybe in childbirth, I don't know."

"You never tried to find out?"

"No. Oh, I did ask questions, of course, but nobody told me anything."

"Why not?"

"Well, I didn't even know I was an orphan until I was about nine," she said. "Then some kid in school made a remark and that made me begin to think about it."

"What sort of remark?"

"About how different I looked."

"Different from what?"

"From my parents," she explained. "They were both short and skinny and kind of dark, whereas, even at nine, I was already pretty tall for my age and, of course, I had this big mane of blond hair."

"No sisters or brothers?"

"No. It was just that I looked so different," she said, "so one day I asked them about it and they told me. They had adopted me right after I was born, which is strange, because they aren't in my earliest memories at all. They wouldn't tell me where and they wouldn't tell me anything else about it."

Their names were Albert and Mimi Bergman, she informed me, and they had lived in Chicago and Miami, Florida, and also in California before moving to Louisville, Kentucky, where Linda had spent most of her childhood. "That's where I fell in love with horses," she said. "The other animals just sort of came along afterwards. When I was about sixteen, I ran away to the racetrack. I was too young and they got me back, but not for very long."

"I'm getting a message in here," I said. "You didn't like your adoptive parents."

"I hated them. Actually, I despised them more than I hated them."

"Why? Were they abusive or mean?"

"Mean, yes, but they didn't abuse me. Well, there was this one time—" She interrupted herself and pulled away from me, sat up in bed with her back against the brass railings of the headboard, her knees pulled up to her chin, as if protectively rolling herself into a ball. Her eyes gleamed with tears in the dim light of the room. "Do you really want to hear this?"

"Not if it pains you too much, no."

"He got into bed with me, but before he could do anything my mother came in and began screaming at him. I was thirteen then. It was horrible."

"I can imagine. And he never tried that again?"

"No, but not because he didn't want to. He was afraid to."

"Because of her?"

"No, it was something else," she said. "I remember when she was screaming at him, she said something about somebody taking care of him or having him taken care of, something like that. And he stopped right away. I remember the look on his face. It was incredible. It was all this rage and fear and he was shouting at her and threatening her, but it didn't have anything to do with her. It had to do with something or someone else. I'd never seen such hatred on a person's face before and I became hysterical. I mean, I didn't realize until later what he wanted to do to me. I only figured that out for myself much later. He hadn't had a chance to touch me or anything and I was pretty naive, I didn't know anything. No, I was terrified by the rage, the hatred I saw on his face when she was screaming at him. He stayed away from me after that.''

"And you never talked about it with your adopted mother either?"

"No. I despised her, too. She was so weak. But not only that—she was as conniving and mean as he was, only she was weak and afraid.''

"Of what?"

"Of him, of everything, Anyway, shortly after that episode they sent me away to boarding school in the East and I didn't see much of them anymore. I wouldn't even go home for holidays or anything. I'd go and stay with friends.''

"Didn't they make you? What did you do for money?"

"Well, that's another thing. I always had my own money. They always sent me money and paid all my bills and everything, but the money came from a bank in Chicago. It turned out that I had a trust fund and these checks arrived. If it had been up to him, he'd have kept the money, I know that, but he had to give it to me, the allowance part of it, once I went away to boarding school. I never found out exactly what the arrangement was, but I'm sure they were paid to raise me and take care of me and that money would have stopped the minute they tried to do anything wrong with it. It must have been quite a lot of money, Lou. I mean, Albert and Mimi were the two meanest, tightest people I've ever known. All they thought about all the time was money."

"What did they do?"

"He was in real estate and he was also a private moneylender and coin dealer," she said. "He was really money-mad. He was a real shark. She used to help him. They had an office in downtown Louisville and they worked out of there. I went there once with Mimi, when some babysitter didn't show up—I must have been five or six—and all I remember is Albert back there in sort of a cage where you had to press a button just to get in to see him and it was dark and kind of dingy, sleazy, like everything about them, everything they touched. I didn't stay long. Albert was screaming about how he'd been cheated and he'd get even someday and I began to cry and he made her take me home. God, I hated him so. After I got to be eighteen, I never saw either of them again. They tried to stay in touch, but I wouldn't have anything to do with them."

She had left school after graduation and come back to Louisville, but not to live with the Bergmans. Mimi cried and both of them tried to persuade her to come back home and go on to college, but all she could think about was getting away from them for good. She was still receiving an income from her trust fund, so she rented a small apartment downtown and went to work in a bank as a teller, which was how she happened to meet Mike Cameron. He was heavily involved in a couple of redevelopment projects in the area and he used to come in and out of the bank on business. "He invited me out to dinner," she said, "and that's how it began."

"Was he always as charming and friendly as he is today?" I asked.

"Oh, Lou," she answered, with a little giggle, "he can be so nice, you don't know."

"No, I don't, but I have to believe you, because

otherwise I can't account for your being married to him."

"He just overwhelmed me," she explained. "I'd never had anyone or anything in my life before and he simply came into it and opened up everything for me. I mean, Lou, you have to understand, I was tall and kind of gangly and awkward all through my childhood and had braces on my teeth. I was very shy and I didn't know anything. And I was lonely."

"You? You must have had a thousand guys after you by that time."

"A few," she said, "not many. I was going out on dates, sure, but mostly men just wanted to sleep with me—"

"Understandable."

"Oh, Lou. Anyway, there wasn't anyone in my life then and I was really lonely. Michael took me out that first time to a very nice restaurant, up the river and right on the water, and he was very correct and polite and it was all sort of wonderful. After that, we began dating . . ."

"As the euphemism goes."

"What does that mean?"

"Oh, I'm sorry, Linda. I guess I just don't like your husband much. Or maybe I'm jealous of him."

"Jealous? Why?"

"Because he's had you for—how long now?"

"Ten years."

"That's a long time. When did he begin to change?"

"Change? He's never changed, Lou. He's always been this way, kind of crude and tough. But never with me. I knew he was a tough guy in business and he had all these macho guys who were friends of his—still has them, he hasn't changed in that way, and neither have they—but with me he was always, well, correct."

"You mean he didn't slap you around."

"Lou, why are you so negative?"

"Because I don't like the way he treats you."

"How's that?"

"As if he owns you. You're just another of his possessions, aren't you? Like his grizzly-bear rug and his guns. Maybe one day he'll stuff you and mount you on a wall."

She laughed. "You're funny." Then she turned serious. "Oh, Lou, you don't know what it meant to me to have someone in my life who wanted me so much and gave me everything. I told you, he simply overwhelmed me. I couldn't resist him, that's all."

"And so you got married."

"Yes, about three months later. And would you believe it?"

"What?"

"I never went to bed with him before we got married."

"Why not?"

"He never pushed me or put any pressure on me. I think he was . . . sort of in awe of me."

"I can believe it, Linda. Michael isn't exactly Kevin Costner or Robert Redford."

"Oh, he had all the women he wanted. I mean, he had money—"

"He could buy the women he wanted, that's what you mean, isn't it?"

"I—I suppose so."

"And then he bought you."

"Is that what you think?"

"He did, didn't he? I'm sure you weren't aware of it, Linda. I can understand what it all meant to you, but from his point of view that's exactly what he did."

"You really hate him."

"No, I don't hate him, Linda. I don't like him, mainly because I just sort of generally don't care for the type, but I don't hate him. I can tell you one thing

—I never would have sold him a piece of Mad Margaret if it hadn't been for you."

"I guess I knew that." She suddenly sat up and turned to me, wide-eyed with alarm. "Oh, my God, Lou, what time is it?"

I retrieved my wristwatch from the nightstand and snapped on a reading lamp. "Quarter of eleven. We have plenty of time."

"No, we don't," she said. "I told Michael we'd be home by noon. He wants to take me to lunch, some new place he told me about in Fairbanks Ranch."

"Oh. Well, I guess we'll see Maggie another day. We don't really have time now."

She stared at me and I could see the fear in her eyes. "What will I tell him?"

"Tell him my car broke down and we never got there," I said. "We had to call the auto club or something. By the way, the filly's fine. I called Sovereign yesterday. The heat is out of her legs and she's doing terrific, eating up a storm."

"Oh, I'm so glad."

"Anyway, I'll take you back and we'll go out there again together. How about tomorrow?"

She shook her head. "No, Michael might think it's strange—"

"Screw Michael."

"Please, Lou—try to understand."

"You tell me when."

"Yes, I will. I want to so much."

"Linda . . ."

"Lou, it's late—"

"No, it isn't, not if we're not going to see Maggie."

"Oh . . ."

"Linda—"

"Yes . . . yes . . . oh, yes . . ."

A long, leisurely, easy move this time, once around

the oval, together gently in the morning light, with the
filtered rays of the sun casting an orange glow against
her skin. She reached out gracefully, unhurriedly,
rhythmically, over me this time, with sweat bathing her
shoulders and neck, but only from the heat, not from
the strain of it, her long neck flung back, her golden
mane cascading behind her. The sense of urgency was
gone, replaced by the need to maintain form, to remain ready and eager and in touch. We finished together again and pulled up gradually, then came back
along the outer rail, completely in harmony with each
other, as if we had always been one . . .

chapter 6

SWERVING

Charlie Pickard had told me that Sovereign Acres was a beautiful place, but my first sight of it took my breath away. I had turned off the highway a couple of miles beyond Ramona and driven into the hills along a private paved road that wound for several miles through an unprepossessing countryside of rocky slopes covered mostly by chaparral. Even though there were no signs to advertise Sovereign's presence, I guessed that they must have built the road and widened it to accommodate its horse vans and other traffic, because, as I proceeded, the mountains closed in on me until I felt hemmed in by them; above me on either side loomed precipitous cliffs armed with huge boulders that, I felt sure, could easily be dislodged by the slightest movement of the earth. I wondered if there were another exit, because otherwise a slide could trap everyone depending on this one access.

Suddenly, the road veered right around a sharp corner and debouched into a small valley of gently rolling meadows entirely surrounded by the mountains. Fields of lush grass were divided by white wooden fences into an irregular patchwork of paddocks and enclosures, all of them containing horses, around scattered rows of large rust-colored barns with angular roofs. To my right, a village of whitewashed wooden cottages huddled along the shore of a small lake, framed by stands of oak and sycamores, while in the distance, rising from a knoll above the whole sylvan setting, an enormous white pillared mansion with a domed roof dominated the entire scene. The spectacle was so unexpected and astonishing that I stopped the car long enough to take it all in before proceeding slowly into the valley through a tall set of iron gates on which the letters SA had been mounted in gold.

I drove another fifty yards or so to an open area in front of an old stone water tower covered by a blanket of green ivy, then followed signs that took me to an administration building, the largest of the cottages at the edge of the village. Inside, sitting behind a plain wooden desk flanked by a computer in the front room, I encountered my first human being, a cheerful-looking California golden girl dressed in a green-and-white jump suit with the Sovereign logo sewn in gold above her left breast pocket. "Hi," she said, favoring me with a dazzling array of flawless teeth, "how may we help you?"

"My name's Anderson," I said. "I'm here to see my filly, Mad Margaret. I called yesterday."

Golden girl consulted her appointment book, then looked up at me again. "Oh, yes, Mr. Anderson," she said, with the professional enthusiasm of a football cheerleader, "we've been expecting you. We thought you'd be here earlier."

"I had car problems," I said. "Then I had to take my partner, Mrs. Cameron, home first, as it was too late for her. If you just point me in the right direction, I'm sure I can find my way."

"Oh, you see the work around the barns is over for the day," she said, "and the tours have ended at noon—"

"I don't need a tour," I explained. "I'd just like to see my filly, maybe find out from someone how she's getting along."

"Oh, yes, well—I think Win is at lunch, but I expect him back around two or two-thirty."

"Who's Win?"

"Oh, yes—Win Freeman, he's in charge of the operations here," she said. "He's the one to talk to about your filly. What's her name?"

"Mad Margaret."

"Oh, yes . . ." She turned to her computer and punched out a little melody on it, then studied the screen intently for a minute or so. "Oh, I see now—she's in forty-eight."

"What's that?"

"The barn number."

"Can you show me where that is?"

"Oh, sure, I guess so," she said, looking a little flustered, "but if you could wait till Win gets back—"

"I just want to walk around, stretch my legs a little," I said. "I've been in my car all morning, practically."

"Oh, well, I guess it's all right." She came out from behind her desk and accompanied me to the door. "You go straight down that road about half a mile," she said, pointing in the direction of the mansion. "The last turn you can make before the driveway up to the house, you go left and it's the second barn.

She might be out in the paddock with the other fillies and mares. And I'll tell Win you're here when he comes back."

"Thanks. By the way, whose house is that?"

"Oh, that's Judge Hunter's place. Isn't it wonderful?"

"Very impressive."

"It's modeled on some old Italian drawing of some old villa somewhere," she said. "It has thirty-nine rooms. The Judge began building it when he first bought the ranch. I've never been inside it, but I hear it's fantastic. On Kentucky Derby day, the Judge and Mrs. Hunter throw a big party for everyone on the ranch, so I guess I'll get to see it next year. I've only been here a couple of weeks now."

I thanked her again and set off down the road toward the mansion, whose dome, painted the Sovereign colors of green, white, and gold, sparkled in the afternoon sunlight. In the fields on both sides of me horses grazed, all broodmares with foals by their sides. I had never been on a horse farm before and I found the spectacle moving. I had been in this game as a mere horseplayer, just another guy who went to the track to bet on horses, then had fallen in love with the whole world of racing, beginning with the animals themselves, and become a regular on the backside among the professionals. Now, suddenly, I was being exposed to the source of the whole business, the geography of creation itself.

Several times I paused to take in the whole scene —the rolling meadows, the white fences pasted like ribbons across the landscape, the sharp blue of the lake to my right, the dark mountains thrusting savagely upward toward the sky and throwing the gleaming multicolored mansion into sharp relief—and to my amazement felt myself close to tears. I think it was the innocent beauty of the animals themselves that touched me most in this setting, so far removed from the clamor and excitement of the racetrack, with its often cruel indifference to anything except the outcome of the racing itself and the payoff numbers flashing on the tote board. Just before turning left on the road below the mansion, I paused at the corner of a fence to admire a group of mares grazing only a few feet away from me with their foals beside them. Suddenly, for no evident reason, one of the foals broke away from its mother and bounded out into the open field, kicking up its hindlegs and tossing its head about as if in ecstasy simply at being alive. Soon, however, its courage deserted it and it came trotting back, pressing itself closely to its parent for protection, presumably from me. I laughed and clucked to its mother, hoping to lure them closer, but she showed not the slightest interest, keeping her muzzle buried in the succulent grass.

"Where are you headed? May I give you a lift?" a man's voice called out behind me.

I turned and found myself looking at the strong-jawed, lined face of a gray-haired man gazing at me from behind the wheel of a dark green Jaguar sedan. His left eye was covered by a black patch, but his right one was large, gray, and extraordinarily luminous, focused on me with the intensity of a laser beam. "I was headed for Barn forty-eight," I said. "I came to see my filly."

"Who might that be?"

"Mad Margaret. My trainer, Charlie Pickard, sent her down here for a few weeks. She has tender shins. I'm Lou Anderson."

The leonine head nodded and smiled. "Yes, I saw your name listed for this morning. You're a little late. Mrs. Cameron with you?"

"No, we had car trouble and I had to turn around and drive her home," I explained. "She had a lunch

87

date or something. I came back because I want to see
how Maggie's getting on."

"Pretty good, from what I hear. I talked to Cameron when he called up about her, but all I know is
what Win tells me."

"You're Judge Hunter."

"Jed. Jed Hunter," he said, smiling. "Come on,
get in. I'll run you down there. I hear from everybody
that this is quite a filly."

"Yes, she is," I said. I got in the passenger seat
next to him and he eased the big car toward a cluster
of barns about another half-mile down the road. "This
is very nice of you, but I was enjoying the walk. You
have a beautiful facility here."

"Thank you. It's been my lifelong dream to have a
place like this," he said, in a dark, musical baritone.
"We've had the land for a long time and are adding to
it year by year, but it was a while before I could even
get to the house. The horses came first, of course, and
the building came along with them. There wasn't anything here but brush and rocks when we started, but
there's plenty of water in the southeast end of the valley, so that made it all possible. We dammed a little
stream there and put in the lake as a reservoir. You
from California?"

"Not originally," I confessed, "but I've been out
here about twenty years now."

"That's long enough. Makes you practically a na-
tive. So I guess you know about the droughts and the
water problem in this state. Without the water none of
what you see here could have existed. We'd have had to
pump it in from too far away. We also normally get a
good spring runoff from the mountains, but in recent
years not enough for this operation. Here we are." He
parked in an open space at one end of a large airy
barn with a triangular roof raised above the stalls containing the horses. "You know what stall you're in?"

"No, I don't."

"Well, we'll find her."

We got out of the car and I had another look at Jed Hunter. He was tall, at least six-four or -five, and he stood very straight, like a retired military man. He was dressed in a custom-tailored dark gray business suit, cut in the Western style to fit snugly on his lean, muscular frame, with black boots, a string tie with an ornate silver clasp in the shape of an SA, and a wide leather belt with a large silver buckle, also in the shape of an SA. He was a walking advertisement for his enterprise. He also exuded an aura of tremendous self-assurance and authority, enhanced by the dramatic black eyepatch and his thick head of iron gray hair above a broad, noble-looking forehead and strong jawline. He must have been an intimidating figure in the courtroom, though I had no idea whether he had actually ever been a working judge or whether the title was in some way honorary. At least he looked the part and in Southern California appearance and substance are easily confused.

"Well, Luke ought to be around here someplace and he'll know," Hunter said. "The trouble is, this is the slow part of the day, as you probably know if you've been around horses at all."

"The work gets done early, like at the track," I guessed.

"Yes, and this time of year is breeding and foaling season," Hunter said, "our busiest time. We had three babies this morning and that kept everybody pretty busy. No problems, luckily—three nice easy births, nice-looking foals, everyone of them."

"How big is this operation?"

He smiled. "It seems to get bigger by the minute," he said. "We have about eight hundred broodmares now and a dozen stallions and I guess there's no end to it."

"Well, you have the space for it."

"About two thousand acres, but there isn't any room to expand," he said. "We're using pretty much all of it right now." He strolled into the barn entrance and I followed him. "Where the hell is that old reprobate?"

"Is there any other way to get in and out of this valley besides the road I came in on?" I asked.

"Which way did you come?" He peered into the shadowy interior of the stable. "Luke!" He looked back at me. "From Ramona?"

"Yeah."

"There's another road in and out from the desert, about a mile behind the house," he said, "but we don't use it much. It's pretty steep and full of curves. It works out to a detour of about sixty miles if you need to go up to L.A."

"Well, I guess you have to worry about earthquakes then," I said. "It could seal you off here for quite a while."

"I suppose it could, but I've never been a pessimist, Mr. Anderson," he said. "I just figure that if I go after something hard enough I'll get it. I always have and everything else takes care of itself." He glanced back at me as we walked along a row of stalls and smiled. "Are you worried your filly will get trapped in here?"

"Something like that. She's the only equine asset I have."

"I wouldn't worry," he said. "We're quite a ways from any of the major fault lines. We did a study before we began to build in here. The road gets temporarily blocked from time to time by big boulders and rockslides, but we have good equipment and we get it open again, usually in a matter of hours. This your filly?"

As we talked, Judge Hunter had been leading the way, peering into each stall as we passed by. Now, almost at the end of the row, he had led me to one containing a strong-looking chestnut filly with a small, triangular white blaze between her eyes. It was my filly, all right, and she looked wonderful, standing peacefully facing us in the soft light filtering down from a row of windows directly below the high roof. Her legs were encased in thick protective bandages, but her coat gleamed and her powerful muscles rippled as she now bobbed her head up and down as if in greeting. "Hi, Maggie, how are you doing?" I said cajolingly, leaning in over the half-open stall door. "How are you, sweetheart?"

Horses are supposed to be stupid, so I don't know if Maggie recognized me, but after a moment or two she moved toward me, thrusting her beautiful head out over my shoulder. I patted her neck and reached up to scratch behind her ears, then I looked around for a sack of carrots, all the while continuing to talk softly to her, getting the message across that I was the one person in the whole world she could trust more than any other.

"Looks like you've got a way with horses," Hunter said, with the hint of a smile. "Oh, there he is. Luke, come on down here."

A sturdy-looking man of about fifty with pink cheeks and the stub of a spent cigar clamped into a corner of his mouth was coming toward us from the far end of the shedrow. He was also dressed in the Sovereign working uniform, but wore a stained green baseball cap pushed up off his forehead. He had the air of a man who had been born in a stall and had never passed a single day of his life out of sight of a horse. "Hell, Judge, I didn't know you was comin' down here," he said. "I'd have been here. Sherry called me from the office, so I come on down. Everythin' all right?"

"I guess that's what we need to ask you, Luke,"

Hunter answered. "This gentleman here is Mr. Anderson, who owns this nice filly. He came by to see how she's getting along. I gave him a lift over."

"Aw, she's doin' just great," Luke said, as we shook hands. "We got the heat out of both legs—the right one was the one that was botherin' her the most —and she's doin' real good. So good that we don't let her out too much now, so's she don't put on too much weight. I mean, this filly's a doer. She'll eat anythin' you put in front of her. We're walkin' her every day now and in about another week we'll jog her some, see how she handles it. Them sore shins ain't nothin' but a nuisance, but with a filly like this you don't want to rush 'em or fire 'em or nothin'. You just give 'em time and the good Lord do the rest."

"Sounds like a winning recipe to me," I said. "Do you have any carrots? She loves carrots."

"Sure thang," Luke said, smiling. "Down at the end over there, by the tack room. I'll get you some. You hang on here with the Judge." And he walked away from us, moving like a man more used to being in a saddle than on the ground.

"I can see Maggie's in good hands," I said, my right arm over the filly's neck.

"The best," Hunter said. "You wouldn't know it to look at him now, but Luke was riding and breaking horses back in Texas by the time he was twelve. Then he rode on the quarter horse circuit for a few years, till he got too heavy. He's been working for me for four or five years now. He's the best with young horses. Sounds to me like you don't have much to worry about. We should have your filly back at the track in another couple of weeks, that would be my guess."

"Here you go," Luke said, coming back with a handful of carrots. "I'd break 'em up for her, on account of it ain't natural food for a horse. She nibbles 'em with her front teeth. I give her a couple every mornin' after we get through doin' her." He handed me the carrots and I began breaking them up as Maggie, excited now by the prospect of a feast, began bobbing her head up and down again and thrusting her nose toward my hands.

Hunter laughed. "Well, Mr. Anderson, I'm going to get about my business," he said. "Luke here will run you back to your car."

"Sure thang, Judge," Luke said. "How's Miz Freddie doin'?"

"Much better, thanks, Luke," Hunter said. "Worst damn cold she's ever had. I've never known Freddie to be laid low by one before, but she caught a beaut this time. Her cough's loosening up, though, so she'll be around in a day or two."

"That's good," Luke said. "It would have to be damn near pneumonia to knock Miz Freddie on the head like this one done. You give her my best, Judge, hear?"

"I'll do that, Luke."

Hunter shook hands with me and left, moving swiftly and majestically back toward his car like a man with a high purpose. I found myself wondering if everything he did had this portentous quality about it, as if the fate of nations might depend on how he brushed his teeth or moved his bowels.

I finished visiting with Maggie, who lost interest in me when I ran out of carrot chunks, and followed Luke out to his pickup truck. "I guess you've been busy," I said, as he drove me back toward the administration building.

"Oh, yeah," he agreed. "This time of year, with all them mares in foal and breedin' and such, we don't get much sleep. The Judge, though, he's right there with us. Ain't much gets by him."

"Well, this is certainly a beautiful place he built here. I guess he's a good man to work for."

"They don't come no better than the Judge," Luke said, "and this place he built here, why, it's state of the art. You seen the barns, so I guess you know. Lots of space and light for the horses, the best feed, the best care you can have. That's Judge Hunter for you, top of the line all the way. He didn't pinch no dimes buildin' here, that's for sure. It's like he set out to put up the best damn horse farm in the world and he done it. You couldn't have sent your filly to a better spot."

As he turned a corner of the road, another pickup came toward us and its driver waved Luke to a stop, then pulled up alongside. A handsome boyish face with bright blue eyes, long blond hair, and a mustache thrust itself out the window. "Hi," it said to me, then addressed Luke, "You better head on over to the breeding shed, Luke. They're having some problems with the mare Old Red is supposed to cover. She doesn't want any part of it. Maybe you can do something with her. Harry asked me to find you."

"Sure thang," Luke said. "I'll drop off Mr. Anderson here and come right on over. That Miss Tillie?"

The young man grinned, revealing a row of perfect-looking teeth and a set of dimples. "Who else?"

"Damn, every year it's the same with her," Luke said. "She just don't like them studs. She darn near kicked one to pieces one year."

"One of those women who hates men," I suggested.

Luke laughed. "Must be," he said. "Okay, Win, I'll be right on over. This here's Mr. Anderson, by the way. He owns that nice chestnut filly in forty-eight."

Win smiled. "Oh, sure. She's a nice filly, beautifully balanced. Good to meet you, sir," he said. "I'm Win Freeman."

"He doesn't look old enough to be the operations

boss here," I observed to Luke, after we drove away from Win.

"He's late twenties, I guess, though he sure don't look it," Luke said. "He's a good horseman. Got to be or the Judge wouldn't have hired him like he done. Brought him in here from Florida. He's a darn nice fella, a little strange."

"Strange? How?"

"Keeps to himself, kind of a loner. And he and Miz Freddie don't get along too good."

"Why is that?"

"Beats me. Ain't nothin' Win has done, I don't think. But from the first day he come here, she don't give him the time of day. And one time I heard her screamin' at the Judge about how could he do this to her and all that and it all had to do with Win bein' here, I think. She was carryin' on somethin' dreadful, right out there in front of the house one mornin' about two, three days after Win come in here, so's practically the whole world could hear her—she's got a voice on her like a damn trumpet when she gets mad—and the Judge, boy, I never seen him so mad. He just done turned on her finally and told her to shut the hell up. That's all he said to her, but it was in this voice he has that's like the thunder of doom, and, boy, she just clammed up but good. Her face was just white and all and I know she'd have liked to chew him out some more—her eyes was all flashin' and teary and such— but she didn't say another word. She just turned on her heel and walked back into the house and slammed the door. I was there on account of I had to pick up the Judge and go on into town with him, so I couldn't help overhearin' it all. It was somethin', but the Judge —well, you met him. He's not a man you wanna go messin' with, even if you are his wife and all. I mean, the Judge has a way, you know what I'm talkin' about?"

"I guess I do. It's strange, isn't it? I wonder what it is about him."

Luke shook his head. "There's just somethin' about that boy that sure pisses her off," he said. "Anyway, Win, he don't go near her now. He does his work and he's good and he and the Judge are real close, get along just fine. Maybe someday Miz Freddie'll get over whatever it is that's buggin' her and she'll make her peace with him. One thang's for sure—the Judge ain't gonna fire Win or anyone just 'cause Miz Freddie don't like him. He lets her run the house, but when it comes to the ranch and the horses ain't nobody tells the Judge what to do."

"I guess he must have been pretty formidable in the courtroom, too," I said.

"So they tell me, but I don't know nothin' about that part of it. They say, though, that he could have gone on to the Supreme Court, if he'd have wanted to. Only with the Judge, this place matters more to him than anything. Even when he was still a judge and all, he was always around the horses and workin' on buildin' this place. It's number one with him, which is good for us."

"And good for racing," I added.

"You betcha," Luke agreed, as we pulled up in front of the administration building. "This all right?"

"Perfect. Thanks a lot."

On the drive back I thought a lot about Judge Hunter and his state-of-the-art horse operation. Something about the whole scene bothered me, but I wasn't sure what. Perhaps it was all too perfect and so isolated, as if Hunter had set out deliberately, by all but cutting himself off from the outside, to create a world of his own that he could control and dominate and in which every human being in it had to dress the part and submit himself to a set of rules and customs as laid down from on high. I was used to a more relaxed scene around horses, a setting in which informality was an accepted norm and no one wore a uniform, but then I'd never been on a working horse farm before, so I had no way of comparing the operation at Sovereign to anyplace else. I also found myself wondering what it was about Win Freeman that could have aroused such hostility from Mrs. Hunter. He seemed like an affable type and handsome enough to be a movie star, so handsome, in fact, that he reminded me strongly of someone, but I couldn't imagine who. In any case, what did it matter? The main purpose of my visit had been accomplished. I had seen Mad Margaret and found her in good hands and doing well. Now I would call up Linda and tell her about my visit, which would also give me an excuse to talk to her.

When I got back to the motel, I found a message from Linda saying that I was not to try and contact her, but that she would call me sometime between five and six o'clock. I was to wait for her call, because it was important. It was then only about four-thirty, so I changed into my warm-up suit and went for a run along the beach. The tide was coming in, so that, as I ran along the water's edge, I'd occasionally be caught by an incoming wave. I took off my sneakers for the last part of it and splashed ahead barefoot through the cold water. I didn't break any world records, but it felt good and I was breathing hard from the effort by the time I returned to my room. No sooner had I shut the door than the phone rang. It was exactly five o'clock.

"Lou? Oh, I'm so glad." Her voice sounded hushed and breathless with alarm.

"Linda, what's the matter?"

"I think he knows."

"About today, you mean?"

"Yes."

"You didn't tell him?"

"Of course not, but I'm sure he knows."

"How could he know?"

"Well, he called the ranch."

"I know that. They told me he had. But didn't you—"

"Yes, yes, I did. I told him your car broke down, that we had to call the auto club and all that, but I don't think he believed me. I *know* he didn't."

"Did he accuse you or something?"

"No, he's not like that. He was up and getting dressed when I walked in and I told him our story and he didn't say anything at all. Then, later, in the kitchen, when he was having a coffee, he dropped a couple of remarks . . ."

"What kind of remarks?"

"About you. About us. Nothing direct, Lou. Nothing specific. Just hints. Like about how convenient it must have been to break down in the middle of nowhere and what had we talked about all that time and wasn't it great to be able to spend the whole morning together and all. I don't know, Lou, nothing really direct, you see. But I'm sure he knows."

She was frightened, genuinely frightened, I realized, and her fear succeeded in making me uneasy as well. I decided to be calm and reassuring, even though all I could think about was the man's gun collection. After a few minutes, during which I came up with all the plausible, rational reasons for his not knowing about us, I did manage to calm her down a little. "Just be yourself, Linda," I ended up suggesting, somewhat naively. "Ignore the innuendos and hints, or make fun of them. Try to kid him out of it."

"I don't know if I can do it, Lou," she said. "You don't know Michael when he's like this."

"No, and I guess I don't want to."

"Watch out for yourself, Lou. Be careful."

"You, too. Linda?"

"Yes?"

"Are we going to see each other again?"

"I don't know, Lou. I really don't know." And she hung up. She hadn't even asked me about the filly.

chapter 7

BLOCKED

Joe Devane offered to extend my gig at the Laugh
Hour by a week and I accepted, mainly because I
thought I'd get a chance to see Linda again, but I
couldn't get her on the phone. The first few times
I called, always at hours I thought her husband
wouldn't be there, I was answered by a machine and I
would hang up. Then, finally, on Wednesday morning,
at about eleven, the receiver was picked up by a woman
with a voice like shaved ice, who informed me that Mrs.
Cameron had gone out of town. "Oh, I see," I said,
feeling a little foolish for some reason. "When will she
be back?"

"I don't know. They didn't say."

"Oh. Well. You see, I—oh, you must be Nellie."

"No, sir."

"Oh, I'm sorry."

"I'm Richardene. I'm the housekeeper."

"Welcome to California. I'm Lou Anderson."

"I *am* from California."

"Ah, yes, I see. Well, hello there. Welcome anyway."

"How can I help you, Mr. Anderson?"

"I'm not sure, but I guess I do need help with this conversation. Is Mr. Cameron there?"

"No, sir. They're both away."

"And you have no idea when they'll be back?"

"No, sir."

A loquacious bitch. "Well, I was just calling to tell them about the horse," I said.

"Are you the vet?"

"No, I'm not. I'm a partner with the Camerons in a racehorse."

"I wouldn't know anything about that, sir," the woman said, sounding like a prerecorded announcement. "I thought you might be the vet, sir. He was expected to call today about one of the animals. I'll take your message, sir."

"My message?"

"Yes, sir."

"Ah, my message. Well, just tell them I called and that everything's fine with the filly. Do you know where they can be reached?"

"No, sir, I don't. They're traveling. Mr. Cameron calls in for his messages."

"By the way, what happened to Nellie?"

"Who is Nellie, sir?"

"Never mind, it doesn't matter. Thanks."

"Don't mention it, sir. I'll tell them you telephoned."

After that conversation, I called Sovereign and got Sherry on the line. Her chirpy style proved to be a relief after Richardene, and I learned that the Camerons, both of them apparently, had stopped by on Tuesday morning to see Mad Margaret, probably on their way north. I decided that there was nothing else I could do but allow events to take their course, so I concentrated on giving Joe Devane his money's worth and on my runs up and down the beach. I was determined to get myself in wonderful shape by the time I got back to L.A. and the vigorous physical exercise helped me take my mind off Linda. I couldn't make myself believe that the few hours we had spent together in that sordid little motel room were all the time we were ever going to have. I had the smell and the feel of her still in my senses. I'm easy prey when it comes to sex, because, at its best, it's the highest form of magic.

On Friday morning, Alden Berry called me and invited me to drop into his office, which was located in downtown La Jolla, the city's most fashionable older suburb. He told me that his client, Michael Cameron, had a proposition to make to me and that I would probably find it attractive. "Why can't Mr. Cameron call me directly about it?" I asked.

"Because he's still tied up out of town, in L.A.," Alden Berry informed me, "and he may be there for a while."

"Yes, I tried to reach them."

"Shall we say three o'clock?"

His office, on the fifth floor of a nondescript older building near the water, was small, just large enough to accommodate him and a secretary, but it was luxuriously appointed. The walls of his waiting room were decorated with Currier and Ives Civil War prints and the two easy chairs, the table, and the divan appeared to be genuine French antiques. Alden Berry's own private office contained modern, more functional furnishings, but his walls were graced by a large original Mondrian, two Klees, and four small Kandinskys, abstracts of line and space celebrating the precise meaninglessness of life. A wide picture window provided a view over the ocean toward an empty horizon that filled the room with light. Seated at his desk, Alden Berry seemed at first to exist merely as another abstraction, a bland, inscrutable figure in a geometrically conceived still life. He did not offer to shake hands, but nodded as his secretary ushered me in and indicated I should take a seat facing him.

"Mr. Cameron, who is my client, will accept thirty thousand dollars for his share of the filly, Mad Margaret," he said, gazing calmly at me out of those pale, expressionless eyes.

"You mean he wants to sell his share back to me?"

"That's right," Alden Berry said. "Under the circumstances, I think it's a very fair offer."

"Fair?"

"Yes. You make ten thousand dollars and own a hundred percent of the horse again."

"I don't think I can do that," I said.

"Why not?"

"Because I need the money, frankly. Of course, if I can find another buyer for Cameron's share—"

"Not acceptable," Alden Berry said. "Cameron wants to sell immediately. This offer is conditional on an immediate sale."

"May I ask why?"

"Oh, come, come, Mr. Anderson, surely you understand."

"I'm afraid I don't."

The lawyer sighed and leaned back in his chair, shut his eyes briefly, as if quickly organizing his thoughts, then opened them again and focused them brightly on me. "I imagine that the fact you are having an affair with his wife may have something to do with it," he said.

"That's ridiculous—"

"Is it?" The lawyer shuffled through some papers on his desk, then leaned over to glance at one of them. "The motel is owned and run by a couple named Pearl

103

and Henry Mandville," he said." He's sick, but she's at the desk most of the time."

"What motel is that you're talking about?"

"Really, Mr. Anderson, this is just wasting time."

He was right, of course, but I had to stall long enough to figure out what to do. "So let's waste some time," I said.

"All right." He looked at the sheet of paper again. "The place is called the Crossroad Motel, just off the back road to Ramona. I can give you the exact address, if you so desire, but there's no need, is there? You registered there last Sunday morning as Harold Houdini and spent somewhere between two and three hours in the cabin with Mrs. Cameron. I had the number of the cabin also written down, if I can find it." He consulted the paper again. "Sixteen, the one at the very end, I was told." He looked at me again. "Really, Anderson—Harold Houdini."

"I guess I was a little overconfident."

"You guess."

"May I ask you something?"

"Why not?"

"I would have to believe, from Cameron's instant assumption of guilt when Linda explained what occurred, that this isn't the first time this sort of thing has happened."

"Is that your question?"

"Yes."

The lawyer nodded. "Many times."

"Are you telling me she's some sort of nymphomaniac?"

"I'm certainly not going to discuss my client's sex life with you, Anderson."

"Why not? Isn't that what we're doing?"

"No. We're discussing your reacquisition of Mr. Cameron's share of your racehorse."

"And I've already told you I can't accept his offer.

I'll try to find a buyer and Cameron can, too. She's a nice filly. There shouldn't be too much trouble.''

"I'll inform Mr. Cameron of your decision. He's not going to like it, as he wishes to clear this matter up immediately.''

"That's too bad about Cameron," I said, getting up to leave.

"One other thing," the lawyer said. "You are to make no effort to contact Mrs. Cameron or to see her again.''

"I can't guarantee that.''

"It would be too bad, Mr. Anderson," the lawyer said. "There could be unpleasant consequences.''

"Such as?''

"Mr. Cameron is prepared to do whatever may be necessary in order to ensure that you do not attempt to see or speak to his wife ever again.''

"He's a scary guy, all right," I had to admit, as lightheartedly as I could manage it. "What if she contacts me?''

The lawyer shrugged. "I doubt that she will.''

"How can you be sure?''

"I think I tried to explain to you that this sort of behavior on her part has occurred before," Alden Berry said. "Mr. Cameron has had to deal with this a number of times. He knows how to deal with it, believe me.''

"What does he do? Drug her? Kill people? I suppose you know she's afraid of him.''

Alden Berry sighed, like an adult reluctantly compelled at last to explain the facts of life to a child. "Linda Cameron is an unbalanced personality," he said. "She's on medication much of the time and has been under the care of doctors and psychiatrists for years. She fantasizes and sometimes she has impulses she finds it impossible to resist on her own. She is a sick woman whom her husband has had to care for for years now. I suggest you accede to his wishes in this matter. Regarding the horse, contact me when you find a buyer. I don't have your home address or phone number. Please leave them with my secretary on your way out."

I was too shaken to answer him, so I simply let myself out of his office. Alden Berry did not move from his seat, but kept his pale gaze focused on me until I had shut the door behind me.

Business was slow at the Laugh Hour my last few days there and I felt badly about it, because I liked Joe Devane and I didn't want to see him go under. "Hey, don't you worry none," Joe said to me on closing night, as I was packing up my stuff in the dressing room after my last show. "I got Alice Little comin' in here next week for a gig."

"The old blues singer?"

"You got it, baby. She's gonna kill the people."

"She's wonderful, Joe, but is she that big a draw? She's been around longer than Peggy Lee."

"Hey, man, at this point in time I don't give a hoot in hell what happens," he said, grinning. "We gonna make some music in here, wake up this hick town."

"I wish you luck, Joe."

"I'm gonna need it, ain't I?" He laughed, then began to cough until I thought his lungs might come up through his mouth. I got up to help him, but he waved me away, staggered over to a chair, and sank into it. After what seemed an eternity, he finally got control of it and looked up at me with tears streaming down his cheeks. He was still smiling. "I'd walk a mile for a Camel," he wheezed, wiping his eyes with the back of his hand.

"Joe, you've got to see a doctor."

"I have seen 'em," he said. "They all tell me the

same thing, man. No use throwin' any more money away on them folks." He heaved himself to his feet again, leaning against the wall with one hand. "Someday, Shifty, if I live long enough, you gonna show me how you do all them tricks of yours." He shook his head. "That one you do with them cigarette papers . . . Say, if I'd have known that one, I could have maybe made all my smokes disappear. You want to show me that one, Shifty?"

"Any time, Joe."

He started to move toward the door. "There's a fella out here wants to see you," he said.

"Who is he?"

"I don't know, but he ain't good folks, Shifty, you know what I'm sayin'?"

"What do you mean?"

"He's either a cop or a mob guy. Sometimes you can't tell 'em apart. You in some kind of trouble, Shifty?"

"I hope not, Joe. Thanks. Where is he?"

"Sittin' out front, waitin' for you. He asked me to tell you."

"Maybe he's the president of my local fan club."

"I don't think so, man. You want me to sneak you out of here? There's a door into the alley."

"No, I better see what he wants."

"You be careful. I don't want nobody beatin' you up till you show me how you do them things you do."

"I'll be careful, Joe. And thanks for everything."

He pushed himself out into the hallway and shuffled back out front. I heard him start to cough again and hoped he would get to the oxygen he kept in his office in time, then I finished packing up. When I emerged into the main room, suitcase in hand, and headed for the exit, a stocky, bald man in his midforties rose up out of his seat against the wall and confronted me. At first glance, he didn't look ominous or formidable. He had a round face with a stubby nose and small dark eyes set fairly close together under bushy black eyebrows and his expression seemed affable enough. "Anderson?" he said, without offering to shake my hand. "We got to converse."

"What about? Who are you?"

"It don't matter who I am," he said. "We got to talk. You want to do it here or you wish to have a libation somewhere, it's up to you."

"A libation? I usually like to know the names of the people I drink with. My first name's Lou. Most people call me Shifty."

"Yeah, I know. So I'm Don. You happy now? Can we discuss matters?"

"How about over here?" I said, indicating a table toward the back of the room. "It's quiet enough."

"Sure."

He sat down first, folding his hands in his lap and regarding me placidly, as if I were a minor constituent of his whom he was obligated to deal with but was bored by having to do so. I did not order drinks, but waved the waitress away; I was no more anxious to prolong the meeting than he was. I also noticed that he had almost no neck and that he seemed to be a small mass of hairy muscle under his ill-fitting black suit. "How can I help you, Don?" I asked.

"You don't help me," he said. "You help yourself."

"How do I do that?"

"The offer Mr. Cameron made to you was a good offer," he said, speaking in a pleasant enough but colorless voice, as if he had memorized his lines but had no talent to make them expressive. "He desires you to know that he is not prepared to be patient in this matter."

"In other words, he wants me to give him back thirty thousand dollars now."

"That is certainly one aspect you could take care of, yeah."

"But I've already explained to Mr. Berry that I can't do that."

"So I was informed. But I wish to impress upon you that you will do that," Don said. "Mr. Cameron would also be very pleased if you was to accept Mr. Gantry as your partner in the horse and Mr. Gantry would be allowed to train it."

"Wait a minute, Don, wait a minute," I said, doing my best to remain calm. "I'm to give him back most of his money and for the ten thousand bucks he allows me to keep he wants me to turn my horse over to Gantry?"

"You keep your percentage in the horse," Don said. "That's only right."

"I'm touched by Cameron's generosity. What did he sell his share to Gantry for? Or is he still part-owner but is using Gantry as a front?"

"I wouldn't know anything about that," Don said. "I only know what Mr. Cameron would like you to do in this matter, you understand, Anderson?"

I stood up. "As Jack Benny used to say, good night, Don."

His right arm shot out and grabbed me by the shirt front. "Sit down," he said. "We haven't finished." He was very strong and he had a good hold on my shirt, so I sat down. "Now, is what I was saying to you clear or would you like me to repeat it for you so that there can be no future misunderstanding?"

"Where did you study English?" I asked. "At the Dale Carnegie School of Elocution?"

He released me. "I was told that you are a funny man," he said, in that same affable, stilted manner. "I can perceive that you are indeed amusing."

"I usually get paid for being entertaining," I said. "Now, to answer your question, this filly is not going to be turned over to D. L. Gantry and the reason is two-fold—one, I have a written agreement from Cameron specifying exactly what the conditions of ownership are and, second, I wouldn't let D. L. Gantry train a goat for me. So please tell Cameron or Gantry or whoever you're working for that there is no deal.''

Don looked sad, as if I had disappointed him, and blinked his little dark eyes at me. "So you are not so bright as I thought maybe you was," he said. "So maybe one of these nights, when you are coming home or walking down a street somewhere, sometime when maybe you are not expecting it, someone will detain you and break a few of your bones, you understand what I am saying to you, Anderson? Like your hands, for instance. I imagine it would be difficult to be a magician if you was to have hands with a lot of broken fingers on them."

I tried to remain cool, but it was difficult. "Let me tell you something, Don," I said, hoping that I didn't sound as shaky as I now felt. "If somebody breaks my hands, then he might as well kill me, because I would have nothing left to live for and I would be sure to do everything in my power to strike back. I am not without resources. I have close friends in the L.A. Police Department who would be very distressed if anything were to happen to me. It is not going to be difficult for me to find out who you are and where you came from and a full record of this conversation will be on the books there along with your picture and a very accurate description of you, so that if anything were to happen to me my friends would know where to look for you. They'll have no trouble finding Cameron and Gantry and the publicity will be fairly sensational for them both. The least that could happen to Gantry is that he'll lose his license, once the stewards and the California Horse Racing Board hear my story. Unless I'm mistaken, Cameron is in enough hot water now with the ongoing investigations into his business activities and the murder of one of his ex-associates. Is this all getting across to you or is it too complex for you?''

Don didn't answer me, but continued to regard me impassively, as if a veil had dropped in front of his eyes and he could no longer see me quite as clearly as before. Perhaps he wasn't used to having people talk back to him.

"So what I think you should tell Cameron or Berry or Gantry, maybe all three of them, is that I will do my best to find a buyer for Cameron's share of the horse and that is all I can promise," I said. "They should not let their personal feelings about me get in the way of business. Can I go now?"

Don shrugged. "So go," he said. "What's keeping you?"

At the exit, I glanced back at him. He was still sitting impassively in place, staring at me out of his little black eyes. I smiled and waved good-bye, hoping that he couldn't see how frightened I really was.

Back at the motel, I found a message from Happy Hal Mancuso, informing me that he had booked me the next day on a local morning talk show, for which I was to receive a five-hundred-dollar fee. I was to perform some magic and I was also to be interviewed about my involvement in horse racing, both as an owner and a player. "I tried to get you on there last week, when it could have done you some good at the club," Hal explained, when I called him at home to get details, "but what the hell, it's five hundred bucks, enough for a few big bets, right, you rotten degenerate? And I can use the commission."

"You must be really hard up, Hal," I said.

"With clients like you, who wouldn't be?" And he hung up on me. It was nice having such a positive force working so hard and unselfishly for me.

The show was called *Sunrise San Diego* and was broadcast out of a station located on one of the endless boulevards that crisscross the flat, high mesas inland from the coast. I showed up there at six A.M., an hour before showtime, and introduced myself to the producer, a harassed-looking woman of about thirty-five, who seemed to be carrying on six or seven conversations at the same time with various subordinates in charge of one department or another. She ushered me quickly into a small waiting room reserved for the show's guests, ordered coffee for me, and revealed that she knew nothing about me except that I was a magician who had been brought in at the last minute to substitute for the ailing author of a series of Mexican cookbooks. "What sort of magic do you do?" she asked, her eyes aglow with concern. "I mean, do you need any special sort of camera angles for your tricks?"

I explained to her, in between interruptions from members of her staff, what sort of magician I was and that all I needed was a camera that could come in close on my hands from time to time. I told her I'd stay away from cards until the end of my stint, when I proposed a little Three-Card Monte. "What's that?" she asked nervously.

"The world's oldest gambling game," I explained, "the one you still see being played on street corners, where you try to guess the right card out of the three being manipulated by the dealer."

"Oh, that one," she said, brightening. "That's great! Can you talk about it, too? I mean, the gambling aspect of it? We had an officer from the police department here yesterday talking about various scams and this would be sort of a continuation, if you see what I mean."

"Three-Card Monte isn't really a scam," I said. "It's a skill. I can do it very slowly and you still won't be able to guess the right card."

"Well, that's fine," she said. "Now, you're our only local guest this morning—the rest of the interviews are from the Persian Gulf—so we need to keep you on the air for ten minutes. I think you can do two or three tricks in all and that should be enough. A lot of people are bored by magic. Your agent said you also know something about horse racing."

"Yes. I even own part of a horse."

"Good, good. Larry—that's our co-host, Larry Gaines—he has a thing about that. He'll be interviewing you and then you do your little tricks and then Larry will talk to you about horse racing."

"Sounds good," I said, taking a sip of my coffee. When I looked up, she was gone, off down the corridor to cope with some other aspect of her show. She was the perfect producer, I thought to myself, for a medium with the attention span of a sparrow.

The show itself went off well. Basically, it followed the format for all morning talk shows—a little news, a little weather, a little sports, a couple of interviews with local personalities, all sandwiched between layers of trivial banter by the hosts, Larry Gaines and Milly Woods, who were both in their thirties, tall, blond, blandly attractive, and insufferably glib. They seemed to know almost nothing about any of the subjects they discussed or the people they interviewed, but covered their willful ignorance with childish jokes and patter. I had been informed it was the highest rated morning talk show in the area.

When it was my turn, toward the end of the hour, Larry Gaines introduced me as "a master magician who is also going to tell us how to win at the horse races." He asked me a couple of perfunctory questions about my craft, wondered aloud if I could make his mother-in-law disappear, then used my exhibition of Three-Card Monte, one of the great classical maneuvers of close-up, to get around to the topic he really wanted to discuss. "That's very interesting, Shifty," he said, beaming with insincerity. "It looks to me about as hard as picking winners at the racetrack. Now, if you can tell us how to do that, that's real magic."

"If I could do that, Larry, maybe I wouldn't have to work for a living," I said, smiling falsely.

"Ha ha. Well, it's pretty hard to do, isn't it?" Larry said. "Especially since there's so much dishonesty in racing."

"Gee, do you really think so, Larry?"

"Well, sure, Shifty. I worry a lot about that when I go to the races."

"Let me ask you something, Larry," I said, smiling sweetly. "Do you keep your money in a bank?"

"Well, sure, I guess we all do, ha ha."

"And I guess you carry insurance—on your house, your car, your life, right?"

"Well, of course, most of us do carry insurance. Now, Shifty—"

"Excuse me," I continued, cutting him off. "What about stocks and bonds, mutual funds, that kind of thing? You have investments in the American Dream, right, Larry?"

"I guess many of us do. What are you driving at?"

"Here you are, involved in deals with the biggest thieves in the world," I said, "and you're worried about being cheated in a horse race."

Just out of camera range, Milly Woods was laughing, as were several members of the crew, and poor Larry was obliged to play along, although I was sure he would have been quite happy to see me drop dead right in front of him. He quickly ended the interview without giving me another chance to make a fool of him, took the show into its final commercial break, then summoned Milly Woods back on camera for the closing segment. I was ushered offstage. One of the crew gave me a thumbs-up sign as I left, but nobody else even looked at me. I had committed the cardinal sin of making the star of the show look bad, which also undoubtedly meant that I would never be appearing on it again, but I didn't care. I had earned my five hundred dollars.

Back in the waiting room, as I was collecting my things, the producer (whose name I never did find out) stuck her head in the door. She did not thank me for my appearance and looked more harassed than before. "You have a call," she said, pointing to a phone by the sofa against the far wall. "You can take it over there." Then she disappeared again, closing the door behind her.

It was Linda. "Oh, Lou," she said, "you were so wonderful. I had to call you. I saw the show."

"Linda, I've been trying to reach you—"

"I know, I know. Listen, I can't talk to you now. I just wanted to tell you you were wonderful."

"Wait. Don't hang up. Are you back?"

"Back? I haven't been away."

"Your housekeeper, what's her name—"

"Richardene."

"She said you were traveling with your husband."

"She's a liar. I've been home. They won't let me go anywhere."

"Linda, what can I do?"

"Nothing, Lou."

"Are you all right?"

"Yes, yes, I'm all right. It's just that Michael knows—"

"Yes. His private investigator dropped in to see me last night at the club."

"Oh, be careful, Lou. Michael's in a rage about everything these days. They're not letting me out of their sight. He's hired this woman—"

"Richardene."

"Yes. Michael fired Nellie. Oh, Lou, be careful."

William Murray

"This guy named Don said he was going to break my fingers if I don't turn the horse over to Gantry. Linda, you—"

"I can't talk anymore," she said, interrupting me. "They're listening in. They watch me all the time. Lou, be careful, please. Do you know Win?"

"Who?"

"Win Freeman. He works at Sovereign. I saw him there. Lou, there's something about him, as if we know each other. He wanted to speak to me. It was so strange. Lou, I have to hang up. She's back in the house, I can hear her. Good-bye, Lou. Be careful."

And the line went dead.

chapter 8

MOVES

I found Charlie Pickard in the track kitchen, which at Hollywood Park is located next to the backstretch, with a terrace overlooking the racing surface. It was convenient for the horsemen, who could thus pop in for a coffee or breakfast without having to walk very far. Charlie was at a small table toward the rear, talking to a middle-aged man in slacks and a gray checked sports jacket whom I recognized as one of his owners. "Jesus, Charlie, all you ever give me is bad news," the man was saying, as I pulled up a chair and joined them. "How come all I ever hear from you is bad news?"

"You just haven't been very lucky, Mr. Green," Charlie said. "Hello, Shifty. You know Abel Green?"

"Yeah, sure, we've seen each other around," I said, shaking Green's hand. "How are you?"

"I'm fine. Only my horses aren't so fine," he said,

grimacing. "Every time I ask Charlie here about one of them—"

"He's only got four," Charlie interpolated.

"—he tells me some disaster story, like one of them has something wrong with him or can't run or something."

"These aren't million-dollar yearlings, you understand," Charlie said. "These are cheap Cal-bred claimers running at the bottom of the barrel. These are horses with enough problems to keep a vet in clover for years."

"So how come you're training them, if they're so terrible?" Green asked. "Answer me that, Charlie."

"Because you took them away from that English comedian, Bellwood, who you say can't do any good with them, and you give 'em to me," Charlie said. "I didn't promise you miracles, Mr. Green. I said I'd try to get them sound enough to run a couple of decent races for you. That's what I'm doing. If you don't like what I'm doing, there are other guys back here who will take 'em off my hands."

"No, no," Green said, "I know you're a good trainer, Charlie. Only I get so tired of hearing nothing but bad news." He looked at me for sympathy. "We got this old claimer called Delmonico, once had some class —he's supposed to run in the ninth tomorrow and now Charlie tells me he's got to scratch him. He's got a curb that's acting up, whatever the hell that is. What the hell is it?"

"Basically, a strained ligament—" Charlie began.

"I mean, why can't you give me some good news once in a while?" the owner said. "There must be something good you can tell me. Tell me some good news about this horse."

Charlie thought it over for a moment or two. "Well," he said at last, "you got partners."

"Jesus Christ, listen to this guy," Green said, pushing himself to his feet. "That's his idea of good news."

"Hey, I got to toughen you up," Charlie said.

"No, don't do that," the owner replied, as he moved away from us, "please. I'm tough enough already. I'm so tough I'm gonna stiffen up until rigor mortis sets in." And he was gone.

Charlie looked at me and shrugged. "You buy cheap, you get cheap," he said. "So how was San Diego, Shifty?"

"Interesting. Sovereign Acres was especially interesting," I said and then told Charlie all about my visit.

"You met Luke Davis, I heard."

"Yeah."

"He's the reason I sent the filly there," the trainer explained. "He's an absolutely top guy with young horses. I've known him ever since he used to break yearlings back in Florida. How's he gettin' on at Sovereign?"

"I think he's got a pretty good setup there," I said, "even though he seems a little out of step, if you know what I mean."

"Yeah, that's quite an operation," Charlie said. "It took old Jed Hunter a lot of years to realize his dream and there were some big fights early on over water rights, I heard. Anyway, Jed runs a tight ship now, but it's a state-of-the-art facility, ain't it? And the horses get the best of care, that's the main thing. I guess that's how come Luke's latched on there. He's no good around a racetrack, but on a farm he's the best there is."

"What's the matter with him at the track?"

"He was a bettin' junkie, like you," Charlie said, "only he couldn't stop. All he could think about was gettin' a bet down on every race and everything else in his life went to hell, includin' his marriage. Sovereign's the perfect place for Luke. There's no distractions, just the horses." He stood up. "Want another cup of coffee? I'm pretty much done for the day."

"Sure. Cream, no sugar."

When Charlie came back with the coffees, I also told him about Cameron and Gantry and Alden Berry and Don. The trainer didn't answer right away, but sipped his coffee in silence, then glanced sharply at me. "What's goin' on, Shifty?" he asked. "It ain't even been three weeks and already you and Cameron ain't gettin' along. What happened?"

"You don't want to know, Charlie, and I don't want to tell you. Let's just say we don't like each other."

"You made a move on his wife, didn't you? I figured you would."

"It wasn't quite like that, Charlie. Out of respect for the lady, I'd rather not talk about it."

"Well, Gantry was over to the barn yesterday," the trainer said. "He wanted me to know that he had nothin' to do with takin' the filly away from me."

"He isn't taking her away from you, Charlie. I decide who trains Maggie, nobody else." I leaned back in my chair. "Boy, they've got a lot of nerve. They must have told Gantry I'd agree to their proposal and he considers it a done deal. I guess I'll go talk to him. What did you tell him?"

Charlie shrugged. "Didn't have nothin' to tell him, Shifty. I hadn't heard from you. I didn't know what to think."

"Where's Gantry's barn?"

"Couple of rows directly in back of mine," Charlie said, "but you can find him out there." He cocked a thumb in the direction of the stand outside the window. "He's still got horses out on the track."

"Okay," I said, standing up, "I'll go talk to him. I don't want him laboring under any misapprehensions. The other thing I'd like you to do, Charlie, is get the filly out of Sovereign and back here, where you can keep an eye on her. I believe you about Luke, but I don't trust that operation down there. Hunter may be involved with Cameron in some business deals and I know Cameron's under investigation here. He may be into some shady stuff with Rhineland. That's Tony Huge."

"I know, I heard."

"So, things being as they are between me and Cameron, Charlie, I'd rather have Maggie right here, where you can keep an eye on her, even if it does cost more. I don't know what these people are capable of, but I'm getting a little paranoid about them."

Charlie regarded me impassively, then said, "You ought to learn to keep it in your pants, Shifty."

"Charlie—"

"Okay, sure, I'll bring the filly in," he said, waving away my protestations. "I can probably get her back in light training in another week or two and I'll give her to May to look after."

"Oh, good, she's still with you."

"You bet. She's turned out just fine and she works real well with Eddie. She loves that filly more than you do."

"Okay, Charlie, I'll go talk to Gantry."

"Don't go gettin' mad," Charlie said, as I walked away. "I don't need no enemies, Shifty. Gantry's got too much clout in the racing office."

I went outside to join the horsemen in the guinea stand, but Gantry was not among them. I was about to ask for him when I spotted him out on the track. He was riding a sorrel pony and making a performance out of it, moving back and forth in front of us and seemingly intent on what his horses were doing. Like everything involving the man, however, it was more theater than substance. Unlike most of the other riders at this hour of the morning, he was impeccably dressed in designer jeans, handmade Italian boots, spotless chaps, and a pink vaquero shirt that looked as if it had been custom-tailored on Rodeo Drive. He sat straight up in the saddle, an ornate Western job that must have cost at least two thousand dollars, and made sure not to move too fast so as not to disturb his carefully coiffed wavy dark locks or displace his Swiss-army sunglasses. "What's with Gantry?" I heard an old horseman next to me ask a companion. "He's puttin' on some kind of damn show out there."

"Aw, shit, it's just Lane doin' his con number on some new owners of his," the friend answered. "Look at the sonbitch, he can't hardly even sit right on a horse. If that sorrel was to break into a gallop, old Lane would be sittin' on his ass in the dirt out there."

I waited until Gantry finished his training chores, then followed him on foot back to his stable. I had to admit to myself that his setup was impressive. He had forty or fifty horses on the premises and his shedrows were immaculate, protected by spotless zebra-striped awnings and bounded by strips of sod imported to lend an air of rural charm to the ordinarily shabby backstretch surroundings. His stablehands were all neatly dressed in one-piece black-and-orange jumpsuits, were all clean-shaven, and apparently were never allowed to sit down. No music blared from portable radios, no one drank coffee, no rub rags hung from sagging clotheslines, and every bale of hay, every piece of equipment, had been neatly stacked or put away. It looked like a set for a brochure designed to attract prospective buyers, which, of course, is precisely what it was. Gantry had more wealthy owners than any other trainer in America and most of them were people who had never before owned racehorses. They were used to corporate boardrooms, luxuriously appointed private offices, limousines, and first-class air travel. To them, D. L. Gantry must have seemed the horse trainer of their fantasies, a kindred spirit who understood the trappings as well as the power of money. Gantry had built his reputation with their wallets and in appearance, at least, he gave value for their trust; in everything he did he conveyed an image of corporate expertise. The fact that most of his expensive charges broke down before the end of their three-year-old racing careers did little to tarnish the picture. What the ignorant rich folks wanted were silver trophies for their walls and these Gantry could supply in abundance. He flew his two- and three-year-olds all over the country to grab off stakes races everywhere and he had never been known to back off a horse until the animal fell apart or dropped dead in front of him. Turning Mad Margaret over to him, I figured, was equivalent to sentencing her to an early breakdown.

Gantry had just dismounted when I showed up. He was clearly surprised to see me, but did his considerable best not to betray it. He ushered me into his office, which contained a comfortable leather sofa, two armchairs, a computer, a TV set, and blowups on the walls of some of the trainer's more notable victories. "I understand there's some difficulty about the filly," he said, as he shut the door behind us.

"No real difficulty," I said. "I would prefer to think of it as a misunderstanding."

"Mike Cameron told me a few days ago that the horse would be turned over to me," the trainer said, flashing me a quick, ingratiating smile, his eyes still hidden behind his omnipresent dark glasses. "Then yesterday I got another call, this one from his lawyer. You know him?"

"I've met him. I presume you mean Alden Berry. What did he say?"

"That you had changed your mind."

"No, that's not accurate. By the way, did you buy Cameron's share?"

Gantry looked genuinely astonished. "You don't know?"

"I was told Cameron wanted out," I said. "First I was asked to return most of his money and to take back full ownership of the filly. Then somebody else came to see me, at the club in San Diego where I was working. This guy, obviously a hired goon, not only insisted I give Cameron his money back, but there was no further talk of reacquiring full ownership. And part of the deal was having to turn the horse over to you."

Gantry leaned back in his chair, as if to get a better look at me. He tapped the points of his fingers together. "This is very strange," he said at last. "I agreed to pay Mike Cameron fifty thousand dollars for his share of the filly on the condition that I would train her and I was told that you had okayed the deal."

"You were told wrong, Lane," I said. "Let's see— thirty thousand from me and fifty thousand from you makes eighty. Cameron has a way of turning a quick profit. Have you paid him the money?"

"No, not yet, but I assumed it was a deal. I told him I'd pay him as soon as the filly was turned over to me and I was assured it would be a matter of days."

"I guess I've got to admire Cameron's bravura," I said. "He nets forty grand for doing nothing."

"That's a form of pinhooking," Gantry said. "It's done in this business all the time. I've done it myself and there's nothing wrong with it. But maybe you ought to know that Mike intends to keep a small percentage."

"Oh, really? How much?"

"Ten percent of my share, just to keep a little interest in the horse. I told him she's got real potential and I believe that. He wants to be a part of it."

"That's truly heartwarming," I said. "Look, Lane, I have no quarrel with you, but Mad Margaret is going to stay with Charlie. I don't care who owns the minority share in her, the agreement is that I call the shots on this horse. So I suggest you restructure your deal with Cameron based on this reality. I'm going to assume that Cameron owns forty-five percent of Maggie, because that's what it says on the partnership agreement on file with the California Horse Racing Board. If you want to buy a piece of her, that's between you and Cameron, but it's all got to be legitimate and above board, otherwise I'm going to the stewards and tell my version of the story."

"I own shares in a number of horses, as you probably know," Gantry said, "but only in ones I train myself. It seems to me that whatever your differences may be with Mike, there's no problem if you turn the filly over to me. I'm not knocking Charlie Pickard when I say about him that he's an old-fashioned horseman, whereas with me you have a real chance to make a top horse out of her. We would integrate her into our program here and give her the very best treatment, so she'd have a shot at the big money. We run a tight ship here and our record speaks for itself."

"You're the best at what you do, Lane," I said, "no doubt about it. But this filly is going to stay in Charlie Pickard's shedrow." I stood up. "I'd appreciate it if you could let me know what you and Cameron decide to do. He and I aren't on speaking terms."

"Well, I'm sorry you feel that way," Gantry said, as we shook hands. "I'm in almost daily touch with the Camerons, so I'll tell them. I don't think I'll want to buy a share if I can't train her. You understand, don't you?"

"Absolutely," I said. "I appreciate your leveling with me."

I spent my first afternoon back at the races in familiar company, with Jay, Arnie, and Angles, but it was not an exciting day, mainly because I couldn't isolate a horse to risk any money on. The boys had so far been having an indifferent meet and an air of frustration pervaded the scene, making Angles more jumpy even than usual. Periodically, he would leap out of his seat and set noisily off in pursuit of information, looking for the angle that would enable him to step out on some otherwise undistinguished animal and make a small coup. To keep ourselves occupied, Jay, Arnie, and I put together a hundred and fifty dollars and tried to bring in a show parlay, but it went down in flames in the fifth race, after we had run it up to about four hundred, so we spent the rest of the card staring glumly at cheap horses in small fields and trying vainly to pretend that we were enjoying ourselves. "I don't know where track management finds these horses," Jay observed after the seventh. "I'd just as soon play the lottery as buy a ticket on any one of these dogs."

Right after the feature, a graceless gallop on the grass course for mediocre fillies and mares, Angles made another foray out into the crowd and returned ten minutes later to tell us that an animal called No Sugar was supposed to win the ninth and final race. "Have you noted who trains the horse?" Arnie asked. "Kuhlmann. How is this paragon of a horseman performing, Jay?"

The Fox consulted one of his big black notebooks. "He's one for thirty-one at this meet and two for a hundred and thirteen on the year. He's a disaster area."

"I once saw him shove a carrot up a horse's ass, because he doesn't know which end of a horse is which," Arnie said. "I'm supposed to risk money on this clown?"

"Very funny, very funny," Angles said. "If you'll look at your paper, you'll see that this filly has been training down at San Luis Rey. The angle is that

Kuhlmann has had nothing to do with her, which is how come she may be a good thing at eight to one."

"The horse is one for seventeen lifetime," Jay said.

"I don't care," Angles answered. "I'm tellin' you, God put this horse in this race today for us to bet on. See?" He showed us a fifty-dollar win ticket on No Sugar.

No one else in our group chose to heed Angles's advice, but we hung around long enough to try and root his horse home. No Sugar did, in fact, run one of her better races and even managed to get the lead at the head of the stretch, with Angles screaming her home, but she faded and finished a well-beaten third. "God must be a show bettor," Arnie observed, as the order of finish was posted.

Angles flung his program to the floor and stamped out of the box. I said good-bye to Jay and Arnie and went looking for my car. As I stepped off the clubhouse escalator, on my way to the owners' and trainers' parking lot, I saw a familiar figure moving ponderously ahead of me like a barge heading upstream and I hurried after it. "Jude," I called out. "Hey, Jude, wait up!"

Jude Morgan turned back to look at me. He was dressed in another of his ill-fitting suits, this one a dark blue job that looked like a tent on him, and his porkpie brown hat sat on the back of his close-cropped gray hair like a halo. He was overweight, but much of it was muscle and it always seemed to bulge out in places no tailor could disguise. The heavy creases that framed his nose and mouth seemed deeper than ever as I approached him and he seemed neither surprised nor especially pleased to see me. He was a black homicide detective in the L.A. Police Department who had become a friend of mine in recent months, especially after we had bumped into each other one day at the races and realized that we shared the same addiction. I had put him on a couple of winners and that also had helped, though he had seen far too much of human behavior ever to allow himself to trust anyone completely. "Well, my man, where have you been?" he asked, as I came up to him. "If I'd known you were here, I'd have consulted you on these horses. None of the ones I picked ran a step."

"It was a horrible card," I told him. "I didn't do any better. Which way are you headed?" He pointed to the far corner of a general parking lot. "I'll walk you over."

On the way, I filled him in on some of my recent adventures, though I didn't tell him anything about my morning fling with Linda Cameron. I concluded with an account of my encounter with Don at the Laugh Hour. By this time we had reached his car, a battered-looking four-year-old Buick sedan. Jude leaned against it and crossed his arms over his chest. "Shifty, my man, what have you got yourself into now?" he asked, a little wearily.

"I guess what I want to know is what I can do about this guy Don."

"Ain't much you can do," he said. "Could you identify him?"

"Yes."

"I'll round up some mug shots for you to look at," he said. "Give me a call tomorrow early, like maybe seven o'clock, at the station. I'll arrange for you to come on down and have a look."

"What about the Tony Huge investigation?" I asked.

"Who?"

"Fazzini, Gaetano Fazzini. You involved in that one?"

"No, that's Eddie Hirschorn's case in Beverly Hills, I think," the detective said. "Why?"

"I think this guy Cameron may be involved in it. I understand there's a big corruption investigation going on."

"Maybe. Why are you so interested?"

"Cameron's the guy who bought a piece of my filly," I said. "He also has to be the guy who hired this Don character."

Jude thought that one over for a while, then turned to open his car door. "Why don't you just stick to magic and playin' horses, my man?" he said, as he lowered himself into the driver's seat. "You're out of your depth in this sort of stuff, Shifty."

"I suppose I am," I said, waving good-bye to him as he backed out of his slot.

I didn't go straight home, but stopped off first at Dudley's, my favorite bar and grill on Little Santa Monica in West L.A. The proprietor, Robert Dudley, a retired English-born jockey with a permanent limp from a bad spill a few years earlier, greeted me warmly and joined me for a drink. He filled me in on all the recent track gossip, since his place had become a gathering ground for horseplayers and other sporting types, and commiserated with me over the poor quality of the recent racing at Hollywood Park. "A lot of horsemen use that track now to lay up their best horses between Santa Anita and Del Mar," he explained, "since the purses there are so much smaller. Anyway, chum, you know how I can tell whether the meet's going well or not? If it's bad, your friend Wolfenden shows up here to hustle." He indicated the pool table toward the rear of the room, where half a dozen young kids were playing friendly games. "He's been in the last three nights, playing Mexican kids for a dollar or two a game."

"That's shameful of Arnie," I said. "You know he used to take on Minnesota Fats and Willie Mosconi and beat them. He must be really hurting."

William Murray

"Tell me about your filly. When do we see her again?"

We chatted for another hour or so, while I ate a steak, drank some house Cabernet, and basked in the pleasant atmosphere of the room, whose walls were decorated with track posters, jockey silks, boots, helmets, whips, and other memorabilia, as well as blowups of celebrated races Dudley had ridden in. I was feeling much more sanguine about my life in general when I left and had stopped worrying about the Camerons, their lawyer, and their hired thug. So I wasn't prepared for the surprise awaiting me at home.

I had barely climbed the stairs up from the carport to my front door than I became aware of a presence behind me. I whirled quickly and found myself looking at the pale, frightened face of Linda Cameron. "Thank God you're here!" she said, falling into my arms. "Oh, Lou, I'm so frightened! Please hold me!"

chapter 9

BOLTED

"Michael's never been like this before," she said, sitting hunched up on the edge of my bed and cradling in both hands the hot cup of coffee I had made for her. "He's always been a hard man, Lou, but he never mistreated me. For the past week I've been like a prisoner."

He had called her every name he could think of, then had locked her into her bedroom for two days, until the arrival of Richardene Leider. The woman was an ex-sheriff's deputy and prison guard, who had been fired from her job for brutalizing her wards. "Alden found her, I don't know where, maybe through that private investigator they hired," Linda said, "but Michael gave her full control over me and the whole household. The first time I tried to argue with her, she twisted my arm up behind my back until I screamed.

Whenever she went out, she'd lock me up again. It's been a nightmare. I never would have believed it."

Michael had hardly been home at all since then, she continued, because he had been so busy up in L.A., mainly on matters relating to the real estate scandal and the investigation. Linda had been left almost entirely to the tender care of Richardene, with whom she'd been unable to achieve any sort of rapport. The woman had not even let her go down to the stable to see the horses. Michael had gotten rid of all the other animals and had fired Nellie back in Houston. "I don't know what he thinks he's doing," Linda said. "He's gone crazy over this. I can't even talk to him, Lou. He won't listen to reason. I told him I'd give him a divorce, I told him I'd move out and that I want nothing but the animals, but he's like a wild man, Lou. I don't know what to do. He's gone crazy. He's scared, he's really scared, and it must have to do with something else, not me. And he's beyond even talking to."

She had escaped by climbing out of a living room window while Richardene was in the house. By the time she reached the road, the woman was in pursuit and would have caught her, if it hadn't been for Thor. The big Doberman had come bounding around the corner of the house to join the action. "I know the commands, obviously," Linda said, "so I used them. He went after the woman and stopped her. She has a gun, but didn't have it with her, and Thor brought her up short. I ordered him to hold her in place, which the dog is trained to do until either the police come or he receives a release order. For all I know, she's still there." The idea brought the ghost of a smile to her face. "I walked three miles into Rancho Santa Fe, got three hundred dollars out of the Versateller, took a taxi into Del Mar and the train up to L.A. I didn't know what to do or where to go, Lou. I don't know anybody here except for Michael's friends and you. So I came to you."

"Well, obviously they'll know where to look for you, so you can't stay here," I said. "I'll make a couple of calls. Maybe one of my friends can put you up for a day or two until we can figure out what to do. You'll need legal advice, so we'll have to find you a lawyer. Got any ideas?"

She shook her head and looked down into her coffee cup. She was dressed in sandals, white jeans, a pink shirt, and a white windbreaker. She looked so vulnerable that it was all I could do not to take her into my arms and make instant love to her, but my conversation with Alden Berry kept me from doing so. I really knew nothing about this woman and I told myself to be careful, not to take everything she was saying to me at face value. What if she had imagined it all? Certainly her story sounded as if it could have been made up. Husbands didn't often kidnap their own wives, keep them prisoners in their own homes, hire sadistic guards to watch over them. What was I dealing with here, reality or a dangerous illusion?

"Have you eaten anything?" I asked. When she shook her head, I offered to make her some soup, but she declined. She finished her coffee and disappeared into the bathroom to take a shower. She had nothing with her, so we would have to go out to buy her a few overnight things. I picked up the phone and called Dudley's. "Robert, I have sort of an emergency," I said, when the owner came on the phone. I told him that Linda was a friend of mine who had been abused by her husband and had run away. She needed a place to stay for a few days, couldn't compromise herself by staying with me, and could he help.

"No problem," he said. "I'll call Ellen and I'm sure it will be all right. The kids are away at school in England and we have a guest room. Do you know where I live?" I wrote down the address, which was up in the old Hollywood hills above Gower, and I told him I'd have Linda there within the hour. "Right," he said. "If I don't call you back, it's okay. I do have to alert Ellen."

"Of course. Thanks, Robert, I really appreciate this."

"Are you involved, Shifty, you rogue?" he asked.

"I don't know," I told him truthfully. "I like the lady a lot, but I think the trouble she's in has very little to do directly with me."

"Right, old boy. Didn't mean to pry," he said. "I'll just phone Ellen now, shall I?"

When Linda emerged from the shower wrapped up in one of my bath towels, she looked so adorable that it was all I could do not to whisk her right into my bed. Instead I poured her another cup of coffee and told her what I'd arranged for her with the Dudleys. She nodded, sipping the hot liquid as she perched on the edge of one of my chairs and looked around the room. "It's you," she said softly. "It's so like you."

"What?"

"This room," she explained, with a smile. "It's just as I imagined it."

"Well, I guess it is me," I said. "Everything I am is right here."

She loved it all—my great posters of Houdini and Giuseppe Verdi, the blowups of great horses in action on my walls, my shelves of esoteric and out-of-print books on magic, the jockey silks pinned in place over my headboard, even the stacks of old programs and racing forms piled into two corners of the room. "I could fall in love with you just by spending enough time in this place," she said, her eyes suddenly filling with tears. "Oh, Lou, what's happening to me? Do you think I'm crazy?"

I sat down beside her and put my arms around

her. "No, I don't think you're crazy," I said, "but can I ask you something, without offending you?"

She nodded and turned to look at me with the innocent, trusting eyes of a child. "Anything," she said. "Really."

"Are you on medication of any kind?"

She looked surprised. "No. Why? I'm not sick. I take aspirins sometimes. What a strange question."

I told her about my meeting with Alden Berry. "He said you'd done this kind of thing many times before. I guess he meant having a fling with some stranger."

She stared at me in amazement. "I've been married to Michael for ten years," she said. "Before you, I've had one other man in my life in all this time. He was my riding instructor in Maryland, when we lived there for a couple of years and Michael was away so much. I've been pretty faithful to Michael, even though I don't love him and maybe never have. I shouldn't have married him, I know that now. But I had nothing, I had no one, and he offered me everything. And at first he was kind to me, Lou, and always generous. He always played around on me, I knew that, but I looked the other way and he never rubbed my nose in it. It's only been during the last few years that he's changed so much, become so bitter and so hard. Alden told you I was crazy?"

"No, but that you fantasized a lot," I said. "He hinted you had a multiple personality."

She laughed. "That bastard," she said. "You know, he's tried so many times to come on to me. Once he even openly propositioned me. I never told Michael, because they were in business together. I should have, I really should have. That little shit!"

I was cheered by her reaction, especially by the flash of anger she had shown me. I couldn't believe any longer in any of Alden Berry's accusations. Some-

thing else was going on here, something Linda represented to them had become a threat. She must have
known something about them and perhaps done something that had alarmed them. I had no way of knowing,
of course, what that might be. "Listen, Linda, I think
you ought to get ready and we ought to go," I said. "I
have this funny feeling that very soon someone is going
to come here looking for you."

She quickly finished drying herself off and got
dressed. I checked the hallway to make sure no one was
waiting for us, then whisked Linda down the back stairway to the carport. As I eased the Toyota out into the
traffic on Crescent Heights, she began to talk again.
"Do you remember me telling you about someone
named Win at Sovereign?" she asked. "I mentioned
him that morning, when I called you at the TV station."

"Yes, I remember."

"I think the trouble started with him, Lou."

"What do you mean?"

"Michael and I went out to Sovereign to see the
filly," she explained. "That was the day after you and I
were supposed to go. I don't think Michael knew yet
about us. He must have told Alden to check into it, but
hadn't yet heard from him. He was very cold to me,
but not hostile. Anyway, we drove out there and this
young guy, Win Freeman, showed us around. Lou, it
was the strangest feeling I've ever had in my whole life.
The thing is, the minute I saw him I felt I knew him,
that he and I were—joined somehow. Have you ever
had that feeling with anybody?"

"No."

"That's what I mean. I hadn't either, until I met
him. It was the most incredible thing. It was like turning a corner and finding yourself confronted by the
ghost of yourself. I almost can't describe it. It was incredibly intense and weird."

"How did he react?"

"That's what was even stranger," she said. "Lou, he had the same feeling I did. I know he did. He even asked me if we had met somewhere. He didn't pursue it, of course, because Michael was right there, but all the while, as he showed us around, he kept staring at me and I kept staring at him and I knew Michael was getting angry, because I guess he thought we were coming on to each other or something. I can't tell you how strange it was. I wanted so desperately to talk to Win, to ask him things. I had to find out where we could have met, but I didn't have the chance. And all the time he looked at me so strangely, with such longing in his eyes. Then, when we got to the stable where Mad Margaret was, he got called back to the front office by Judge Hunter and had to leave. But as he left, he looked at me again and he said, 'We know each other, don't we?' And then he left and I didn't see him again. But you know? I've dreamed about him since, several times. We're always in this big room and we're running, running, trying to get out of it, but there's no door and we can't get out. And then some people come and there are voices shouting and screaming and I'm taken away and . . . and . . . oh, I don't know, I can't remember exactly, but it always ends with me being taken away by someone somewhere. I wanted to find Win again to talk to him, but I haven't been able to. That afternoon Alden called Michael and that's when this all started. Michael locked me in my room for two days till that woman came."

"Where could you have known this guy? When you were kids, maybe?"

"Yes, I think so. I think that must be it. I've got to find out someday, Lou. I don't know why, but I know it's important."

On the way into downtown Hollywood, we stopped at an all-night drugstore and bought some basic toilet articles, as well as a terrycloth robe and a sweater. "I can go to a Versateller tomorrow and get some more money," Linda said. "I'll have to buy some clothes."

"Do you have your own account or is it a joint one?"

"It's my own. I still have the money every month from my trust fund. It's not a lot, but I use it to buy clothes and stuff."

"Good. I was afraid your husband might shut it down."

"He can't. No one can. I can't even touch the principal and I don't know where it comes from, except through this bank in Chicago. It's about twelve hundred dollars a month. It's not much these days, but it's nice to have."

It was about eleven-thirty when I pulled into the driveway in front of the Dudley house, a small California-Tudor bungalow nestled into the shoulder of a hillside above Gower. Below us the lights of Hollywood glittered pink and gold in the soft spring night and a breeze blew through the fronds of the royal palms lining the road. Ellen Dudley, a lanky brunette with a good-humored, strong-jawed English face set off by a nose built like a ski jump, answered the doorbell herself. "Hello," she said, beaming with pleasure, as if she had been eagerly awaiting our arrival all evening, "come in, come in. I've put on the kettle. Are you hungry, love? I've got plenty to eat. With the kids gone and Robert never home the larder's always full. Shifty, you reprobate! Where have you been hiding this ravishing creature? Come in, don't just stand there!" She put one arm around Linda's shoulders and whisked her inside into safety and warmth.

Jamie Horton, the only lawyer in town I knew and trusted, had become a partner in the firm of Harvey, Harvey, and Walsh in Pasadena, the same one she had worked for when I had first met her six years ago. She was now in her middle or late thirties, tall and more attractive than I remembered her, with large gray eyes and a mass of cropped brown curls, but she had still not acquired a sense of humor. I had met her when she had represented a woman I was in love with in a shoplifting case, but she had considered me and my profession as an evidence of weakness in her client's character. And now here I was, once again involved with a married woman in trouble. If anything, her distrust of my motives seemed to be stronger than before. No sooner had Linda and I settled into chairs in her comfortable second-story office, with its pleasant view over a small public park, than she chose to ignore me completely as Linda explained to her what had been going on. She left out the part about our torrid interlude at the Crossroad Motel, but Jamie Horton clearly had the feeling that something fairly crucial had been left out of her potential client's narrative. She looked disapprovingly at me. "And exactly how are you involved, Mr. Anderson," she asked, "apart from your shared ownership in this racehorse?"

"I guess you could say I like Mrs. Cameron but don't care much for her husband," I said. "Do you need details?"

Linda blushed. "I'm—I'm sorry, Miss Horton," she said. "Lou and I—well, we've been involved with each other."

"For how long?"

"Not long." Linda glanced at me in desperation.

I rose to the occasion magnificently. "We spent two hours together in a motel one morning," I said, not looking at Linda. "Unfortunately, Cameron found out about it. Most of the trouble seems to stem from that time."

"I can see that it might," the lawyer said drily.

"We didn't plan it or anything," Linda said. "It just happened."

"Yes, I understand. What is it you would like me to do for you, Mrs. Cameron?" Jamie Horton asked.

"I—I'm not sure," Linda said. "I—I guess I'm frightened. Michael's gone crazy or something."

"He's made her a prisoner in her own home and he's threatened me," I said.

Jamie Horton ignored me again. "Do you want to separate from your husband?" she asked Linda. "Do you want a divorce?"

"I—I think so. It's all happened so fast . . ."

"I suggest you think that aspect of it over for a few days," the lawyer said. "Give yourself some time. What I can do for you now is contact your husband and put him on notice to cease and desist with his threats and potentially criminal actions. If I have to, I can get an injunction, which is, in effect, a formal court order, to do so. I can better advise you on that point after I've talked to him or to Mr. Berry. Then, if you wish to pursue the matter further legally, I can set separation and divorce proceedings in motion. Are you certain that you're being well-advised in this matter?"

"Yes," Linda said. "Tell me what I have to do now."

As the lawyer talked, gently ferreting out additional information from her new client, I sat back in my chair, wondering what I was going to do about the man who had threatened to break my fingers. It hadn't taken long to find out about him, but none of the information had proved reassuring. His face had popped out at me from the second set of mug shots Jude Morgan had dropped in front of me. "So quick?" the detective had asked, as I stepped into his cubicle at the West Side station.

"This is definitely the guy, Jude," I said, dropping the picture on his desk.

"You're sure?"

"Absolutely."

The typed information next to the photograph on the printout recorded a brief but inglorious career in crime. His name was Donald Houps, fifty-two years old, five feet nine and a half inches tall, weight two hundred and five pounds, brown hair, brown eyes, no distinguishing scars or other marks. He had once been a licensed private investigator, authorized to carry a gun, but had been arrested twice for breaking and entering, had served time for assault and battery, had beaten both a kidnapping and a manslaughter rap, but had lost his license and was now regarded as a potential threat to the peace and welfare of the community at large. "So what am I going to do about this guy, Jude?" I had asked.

"Well, my man, I would try to avoid any vexatious confrontation, if I was you," the detective had calmly announced.

"Great, Jude, terrific," I said. "Such a big help. Knowing that I have the forces of law and order on my side has given me a tremendous lift."

"Ain't much else I can do right now, Shifty," he had said. "Get the message over to him that we know who he is and we'll go lookin' for him. If he bothers you again, maybe we can go after him then. You just got to watch yourself, my man."

"Do you have a place to stay?" Jamie Horton now asked Linda.

She glanced over at me and I nodded. "You'll be okay at the Dudleys for a while," I said. "I'll talk to Robert. Then, eventually, I suppose you'll want some more permanent arrangement."

"Yes, I can't stay there forever. I don't have a lot of money, but I'm sure I can make some arrangement."

Jamie Horton looked at me with what I took to be mild distaste. "Meanwhile, it would be better, obvi-

141

ously, if you and Mr. Anderson here were not to be seen together," she said.

"How about if we're just discreet?" I suggested, with a smile. "I'm the only friend Linda has around these parts."

The lawyer shrugged. "Well, you'll do what you think best," she said. "I think the less we do to exacerbate an already tense situation, the better, obviously."

"Noted," I agreed, turning to Linda. "Darling, we'll have to postpone our appearance on *Donahue* until this is over."

Linda stared at me in amazement. "What?"

"Nothing, nothing," I assured her, taking her hand comfortingly. "I never can resist a joke."

Jamie Horton glanced at me as if she had caught me picking my nose at the rear of her classroom, then rose to say good-bye to her client. "Please call me this afternoon, Mrs. Cameron," she said, shaking Linda's hand. "I may have some news for you then." She handed her a card. "It has my unlisted home number on the back. Call me at any time, if you need me. Do we have your number, Mr. Anderson?"

"You used to have it. It hasn't changed."

"Please leave it with the receptionist on your way out," she said, not shaking my hand and turning her attention back to the stacks of paper on her desk. Obviously, she was never going to be elected president of my local fan club.

"You believe these people?" Angles Beltrami asked. "For a lousy twenty-three hundred and eighty dollars, which I don't even owe them?" He turned in his seat to confront us. "I mean, I paid the damn taxes on the house."

"Evidently they perceive that your payment was a little short," Arnie said, scanning the field through his binoculars as the horses moved past us on their way to the starting gate.

"So we got a difference of opinion here, right?" Angles said. "So what right have they to send me this kind of notice? So you know what I do? I figure the angle. Better to go down there and talk to them in person, I figure, rather than mess around. I mean, these people can get nasty, you know what I'm sayin'? Okay, so I go down there and I talk to this broad, which has got a face like a rusty hatchet, and right away I can tell she hates me. I mean, she sits behind this desk negotiating with characters like me, who don't work for a living, and she's gotta hate us, right? So I tell her it was my mother's house and we had to sell it, on account of Mom cooled a couple of years ago, and I can tell right away she don't like what she's hearing, like I'm some kind of freak who don't like his mother. I hated the bitch, but that's another story and I don't need to go into it with this IRS broad. So I show her how I sold the house and my accountant figured the taxes and I paid them and all. And then she says my accountant figured wrong and I owe the government another twenty-three hundred and eighty bucks and I gotta pay it or they're gonna attach my property and varnish my salary or some damn thing. So I tell her I don't have no other property and I don't work. So she asks me what do I do for a living, so I tell her I'm like retired. I mean, I ain't gonna tell this bitch I go to the track, am I? I can see that don't set well, so then she says maybe they'll audit all my past returns for the last five years if I don't pay this money, so I tell her I didn't make no returns the past five years on account of I didn't make no money. So she asks what I'm livin' on and I tell her my savings, which I don't keep in no bank on account of I don't trust 'em. Now I can see she's gettin' really pissed off, 'cause she don't believe anythin' I'm tellin' her."

"Would you?" Arnie asked. "Who would believe you, Angles, if you weren't actually a living presence among us?"

"Shut up, Arnie, I'm talkin'," Angles said.

"Are you making a wager on this race?" Arnie asked Jay, as the horses neared the gate.

"No," Jay answered. "Any one of four horses could win it, so I'm passing."

"Anyway, I tell her I ain't got the twenty-three eighty and I leave," Angles continued, "so now I start gettin' these letters from them sayin' I should pay up or else. I mean, what the fuck am I supposed to do?"

"Tell them you'll pay them when your giant exacta hits," Arnie advised. "Explain to them that you are a serious player and you have this foolproof system."

"Listen, Angles, do you own anything?" Jay asked. "I mean, like property, stocks, bonds, stuff like that?"

"Are you kidding?" Angles answered. "You got to be out of your mind. I don't even own my car."

"So what's the problem?" Jay said. "What are they going to do, attach your wardrobe? Tell them to take a hike."

"Yeah, that's what I figured, only I can't sleep good," Angles said. "I mean, these people can get real nasty. I don't want to wind up in the slammer again. So you know what I do? The other night, about four A.M., I can't sleep, so I remember that the IRS has a twenty-four-hour hot line. So I pick up the phone and I call them."

"At four o'clock in the morning?" Arnie said. "You must have been desperate."

"I couldn't sleep from worrying about what these bastards could do to me," Angles said. "Anyway, some guy picks up the phone and I explain the whole thing to him and then he asks me, 'Hey, man, how much you owe?' So I tell him and he says, 'Twenty-three hundred and eighty dollars? Hey, go out and buy some lottery tickets, man!' I mean, can you believe this? This is the IRS hot line at four A.M. I'm tellin' ya, the whole fuckin' country's goin' down the fuckin' tubes."

"I find it heartwarming that our public institutions are staffed by players," Arnie commented, as the horses walked into the starting gate. "There's hope for the nation yet."

Before leaving the track that afternoon, I called Linda to make sure she was all right and made a date to pick her up for dinner. "Have Ellen drop you off at the restaurant," I instructed her, "just in case I'm followed out of here. I'll go home first, make sure I'm alone, then meet you there about eight."

"Be careful, Lou," she said. "Michael's capable of anything, I think."

"I think so, too," I said. "Don't worry. If I'm late, just wait for me, okay? I'll get a message to you."

It didn't surprise me, when I drew up in front of my house forty minutes later, to find Don Houps waiting for me. He was sitting behind the wheel of a red Ford Escort parked down the street and hadn't yet spotted me. He must have expected me to drive into the carport and come up the back stairs, where he would confront me out of the public view. Instead I parked directly in front of the building and walked back to where he sat. "Hello, Mr. Houps," I said cheerfully. "Been waiting long?"

The little black eyes stared at me as if I had spat on his shoes. "Where is she?" he asked.

"Who?"

"You know goddamn well who," he said. "Are you going to tell me or am I going to have to persuade you of the seriousness of the occasion?"

"Mr. Houps, my friend Jude Morgan of the L.A. Police Department is well informed as to your where-abouts and activities," I said. "I would caution prudence in this matter. Am I using big enough words for you?"

"You don't tell me where the woman is you won't be using words much longer," he said. "Where is she?"

"I told you, I don't know what you're talking about. Now, are you going to leave or am I going to have to summon the forces of the law in all their magisterial splendor in order to prevail upon you? How's that? The English convoluted enough for you? Are there enough rococo flourishes?"

With a grunt of rage, he suddenly opened the car door and came around the hood to get his hands on me. He moved with surprising speed and I barely had time to get one kick in. It was a good one, though, that caught him just below his right kneecap and sent him lurching sideways against the body of the sedan. He tried to grab me with his left arm, but I danced out of reach and began yelling, "Fire! Help! Fire!"

He looked startled, then swiftly limped back to the driver's side and got in. I kept on yelling until he had pulled out from the curb and driven away up the block.

"Shifty, is that you?" Max asked, as he came through the front door of the building, holding a small extinguisher in his hands. "Was that you? What's this fire?"

"It's okay, Max," I said, as two of the tenants now also appeared, along with several neighbors from the house next door and across the street. "It was a mugger. I kicked him and shouted, so he ran away."

"But what's the fire?" Max asked.

"That's what you shout, Max," I explained. "You shout for help, nobody comes, because they're too scared. You shout fire and everybody comes."

"Who told you this, Shifty?" Max asked, amazed.

"My women's defense class," I said. "Kick and shout, just basics, Max. Thanks for coming."

"But the fire engines," Max said. "I already called."

In the distance I could hear the sirens. "I guess we'll just have to explain it to them, Max," I said. "What else could we do?"

chapter 10
LUGGING OUT

Unlike his brother, who had apparently been killed in his sleep, Giorgio Fazzini put up a terrific fight for his life. He had been living in a hilltop house outside the small coastal town of Cambria, a hideaway he had apparently bought some years before under an assumed name. The place, originally a two-story hacienda belonging to an old Hollywood character actor named Vic Maples, had been converted into a fortress complete with a sophisticated alarm system, floodlights, and two trained German shepherds. Giorgio liked to spend weekends there, usually with one or more of the expensive hookers he enjoyed entertaining. It was one of these women who had apparently tipped off the police as to Giorgio's possible whereabouts, which is how it happened that his body was finally found. He had always kept a deliberately very low profile around Cambria, had never appeared in any of the local shops or public places, and in recent weeks, ever since the murder of his brother, had not set foot outside the grounds. He had evidently stocked the house with food and liquor and no one went in or out except his private bodyguard, a professional muscle man named Tony Uccello.

The presence of the bodyguard had been his undoing. Uccello must have left the grounds on an errand of some sort and been surprised by the killer on his return. His throat had been cut, probably as soon as the murderer had succeeded in gaining access to the property. His body was found just inside the gate, almost certainly dumped there from a moving vehicle. Both the dogs had been shot, by which time Fazzini must have known that something was wrong, but not in time to prevent the killer from getting into the house.

The police found evidence of a tremendous struggle. Giorgio must have met his assailant in the foyer or the adjacent living room, because both areas contained smashed furniture and other evidences of a violent encounter, including bloodstains on the floor, carpeting, and walls. Somehow the battle had continued, up the stairs and into the studio, then at last in the bedroom. Giorgio's body had been found sitting up on his king-size bed with his back against the headboard. He was the victim of multiple stab wounds to the chest and abdomen. His throat had also been cut, so completely that his head had almost been severed from his body. He was dressed only in a bathrobe. A .38-calibre Beretta lay on the floor by the head of the bed, under an open drawer of his nightstand. Giorgio had evidently tried to get at it before dying, but had been unable to. The police surmised that he had died on the floor, then had been hauled up into bed as a sort of macabre joke. He had been dead for at least two days.

The police assumed that the motive had been robbery, because every room had been ransacked. A small wall safe behind a picture in the living room had been blasted open and emptied. It was not clear, however, what the killer had been after, because every drawer in the house had been opened, every piece of furniture slashed apart, every rug flung aside, every closet and cabinet rifled. Giorgio's wallet, containing several hundred dollars in cash, and his gold Rolex, had been left on his bureau, perhaps by mistake. Below the safe, a stack of negotiable bonds lay scattered about, while nothing had been removed from the silver cabinets, one of them containing an almost priceless collection of antique stirrup cups. "We figure the guy was looking for something specific," one of the police spokesmen informed the press, "but we don't know what it was or if he found it." There were no clues as to who the killer might be, or at least the police were not revealing any more about the case.

I found out about all this from a story in the *L.A. Times* and I immediately called Linda at the Dudleys. She was upset about it, because she had met the Fazzinis and knew that her husband had been in business with their firm. "Do you think Michael could have done this?" I asked her.

"Killed them? No, Lou, never."

"I don't mean with his own two hands," I explained. "Obviously, this was the work of a professional. No, I mean, could he have hired someone to do this?"

She seemed stunned by the idea, as if I had suggested that her husband ate human flesh or slaughtered babies. "Michael's not a murderer, Lou," she said. "He could never have done such a thing."

"He hired a woman to keep you a prisoner in your own home against your will," I pointed out, "and he's paying a professional hood first to force me into a crooked deal, then to terrorize me into revealing your whereabouts. Where do you draw the line, Linda?"

"Oh, Lou, I don't know, I just don't know anymore." She was crying, but she quickly got hold of herself. "Jamie's set up a meeting with Michael."

"With you?"

"Yes. With the lawyers."

"Where?"

"In Alden's office in La Jolla. We're going down this afternoon and we'll probably drive back after dinner."

"What's the idea?"

"Jamie wants to arrange separation terms, after which we'll institute divorce proceedings," she said. "I'm not going to ask for anything, Lou."

"Don't be silly, Linda," I said. "There are community property laws in this state."

"I told Jamie I just want the animals and enough money to take care of them," she said. "I have an income—"

"It isn't much these days, Linda," I said. "Twelve hundred bucks a month puts you at the poverty line."

"I don't want anything of Michael's, only enough to keep the animals and enough to support myself until I can get a job."

"What kind of job, Linda?"

"Something to do with animals," she said. "I'm good with animals. Oh, and I'm going to ask for Maggie."

"Linda, don't rush into anything. Have you discussed all this with Jamie?"

"Yes, and she sounds like you do."

"Listen to her, for God's sake," I urged. "If you don't want fifty percent of everything and you just want some sort of reasonable settlement, then I'd bet Michael will go along. Why wouldn't he? But don't give all your rights away. You devoted ten years of your life to this guy."

"I know, I know . . ."

"Linda, listen to me. Let Jamie talk, let her handle everything, okay?"

"Okay, okay."

"Tell you what—I'll drive down to Del Mar and get us a room, at the little motel on the beach, all right? Then Jamie can drop you off there after the meeting with Berry. We'll have an evening together and tomorrow morning we can go out to Sovereign and see the filly on our way back to L.A. How does that sound?"

"Wonderful, Lou. Jamie won't approve—"

"Jamie doesn't like me," I said. "She thinks I'm a bad influence on women in trouble."

Linda giggled. "You are. I knew it the moment I set eyes on you. I think I might just fall in love with you, Mr. Anderson."

"Oh, don't do that, Linda," I said. "I'm a man without a future, don't you know that?"

"I only know I want to make love to you."

"That I can arrange," I said. "That I can guarantee."

We hardly slept at all that night. We took long, leisurely gallops around each other, not asking for speed or quick breaks, but concentrating instead on checking off nice even quarters. By midnight we had finished and were lying naked in each other's arms on the queen-size bed in my motel room. An obscenely huge silver moon sprayed light through the window and a soft spring breeze wafted in through the half-open blinds. I held Linda against my chest, allowing her head to rest on my shoulder, her long blond hair spread out on the pillow behind her. "Oh, Lou, this is what I needed," she said. "I've been so afraid, so tense this past week."

The meeting in Alden Berry's office had gone about as well as could be expected. Michael Cameron had begun by remaining in the background, a hulking presence with his back to the wall, while Alden Berry outlined his position to Linda and Jamie Horton, seated in chairs facing the lawyer's desk. "Basically, Alden said that Michael owed me nothing and that, if he wanted to, he could fight me in the courts for years and pay me nothing during all that time," Linda informed me.

Jamie Horton had listened politely to Alden's slick, preposterous opening salvo and then had quietly read a few facts of California law to him. "Mr. Berry, you know as well as I do that I can go into court tomorrow and get an order committing your client to paying enough for Mrs. Cameron to live on until such time as this matter is resolved, even if it does take years," she told him. "On the other hand, my client is perfectly willing to make a reasonable settlement right now that will avoid all this unpleasantness and save us all trouble, time, money, and needless litigation. Why don't you and Mr. Cameron confer and let's see if we can come to an agreement."

She had ushered Linda out of the room and downstairs into a coffee shop on the ground floor of the building, leaving Cameron and Berry alone. Forty minutes later, they had seen Cameron storm out through the lobby and into the street, presumably heading for his car. Then they had been summoned back upstairs and into Alden Berry's office. "On the assumption that your client will indeed be reasonable," Berry had begun, "we are prepared to arrive at an agreement, pending an ultimate resolution at such time as the divorce becomes final."

"Are you prepared to go to arbitration, if there should be a disagreement?" Jamie had asked.

"We have no objection," Berry had answered.

Cameron agreed to pay Linda six thousand dollars a month, out of which she would have to take care of all the animals, since he had no intention of keeping any of them—horses, dogs or cats—himself. Proceeds from the sales of their houses in Houston and California would be divided fifty-fifty. "As you know, my client is under investigation and there may be lawsuits and criminal proceedings," Berry had informed Jamie Horton. "Therefore, we can't make a final agreement until we know the outcome of the litigation. This arrangement is conditional on my client's ability to pay. It's possible his assets may be tied up until some sort of resolution is achieved."

Jamie Horton hadn't wanted to accept the deal. She thought it was insufficient and that Cameron had a lot more money than he claimed to have, but Linda had insisted on accepting the offer. Documents were to be drawn up and signed within a matter of a couple of weeks or so. "And I get to keep Maggie," Linda said, excitedly. "We're selling all the other racehorses, but my share of the deal is the interest in the filly. Isn't that terrific?"

She propped herself up on one elbow to gaze smilingly down at me. I grinned back. "Hello, partner," I whispered. "Want to do a little running?"

"Aren't we coming back too soon?" she asked.

"I'm sound enough. How about you?"

For an answer, she leaned over and kissed me. A bell went off, the gates opened, and we broke into the clear, lying flat against each other and going lickety-split again, gaining position as we hit the first turn. We were unquestioningly becoming stakes contenders.

Win Freeman was standing inside the reception area in the administration building when Linda and I walked in there, at about eight-thirty the following morning. My second impression of him was that we had surprised Linda's double, all dressed up in male clothes, but it was quickly dissipated when he spoke to us. He had a cold, soft voice and a reserved, self-contained manner that was not at all like Linda. He had nothing of her natural vitality and ebullience, but seemed abstracted from life, as if he were motivated by concerns and desires hidden from the public view. Still, the initial impression startled me, because something in the eyes and expression, even in the way he moved his head, seemed so like her that it brought me up short. He had had his back to us, leaning over to talk to Sherry at her desk, and turned when he heard the door open behind him. I heard Linda give a little gasp, as if she, too, had been caught, as I had been, by the sudden, almost blinding similarity, like unexpectedly catching a glimpse of oneself in a distant mirror. He must have seen this look on our faces, because he stared at us for a long moment, puzzled perhaps by our reaction. "Well, hello, Mrs. Cameron," he finally said, "it's nice to see you back here." He looked at me. "Mr. Anderson, isn't it?" I nodded. "I guess you've come to see your filly."

"How is she?"

"Just fine. Luke says there's no heat at all in either shin now and we're having our vet check her out this morning, around ten," he said. "We wouldn't want to ship her back to Mr. Pickard in anything but top shape. The R and R here has done her a lot of good. I'm glad you sent her to us."

He sounded so unlike Linda that my initial feeling on seeing him quickly faded. Everything he said seemed calculated to make a good impression and his tone was flat, almost monotonous in delivery, as if he had been coached. He was dressed in a dark blue business suit, perfectly tailored to show off his trim, muscular frame, and his blond hair was neatly combed back, showing off his blue eyes above a tight, thin mouth all but hidden under his brush mustache. He looked like a clothing ad for the menswear section of a luxury department store. I began to wonder how I could possibly have imagined that he looked like Linda, who was warm and vibrant and outgoing, with all of her emotions near the surface of her life.

"I'll call the barn to make sure Luke or somebody's around," he said, picking up a phone. "We've had a busy day already—two foals born within an hour of each other."

"Oh, that's so lovely!" Linda said. "Can we see them?"

Win Freeman smiled back at her, but his eyes remained intensely serious. "Sure, why not? Luke, this is Win," he said, speaking now into the receiver. "Mrs. Cameron and Mr. Anderson are here to see their filly. I'm sending them right over, okay? Sure, sure, that's fine." He hung up. "Go on over. You know the way, don't you?"

"Yes," I said, "no problem."

"I have a few things to attend to here," he continued, "then maybe I'll join you. By the way, Mrs. Cameron, the Judge would like to meet you. I told him about you."

"Oh, really?"

"Yes, he's very anxious to meet you."

"Well, fine, anytime," Linda said. "And I was going to ask about boarding some horses here for a while."

"Sure thing," Win said. "Thoroughbreds?"

"No, my two jumpers." Her face flushed with embarrassment. "My husband and I have separated. I have to find a place for them for a while."

"That shouldn't be any problem," he said. "If you'd like to stop by the office here before you leave, Sherry can make all the arrangements for you."

"Oh, thanks so much. I've been really worried. I was hoping you could take them."

"If you'll excuse me," he said, smiling, "I'll tell

the Judge you're here. You'll be coming back this way to see Sherry." And he left us to go into an inner office, closing the door behind him.

Luke Davis was sitting on a chair outside his tack room when Linda and I drove up a few minutes later. "Sure is nice to see you folks," he said. "Why don't you wait out here and I'll bring her out, so's you can see how she's gettin' on." He disappeared into the stable and came out a couple of minutes later leading Mad Margaret behind him. "See?" he said. "Put some nice slow gallops into her, then a couple of works, and she's ready to win for you." He grinned and patted the horse affectionately on the neck.

The filly looked marvelous to me. Her coat gleamed in the sunlight and her muscles rippled under her skin as she moved, her head up and her ears cocked forward, her liquid brown eyes alertly taking in the scene around her. Her lower legs were encased in thick protective bandages, reminding me of a ballerina about to stretch herself at the bar. Luke walked her around, so that we could watch her move, admire the incipient power and grace within her. "Isn't she a beauty?" Linda said. "Oh, Lou, I'm so excited! I just know she's going to do something important!"

"She figures to, ma'am," Luke said. "She's just the nicest filly I've ever been around. Just like a big, friendly dog most of the time, but when you take her out on the track and she gets her mind set on runnin', why she's a handful and then some. I never seen her run in a race, but this filly could make a gamblin' man out of me again, I tell ya."

As we stood there in the warm spring sunlight, admiring this miracle of nature that had been entrusted to our care, a big green Jaguar came slowly around the curve of the road and parked a few feet away. Judge Jed Hunter got out from behind the wheel and walked smilingly toward us. He looked even taller and more impressive than I remembered, as if he had stepped out of a Norman Rockwell portrait of a distinguished American. His black eyepatch lent him a somber air, but also contributed to the overall impression he made of utmost rectitude, as if he had somehow paid with an eye for his present eminent position in the world. "Hello there, I'm Jed Hunter," he said, holding out a big strong hand toward Linda. "Win said you folks were here to look at your horse, so I thought I'd better mosey on down to greet you." His gaze focused on me. "We've met, haven't we, Mr. Anderson?"

"Yes, a few weeks ago," I said.

Linda's hand disappeared into both of his and he turned his full attention on her. "Well, you're a sight for a tired eye," he said. "Win didn't begin to do you justice."

I looked at Linda. She seemed paralyzed, as if transfixed, her hand imprisoned in his. "You . . . I . . . ," she stammered. "Have we met?"

"I don't think so," the Judge said, smiling benignly at her. "No, I don't believe we have. I'd have remembered, all right. Where are you from, honey?"

"I . . . I was brought up in Louisville, Kentucky," she said, "but I haven't been living there for a long time."

"I know Michael, of course," the Judge said. "I knew him back here before he moved East and then we've been in a couple of ventures together. I guess you know he helped me build this place."

"No, no, I didn't know," she said. "Michael never discussed his business affairs with me." She withdrew her hand from his, but Hunter never wavered in his scrutiny of her, as if never before in his entire life had he ever encountered so extraordinary a human being. It was a quality all great politicians have, the one that turns constituents to jelly and creates a mass of uncritical, fanatical supporters. "I suppose you know that Michael and I . . ."

"Win told me," the Judge said. "I am sorry about that. I hope you'll be able perhaps to patch things up."

"No, I don't think so," Linda said. "No, I don't think that's possible now."

"Well, in life, I've found, things have a way of working themselves out," the Judge countered. He turned to Luke. "You can put the filly away now, Luke. I guess we've seen what we need to." He focused on Linda again. "Louisville, you say? Your family's there?"

"Just my father," she answered. "My mother's dead."

"And your family name?"

"Bergman."

The Judge stared at her. "Oh, I am sorry about your mother," he said. "And I'm sorry, too, about all this trouble Michael seems to be having with this investigation up in Los Angeles. But I guess Michael never discussed that with you either."

"No, no, he didn't."

"Seems like trouble comes in bunches," Hunter said. "But I'm sure Michael can handle it. He's a smart fellow, I know that. Where did you two meet?"

"In Louisville," Linda said. "I was just out of school, working in a bank back there when Michael was in town. He was building a big shopping mall on the Ohio side, so I saw quite a lot of him at the bank."

"And he didn't have to see too much of you, did he?" the Judge said, smiling broadly. "Was your name always Bergman?"

"What do you mean?"

"Well, I was just curious." He laughed, a little too heartily, I thought.

"I was adopted. I don't know what my real name was."

"No, of course not. Say, I don't mean to pry," the

159

Judge said. "Win thinks he may have known you before at some time, maybe when you were kids, so I just thought I'd ask. You do look a little alike, don't you think?" He smiled. "Maybe you're long lost kin. You know Win is an orphan, don't you?"

"No, I didn't."

"Well, he is. Only he was raised in the East, went to a couple of fancy schools back there, learned a lot of important stuff, then threw his education away by going to work in the horse business. How's that for an inappropriate way to mishandle a good education?"

"I envy him," Linda said. "I always wanted to work around animals, but Michael didn't want me to."

"Bergman, Bergman," Hunter said. "I knew a man by that name once. Do you happen to know if he came originally from these parts?"

"He never told me much about himself," Linda said, "but I think so. He talked a couple of times about having lived in California. I think he was in real estate back here."

"I see. Might be the same man. How's he doing?"

"All right, I suppose," Linda said. "We're not in touch anymore. We never got along too well."

"And your mother? What was she like?"

"Oh, she used to drive me crazy," Linda said. "She worried about everything and she and my father fought all the time. I couldn't wait to get out of there. Luckily, I had my own money and I was able to leave."

"You had a trust fund?"

"Yes. How did you know?"

"I didn't," Hunter said, with a booming laugh. "I just guessed. When folks have their own money, it's often in the form of some kind of trust. I guess your real parents must have made some provision for you."

"Yes, they did. I'm grateful for that."

"And you don't remember anything about your earliest childhood?"

"No, almost nothing. There was the outdoors, lots of sand, with trees and rocks and such," she said, "but nothing else. And there's one memory I have of something very bad happening, maybe a fire. I have nightmares sometimes and it's always about people shouting and screaming and running and that's all I remember. I must have been tiny when my real parents died, I guess."

"Sounds to me like you may know something about Linda's childhood," I observed.

Hunter focused that one brilliant eye of his on me. "Just speculating, Mr. Anderson," he said. "It's interesting, you know."

"Yes, it is," I said. "Linda and Win seem to have come from similar backgrounds and they do look a little alike, don't you think? Might be worth looking into sometime. I wonder how one would go about it."

The Judge laughed. "Oh, I wouldn't waste a lot of time on that, if it were me," he said. "It would be quite a job and often people who have been adopted don't like what they find when they dig back into the past and find out who their real parents were. I wouldn't advise it, really. I just brought it up because of Win. He was struck by seeing you, Mrs. Cameron. I guess you both had the same feeling."

"What was his story, exactly?" I asked.

"Oh, quite different in many respects," the Judge said. "Win's folks were horse people. His real dad was a gypsy horse trainer, an alcoholic who never had much luck in life. His wife died and he put Win into a home and disappeared."

"Where was that?"

"In Florida," Hunter said. "Mostly they lived in Florida, up around Ocala in the horse country. Summers they'd follow the horses north to Maryland and the New Jersey circuits. Win was not much more than two when his dad gave him away. He doesn't remember much about him."

"I guess orphan stories are all pretty much the same," I said.

"They don't all end up as well as these two did," the Judge answered.

"By the way, didn't you say Win went to some expensive private schools back East?" I asked.

"Yes, why?"

"Where'd the money come from for that?"

"Oh, his adoptive parents had plenty of money," Hunter observed. "They were in banking and real estate out on Long Island. But Win must have had horses in his blood, because from the time he was sixteen that's all he cared about. He went to the races one day at Belmont and got hooked and it never left him. Blood will tell, won't it?"

A woman came running up the road toward us from the direction of the main house. She was dressed in a blue jogging suit and moved at a steady if unspectacular clip. As she came near us, she waved, as if about to keep on going, but then abruptly slowed down and walked toward us. She was in her sixties, I estimated, but in very good shape, lean and hard of body, with copper-colored skin. Her gray hair was tied back into a ponytail, her mouth bore a trace of lipstick, and she looked at us through a pair of large, stunningly beautiful green eyes. "This is my wife, Freddie, Mrs. Cameron," the Judge said, as she came up to us. "And Mr. Lou Anderson."

Freddie Hunter stared at Linda as if she had seen a ghost. "I wouldn't have believed it," she said.

"It's pretty striking, isn't it?" Hunter replied. "No wonder Win was surprised."

"I guess you realize we think you two look a lot alike," Freddie Hunter said. "That's what brought me up short just now. I had to come over and see for my-self. I hope you don't think I'm being rude.''

Linda smiled. "Oh, not at all," she said. "I was pretty startled myself when I first met Win. But I guess it's just a coincidence. We have very different back-grounds and come from different parts of the coun-try.''

"Is that so?" Freddie Hunter said. "Well, people do get around, you know. I'd swear you two were brother and sister.''

"We *are* both orphans.''

"You don't say?" Freddie Hunter exclaimed. "My God, this is the damndest thing!" She turned to her husband. "Have you talked to Win about this?''

"No need to," Hunter answered. "It's pure coin-cidence.''

"I wouldn't bet on it," Freddie Hunter said. "If I were you, honey, I'd do a little investigating. It might be fun to find out, wouldn't it?''

"I guess so," Linda said, unconvinced. "I don't know, though. There's a lot about my past I'm trying to forget and I'm not sure I want to know everything.''

"Well, you and I are different, then," Freddie Hunter said. "There's no aspect of life I don't want to know everything about. Certainly, if I had a long lost brother lurking in the bushes somewhere, I'd sure as hell try to find him." She smiled brilliantly at us. "Well, that's your business, of course. Anyway, I'd bet-ter get back on the road here before this old body of mine crumbles into dust. It sure was a revelation seeing you, honey. And not just because you're about the prettiest thing I've set eyes on in half a lifetime." With a wave of good-bye, she broke into a run again and moved away from us.

Hunter watched her go, then turned back to us. "Win tells me you want to board a couple of your show horses here for a while," he said. "We can arrange that."

"Oh, I'm so glad."

"Just stop by the office on your way home. And good luck with this fine filly of yours. Don't listen to Freddie. I agree with you. Some things in the past are better off left undisturbed, don't you think?"

"I guess I'm afraid to know, for some reason," Linda said. "There must have been so much unhappiness."

"Yes, yes, I guess that's right," Hunter said, heading for his car. "Can I give you a lift back?"

"No, that's all right, we'll walk," I said. "We like to look at the horses."

"Yes, of course, why not?" He seemed suddenly abstracted, lost to us, as if reminded of something important he had overlooked. "See you folks." And he quickly drove away up the road where his wife, now a distant blue speck, ran toward the barren hills.

chapter 11

FANNED

"Did you ever hear what happened on the day Harry S. Truman died?" Arnie asked, during a lull between races on the Wednesday card.

"Oh, here he goes again," Angles said. "Do you believe this guy?"

"This is a true story," Arnie said, "not one of your crude dirty jokes, Angles."

"Okay, what happened, Arnie?" Jay asked, as he leafed through one of his notebooks to look up the record of a trainer newly arrived in town with a small string from the East.

"Truman died during the course of a racing day at one of the Maryland tracks," Arnie said, "and so the announcer told the crowd about it. 'Ladies and gentlemen,' he said, 'we are sorry to have to inform you that our beloved ex-president, Harry S. Truman, died this afternoon at his home in Independence, Missouri, where he will be buried next week. In honor of our beloved late president, we would now like to ask you to observe a moment of silence.' The crowd quieted down, all except for one railbird, who shouted, 'Fuck Harry S. Truman, I'm getting buried right here!' ''

"I don't get it, what's so funny?" Angles asked, as Jay and I rocked back and forth.

"Ah, Angles," Arnie said, "it could have been you."

"You know, Arnie, you think I'm some kind of dummy," Angles said. "I'm no dummy. I just don't see what's so funny about that story." He stood up. "Anyway, this is important. I hear the six horse is real live in here, but I'm gonna find out about the change of jock before I risk any money on the bum. They ain't givin' it away here these days." He bounded out of the box with his usual manic energy in pursuit of the elusive angle.

It had been a good week, every day a winning one, and my life would have seemed full to me, if Linda had been around. We had spent the first two days after getting back from Del Mar finding her a place to live. She had ended up renting a small furnished cottage in West Los Angeles. It was sandwiched between rows of apartment buildings and condominiums in a part of town inhabited mostly by young professionals. The property was owned by an elderly Japanese widower, who kept it primarily so he could go on tending the small but exquisite garden he had first planted there thirty years before. His wife had died three years earlier and he had moved in with his son and daughter-in-law a few blocks away, but returned nearly every afternoon to plant, trim, mow, water, and feed his creation. Behind an outer sheltering hedge, a perfectly manicured lawn framed beds of flowers of all sorts, planted so that each passing season brought its quota of colorful blossoms. Pink and white bougainvillea grew up over one corner and tumbled down a trellis at one end of the house, while a small back patio was sheltered at the rear of the lot by a tightly packed row of fat cypresses. Inside, a small living room was dominated by a large functioning fireplace, and there were two bedrooms, a kitchen, a dining alcove, and, behind it, a small studio. "It's perfect," Linda had said to me. "There's even a room for you to come and practice your magic." The rent was high, twenty-two hundred dollars a month, but Linda had signed a two-year lease an hour after seeing it and without having to produce any documents or wait for a credit check. Her enthusiasm for and appreciation of the garden had immediately convinced the old man that he was about to acquire an ideal tenant. I had helped her to move in that very evening, which hadn't been hard, because she still had little more than the clothes on her back. Jamie Horton had contacted Alden Berry about arranging to have her personal possessions packed up and moved out of the Rancho Santa Fe house, but nothing had yet been done about it.

She had left the next day for Houston to see about her animals. Cameron had apparently arranged for all of the cats and dogs to be picked up by the local animal shelter, a euphemism for the city pound, and her concern was to recover as many of them as she could and arrange to have them shipped back to her in L.A. or at least to find homes for them locally. "Lou, you can't simply walk away from your animals, any more than you could walk away from your children," she explained, when I asked her how she could afford to take care of all of them. "And I love them. I'll be back in a few days."

"Hurry up or you'll miss me," I said. "My ship sails in five days."

"Oh, Lou, what will I do without you?" she had asked, falling into my arms.

"You'll have plenty to do," I said. "You'll have all your animals to take care of and your things to get organized. And you'll have to go out to the track to make sure the filly's okay. Don't worry, you'll be busy enough. This is a good job and I can't afford to turn it down."

Hal had booked me on a cruise ship to the Caribbean for a two weeks' stint. I would perform two shows a night in the main lounge and also mingle with the passengers, doing a little close-up here and there, as the occasion arose. The money was good, twenty-five hundred dollars with all expenses paid, and I didn't want to turn it down. I hadn't counted on Linda going back to Houston, but I figured that, at the worst, we might not see each other for three weeks, not an eternity even for new lovers. Until she left, I had seen her every night and our lovemaking had become the most important thing in my life, perhaps the most passionately carnal affair I had ever been involved in. She seemed to have a lifetime of love to commit to me and it came close to overwhelming me, mainly because she seemed so fragile, so vulnerable, almost haunted. She had begun to dream and the dreams were mostly nightmares, out of which she awoke crying and bathed in sweat, terror-stricken. She could never remember any of them clearly, but they seemed to arise out of her earliest memories and always ended in screams, the sounds of running, sometimes the fear of fire or of some other huge calamity closing in on her like a smothering blanket. I had made her promise me to go and see a therapist upon her return, because all I had been able to do for her was hold her in my arms until the fear passed and she could fall asleep again. It had troubled me, but I had reasoned that it could be dealt with and that somehow my growing feelings of love for her would eventually provide a wall behind which she could shelter from whatever horror had befallen her in infancy. Horseplayers are all incurable optimists and I am certainly no exception.

She had called me from Houston a few days later. She had only been able to save one of the dogs and two of the cats, all the other animals having been put to sleep at the shelter. She couldn't leave there, she explained, until she had found a home for the dog; the two cats, both Siamese, she would bring back with her. She had also found Nellie and was making sure that the old woman was happily employed. So the upshot of all this activity was that she would not get back before my scheduled departure from San Pedro that night. She was in tears on the phone. "Michael killed my animals, just as surely as if he'd done it himself," she said. "I hate him, Lou. How could I have lived with him all this time? I hate him so!"

Once again I had done my best to calm her. "Anyway," I added, "you can take some consolation from all the trouble he's in. He was indicted yesterday."

"Yes, I know," she said. "There was an item about it in the papers here."

"He's out on bail, of course, but it looks like they may have the goods on him," I told her. "He's charged with having filed fake bids on city jobs here and of having kicked back to various public officials. The mayor's office is implicated as well. Rhineland Sand and Stone is part of it, but now that both the partners are dead it doesn't look like they're going to get much information from that source. If Michael is found guilty of all the charges, he could get thirty years. His lawyer, our pal Alden Berry, is denying everything, of course. I guess I have to question your taste in men, Linda."

"Where does that leave you?"

"What I mean is, you go from one extreme to the

other," I explained. "First you marry a rapacious, crooked wheeler-dealer, then you choose a horseplaying close-up magician. You're either unlucky or have very poor judgment."

That made her laugh. "Oh, Lou," she said, "come back to me safely. Don't flirt with ladies on board."

"I'll leave that to the Italian crew," I said. I blew her a kiss into the receiver and hung up on her. I remember being so little concerned about her that my one thought was wondering what effect the presence of the two Siamese cats in her life would have on our relationship.

"So how long are you going for, Shifty?" Jay asked me, as we got up to go and bet on the ninth race.

"Two weeks."

"By the way, I meant to ask you, you know this guy Cameron, don't you?"

"Yeah. His wife owns a piece of my filly."

"They're saying he was in with Tony Huge on this deal downtown."

"So I heard."

"Know anything about it?"

"No more than you do, Jay."

"You ever see him?"

"No. He's sold all his horse interests. He and his wife have split and she received his share of the filly as part of the settlement agreement."

Jay turned around to grin at me as we took our places in a betting line. "Hey, not bad," he said. "I've seen the lady."

"No comment."

"Ah, Shifty, you rogue," Jay said, "there's no end to your devious magical ways."

I bought a fifty-dollar win ticket on a five-to-two shot Jay had assured me could not lose, while he boxed the horse with four others in exactas. We got back to our seats just in time to watch the race go off and our selection bounce quickly out to an easy lead in the mile-and-one-eighth gallop over the main track. He stayed there all the way, enriching us all. "Would that it were always this easy," Jay said, as we rose to leave the premises.

"Hey, Shifty, I just made two grand!" Angles exclaimed, bounding to his feet in elation. "This was a great day! Just like the one when my father died!"

"Nice," Arnie said, "very nice, Angles. I guess I don't want to know about your childhood."

"No, you don't," Angles said, rushing away toward the windows to cash in.

"Dinner, anyone?" Arnie asked. "I'm treating. Dudley's at eight o'clock."

"That I don't want to miss," Jay said. "It isn't every day Arnie picks up a tab. Shifty?"

"I can't. I have to pack and be on board by midnight," I said. "We sail early tomorrow morning."

"You won't have to hustle the kids at the pool table tonight, Arnie," Jay said. "How much did you hit for?"

"Enough," Arnie said. "I can smell the flowers in my garden for a while. Very nice, Jay, very good handicapping. When your figures hold up, it's like a miracle."

"The figures never lie," Jay said. "They're the one constant in a cruel world of deception and illusion, the one solid faith to build your life on."

"I guess I'll sell you my piece of the True Cross," Arnie said. "One of these days, Jay, you're going to walk on water."

The cruise proved to be uneventful and financially fruitful. Most of the passengers were middle-aged and elderly couples, who spent most of their time eating and shopping at our various ports of call. They tipped fairly generously and seemed appreciative of my work, but they were a bland audience. By the time we got back to L.A., I was so rested I felt half-dead and I was bored nearly out of my skull. I telephoned Linda from on board as we were docking, but received no answer. I picked up my car and drove out of San Pedro in late afternoon, fought traffic most of the way up the freeway, and finally got home a little before seven.

Max Silverman saw me drive up and came out of his little flat to greet me. "So how was it?" he asked. "You enjoyed yourself?"

"Max, it was very nice and very boring."

"Yes, the Caribbean is an area without culture," he said. "It has no art, no music, and cooking you could die from. Wait, I have mail for you." He disappeared inside his apartment and popped out again a couple of minutes later with a stack of mostly monthly bills. Buried in the center of the pile, however, was a small, sealed envelope addressed simply to "Lou" that had apparently been delivered by hand. "This lady brought it by two days ago, as I was sorting the mail," Max informed me. "She asked me to give it to you. Shifty, this was some lady. I mean, this was a woman to compose sonnets about. Is this a friend of yours?"

"More than a friend, I hope, Max," I said, heading back toward my apartment.

"Some men live their whole lives without knowing beauty," Max said. "It is an aesthetic deprivation that shrivels the soul."

I waited until I was safely inside my apartment before opening the envelope. "Dear Lou," the letter read, in a spidery handwriting scrawled along the page from edge to edge, "I don't know how to tell you this or how to explain anything to you, but I can't see you again—at least not for a while. Something extraordinary has happened to me, something I almost couldn't believe. I have found my soulmate, the person I've been waiting for my whole life. I know you will find this hard to believe, after us, but it's true and I can't help it or myself. Please forgive me. You're a wonderful man and I'll always cherish the memory of our time together. Someday, I know this, you will understand. Linda."

I sat down, feeling as if somebody had just punched me with an iron fist under my rib cage. Then I got up, went into my kitchen, made myself some coffee, and sat down to read Linda's letter again. It didn't improve on a second reading. If anything, the pain increased and for several minutes I had to sit in place, fighting for air. I wanted to stand up and shout and begin breaking things, but all I could actually do was breathe, one small lungful at a time. The coffee helped, but not that much.

I lay down on my bed and stared at the ceiling for a while, then I sat up and dialed Linda's number. No answer. I lay down again, then sat up a second time and called Charlie Pickard at home. "Shifty," the trainer's voice barked raspingly into my ear, "you're back. How was the Caribbean?"

"Boring," I said. "Charlie, have you seen anything of my partner since I've been gone?"

"You mean Mrs. Cameron? No. Why? Something wrong?"

"I don't know, Charlie," I said, hoping my voice sounded a lot calmer than I felt. "She wrote me a pretty strange letter, something about having met her soulmate or something. I was wondering if you'd seen or heard from her. She sounds like she might be having a breakdown of some sort. She was pretty nervous and tense the week before I left."

"She ain't been around the track, at least not in the mornings. Listen, Shifty, about women—believe me, you're better off without them. Get laid, sure, but get them out of the house before breakfast. You'll live longer."

"I'm worried about her, Charlie," I explained. "She sounds more than a little crazy."

"They're all crazy and they'll drive you crazy, if you let them. Listen, maybe she's upset over her husband being in the slammer."

"Cameron's in jail?"

"Yeah, he was arrested five days ago and booked for the murder of the Fazzini boys."

"You're kidding."

"Would I kid you, Shifty? No, they think he had them cooled because they were gonna blow the whistle on him on them real-estate deals downtown," the trainer said. "Anyways, he's denying everything, but this judge put him in a cell. He can't even make bail right now, 'cause the judge made it two million dollars."

"What evidence do they have?"

"Who knows? I only read about it in the papers."

"Well, it isn't Cameron she's gone back to, that's for sure, Charlie."

"Forget her. She's trouble, she'll cost you money. Want to hear some good news?"

"I sure do."

"Your filly's doin' great. I'm gonna breeze her tomorrow, an easy three. You comin' out?"

"I'll be there, Charlie. Thanks."

After Charlie, I called Jay. He was very glad to hear from me and informed me that I had missed a tremendous two weeks of action at the betting windows. "I look at the Form these days," he said, "and the winners jump off the page at me and run around the track like little trained pigs. I've made eight grand since you left, Shifty."

I congratulated him and asked him about Cameron. "Charlie said he's a suspect in the Fazzini murders."

"That's right," Jay said. "They think he killed them both."

"To keep them quiet?"

"Who knows? But this is a big scandal, Shifty, bigger than you can imagine. You know who else's name came up?"

"Who?"

"Judge Jed Hunter. One of these deals involved the building of Sovereign Acres," Jay said. "Something about kickbacks from city contracts going into the Sovereign project. It seems both Cameron and the Fazzini boys were into all kinds of scams. They moved money around from one account to another so it was hard to keep track of where any of it went."

"How would they funnel money back into building Sovereign?" I asked.

"Who knows? There have always been rumors about Sovereign, that it was some kind of a land grab involving water rights and there was a lawsuit some years ago. This is all according to recent stories in the press. It's complicated, Shifty, but now Hunter has released a statement about how he'd worked with both the Fazzini boys for years and always found them to be honest and all that. Bullshit, you know. He said he'd stake his reputation on Mike Cameron's honesty and said he was helping him raise the bail money. Two million bucks is a lot of bread. Cameron's lawyer said it's an outrage and that there isn't any evidence of any wrongdoing involving his client. I love lawyers, don't you?"

"Cameron's got the money. He's rich."

"Sure, all these guys are," Jay said, "but a lot of it is done with mirrors. You know, they own everything in sight, but they're always cash poor. They operate through banks and off big loans. It's not like in the old days, when the rich bought gold and buried it in the ground. To raise two million in cash these days you got to sell something or mortgage it or borrow it off your assets. I don't know exactly how it works, but I do know that much about it, Shifty. You comin' out tomorrow?''

"Yes, I think so. But I haven't even bought a *Form.*"

"Don't bother. Uncle Jay, the old fox, will pick live horses for you."

"Careful, Jay. The track always punishes hubris."

"Who's that?"

"A Greek friend of mine. I'll see you, Jay."

I hardly slept at all that night. My bed seemed achingly empty. I could almost feel the presence of Linda in my arms, the way she had nestled on my shoulder after our lovemaking and the golden sheen of her hair as it spread out over my pillow and the soft, warm breath of her as we lay with our arms around each other and talked. It was well after three when I finally dozed off and I was awake again by the time my alarm went off at six-thirty.

"You don't look good," Charlie said. "If you was a horse, I'd lay you up."

"I haven't had much sleep," I said.

"We ready, boss?" Polo Rodriguez asked, coming up behind us. He was standing outside the barn, waiting for the filly. It was going to be a beautiful spring day, with no early-morning fog for a change, and the sun felt good against the back of my neck and on my shoulders.

"Here she comes," Charlie said. "Now remember, Polo—once around, nice and easy, then breeze her three."

The boy grinned. "If she let me."

"She's tough," Charlie said to me, "always ready to go. She don't know she ain't in shape to run a race yet."

May Potter emerged from the shedrow, leading

Mad Margaret out into the bright sunlight. The filly was full of herself, her ears cocked alertly forward, her chestnut coat gleaming. From time to time she'd toss her head up and down, as if to get rid of May's tranquilizing hold on her. I know what I'm doing, she seemed to be telling us, get rid of this kid here and I'll really show you something. May held on, talking softly to her the whole time.

Charlie saddled her, taking extra care with the cinch to make sure the equipment wouldn't slip during the workout, then gave Polo a leg up. Maggie tossed her head back and grunted with what I took to be pleasure. "Look at her," the trainer said admiringly, "she thinks she's gonna go out there this morning and blow everybody away."

"She looks great," I said, so excited by the sight of her that I temporarily forgot about Linda and my lack of sleep.

"She's a real racehorse, this filly," Charlie said. "She was born to run."

We followed her out toward the track, then went up into the guinea stand to watch her gallop. No sooner had we reached the rail than she went past us in the middle of the track, her beautiful head tucked low and her neck arched against the tight hold Polo maintained on her. She seemed about to explode, as if at any moment she would shake the boy off her back like a bothersome insect and take off on a wild run of her own. But Polo knew her well and would allow her just enough rein to keep her interested. Horse and rider swung out into the turn, moving like a mirage off into the morning light, a study in repressed power and grace.

"Them shins of hers is real tight now," the trainer said, "cold as ice. If we stay on schedule, she may run for us once at this meet. She'll definitely be ready for Del Mar."

We stayed in the stand long enough to watch her navigate once around the oval, then breeze for three furlongs with the boy practically standing up on her. We went down to the gap as Polo turned her head back toward the barn. "Good," Charlie called out. "Thirty-six and four."

"Man, she's a handful," Polo said, grinning as they came up to us. "She wants to go from the moment she hits the track."

"Ain't that too bad," Charlie said. "I just hate to have a horse in the barn that all it wants to do is run all the time. Gets me to thinkin' we might make some money with her and that ain't good for my peace of mind." He winked at me. "Want some coffee?"

We went into the track kitchen, picked up two cups of hot brown water, which is the closest any track kitchen can ever seem to come to making real coffee, and sat down at a corner table in a patch of sunlight streaming in through the plate-glass window. D. L. Gantry saw us and got up from a large table in the center of the room to join us. "That was your filly out there, wasn't it?" he asked, pulling up a chair. "She looked awful good."

"Yeah, Lane, but we got a ways to go with her," Charlie said. "You still got some of those Cameron horses for sale?"

"I kept three of them," Gantry said, "but I got one I want to get rid of. He's not much, but he should win at the forty or fifty thousand level. You know the one I'm talking about?"

"No."

"The three-year-old roan with the black shoulder patch," he explained. "He doesn't have a lot of speed, but he'll be all right when they stretch him out."

Charlie turned to me. "How about it, Shifty?" he asked. "Want another horse? This is one of the ones Lane bought for your friends."

"No, thanks," I said. "Can't afford it."

"I'll see if I can talk Abe into buying him," Charlie said. "He could use another claimer in his string."

"Why don't you buy the man a good horse, Charlie?" I asked.

"Any one of Lane's castoffs is a better horse than Abel Green has," Charlie said. "Besides, he don't deserve a top horse. Abe's a cheap claimer at heart himself." He looked at Gantry. "I think we can come up with forty for him. I'll call Abe and let you know."

Gantry shook his head and sighed. "It's a funny thing about this deal," he said. "It's the first time I ever got a man out of the horse business before I even got him into it. Not one of his animals has even run a race. And I bought him some nice stock, too."

"I guess it don't matter too much to Cameron now," Charlie said. "He's worrying about the gas chamber."

"His wife still own part of the filly?"

"Part of her," I said. "Why?"

"I saw her down at Sovereign yesterday," Gantry said. "I said hello, but I don't think she recognized me. Is she living down there?"

"I don't know," I said. "I've been away and I haven't spoken to her recently. What was she doing?"

"Working with those two jumpers of hers," Gantry said. "I guess she's taking personal care of them, the grooming and all. I said hello, but she sort of looked right through me, so I kept on going. I went down to look at some yearlings. They've got some pretty good stock down there now. The Judge has put a lot of money into his breeding program."

"What made you think she might be living down there?" I asked.

"I don't know, she seemed pretty much at home. Win was with her and they seemed awful close."

chapter 12

ON THE WRONG

LEAD

Jamie Horton hadn't heard from Linda and was actually glad that I had called. "I've been trying to reach her, because I have papers for her to sign," the lawyer explained. "And you say you don't know where she is either?"

"I think I do," I said, "but I thought I'd check with you first."

"She left me her number in Houston and I called her there, but she'd already left. When I called her number here, no one ever answered. Then I tried you, but your answering machine said you'd be out of town for a couple of weeks, so I didn't bother to leave a message. I thought Mrs. Cameron might have joined you somewhere."

"No such luck," I said. "Look, Jamie, something a

little strange is going on and I'm going to try and find her. I'll tell her to call you."

"Thank you. I appreciate it. I'm supposed to return all these documents to Mr. Berry as soon as Mrs. Cameron has had a chance to look them over."

The next morning I waited until after the rush hour and then drove south to Sovereign Acres. It was about eleven o'clock when I arrived and parked in front of the administration building. Sherry looked up and smiled brightly at me as I walked in, but gave no hint that she had ever clapped eyes on me before. "Hello there," she chirped, "welcome to Sovereign Acres. How may I help you?"

"I'm looking for Linda Cameron," I said.

"Oh, dear," the girl replied, looking alarmed. "I —I really don't know how I can help you. I—oh, dear . . ."

"I know she's been here," I said. "It's very important I speak to her. We have a horse together and I have to locate her. Is Win Freeman around?"

"Oh, my goodness," the girl said. "No, he's—I mean, they're—what did you say your name was?"

"I didn't. Anderson, Lou Anderson. We met a few weeks ago, Sherry, when our horse was boarding here, in Barn forty-eight."

"Oh. Oh, yes, I remember," the girl said, looking wildly around for help. "Oh, dear. I do think you should speak to somebody else. I really don't know what I can tell you."

"Well, Sherry, you could start by telling me whether Mrs. Cameron is here or not. That would be a fine and useful beginning."

"Oh. Ah. Yes. Well, you see—no, I can't. I can't do that."

"Has she been here?"

"I can't tell you that. I'm not authorized—I mean, I just don't know."

"You don't know?"

"No, I don't know." She took comfort from her assumption of ignorance and made a brave effort at a smile. "Perhaps you could call back—"

"No, Sherry, I drove all the way down here because I was told on good authority that Mrs. Cameron was here," I said. "Now, why don't you rack your memory and see if you can't remember whether you saw her here or not. She's a tall, very beautiful lady of about thirty, with fair skin and long blond hair. She has two show horses boarding here."

Sherry's resistance hardened into a pout. "I told you, I'm not authorized," she said. "I can't say anything else."

"Well, what about Mr. Freeman?"

"I'm sorry," the girl said, her mouth tightening into a thin line. "I'm not going to say anything more."

"You haven't said anything at all, Sherry," I said. "Are the Hunters here?"

"The Judge went into town," she said. "He's due back this afternoon. Mrs. Hunter should be home, but I haven't seen her." She turned to her computer and began to punch numbers into it, a way of dismissing me from her thoughts, I presumed.

I left her office, got back into my car, and drove down to Barn 48, where I found Luke Davis sitting in his tack room with his feet up on his desk and reading the *Racing Times.* "Well, howdy," he said, getting up to greet me. "How's the filly doin'?"

"Very well, Luke," I told him. "She breezed an easy three furlongs yesterday and she's looking terrific. Listen, I heard that my partner, Mrs. Cameron, might be down here, but I can't find her and Sherry isn't being very helpful. What's going on? Has something happened?"

"Aw, Jesus, you don't know?"

"I haven't heard a thing, Luke," I said. "I've been

away and I just got back. I gather something's been going on. Mrs. Cameron's lawyer hasn't even heard from her and it's urgent. What's going on?"

Luke stuck his head out the door and looked up along his shedrow, then turned to face me. "Ain't anybody supposed to talk about it, but there's been some kind of shit storm around here. That Mrs. Cameron, she came on down here a couple of weeks ago to work with them two jumpers of hers and Win took care of her." Luke grinned conspiratorially. "Now remember, I didn't tell you nothin', right?"

"Right, Luke. Go on."

"Next thing anybody knows, they're rollin' around in the hay together and I ain't just spoofin' you. First time they got together was in the barn where she keeps them two horses of hers. They got it on in one of the stalls in there."

"How did anybody find out about it?"

"Hell, there wasn't no way you couldn't see it," Luke continued. "They was together every damn minute of the day. She followed him around like a little old puppy dog. It got embarrassin' after a while. So Judge Hunter, he calls Win into his office up at the house to talk to him about it, but it didn't do no good. They just couldn't keep their hands off of each other. It got so everybody was talkin' about it, how she just moved in with Win and all. He's got a cabin, you know, down there right on the lake and she just set up housekeepin' in there with him. The Judge, he just about had a fit and the word was that Miz Freddie was so mad she was gonna leave the farm, fly off to New York or somethin'. The thing was, Win just about stopped workin' at all when he and the lady started foolin' around, didn't do nothin' he was supposed to. So two days ago they left."

"They left?"

"Yes, sir, just picked up and went, without sayin'

good-bye to no one. I never seen the Judge so upset before. He was runnin' around here askin' questions and stormin' about the place. You don't want to go makin' the Judge angry, you know. He's got a temper on him that won't quit. I wouldn't want to be in that boy's shoes when the Judge catches up to him, no, sir.''

I said good-bye to Luke, got back into my car, and started to drive away from Sovereign Acres. Out of my left window I could look up the slope of the hill toward the main house. The building, with its impressive dome and white pillared facade, looked suddenly huge and empty, as if it had been abandoned by its creators. On impulse, I suddenly turned left into the driveway leading up to the house and came to a stop by the front door. I got out and rang the bell. As I waited, I looked back over the ranch, with its acres of fenced pastures and stables, at the lake and the cluster of bungalows at one end, the scene framed by the bleak crags of the surrounding mountains, and the sight rang a small bell in my head. The scene reminded me of an illustration in one of my childhood books, a saga of knight-errantry whose title I had forgotten, but whose images remained vivid in memory. It was from just such an enchanted setting that heroes mounted on horseback had left to seek out dragons to slay and villains to conquer. Why couldn't I recall exactly what book it had been? I was so lost in the recollection that I didn't hear the front door open.

"Yes? Can I help you?"

I turned and found myself confronted by an old Indian woman dressed entirely in black. Her face was deeply wrinkled and devoid of makeup, with a strong chin and firm-looking mouth. Her long white hair had been pulled back into a bun and her eyes peered out from under heavy lids like those of a hawk. "I'm looking for Judge Hunter," I said.

"Not here," the old woman answered. "You try

down there." And she pointed to the administration building.

"I did. The girl didn't seem to know anything. My name's Lou Anderson. I'm looking for my partner, Mrs. Linda Cameron."

The old woman gazed at me impassively for a moment, then she took a step back. "Come in," she said. "I tell Mrs. Hunter you're here."

I entered and found myself confronting a huge circular staircase leading to the upper floors, then turned left and followed my guide into a small foyer off the main entrance hall. "Wait here," the old woman said, leaving and shutting the door behind her.

I looked around. The room was small, but with a high ceiling. Bookshelves soared upward full of leather-bound sets on all aspects of the law. One wall was covered with oil paintings of great racehorses, mostly English, mounted in tight array, while against another wall a set of glass-enclosed cabinets contained gold and silver trophies won by various Sovereign horses over the years. Properly impressed, I sat down in a leather armchair to wait. Although it was midday outside, the only light in the room came from a narrow window high above me, and a large floor lamp had been turned on in one corner to ease the gloom. I had the strange feeling that I had been whisked into another time frame, as if in this room only the past counted and nothing would be allowed to disturb it.

Ten minutes later, the door opened and the old Indian woman stuck her head in and indicated that I was to follow her. "Mrs. Hunter wants to see you," she said. "This way."

She moved quickly for a woman of her age, with long catlike strides that whisked me through a series of elegantly appointed rooms full of bright colors and living plants and as cheery as the waiting room had been gloomy. There were vivid Impressionist paintings of pastoral scenes on the walls, but I had no chance to take in details. I retained only an impression of comfort and elegance, with the sun streaming in through the half-open blinds over the windows and bathing the interiors in golden light. The old woman opened a set of atrium doors onto a back patio, then shut them behind me as I stepped outside.

Federika Hunter was sitting on a padded iron garden seat facing me, her face half-hidden under a broad-brimmed straw hat and a pair of sunglasses. She was dressed in a handsome orange pants suit and espadrilles and a set of garden shears rested on the coffee table beside her. Behind her, extending the full length of the house and down the slope behind it, sprawled a huge garden full of roses, hundreds of bushes, with blossoms of all colors and sizes in effulgent flower. She saw the impression the sight made on me and smiled. "My one extravagance, Mr. Anderson," she said. "My husband rages at me about it, since roses require a lot of water and water is a scarce commodity around here these days, but I ignore him. It's a passion of mine, you see."

"They're pretty spectacular," I said. "How many different kinds do you have here?"

She shrugged. "I don't know," she said. "Over a thousand, I'm sure. Please sit down. Would you like something to drink?"

"No, thank you. I'm sorry to disturb you," I said, "but I'm a little desperate."

"About Mrs. Cameron?"

"Yes. She seems to have disappeared. Her own lawyer hasn't heard from her. I gather she's been here and left."

"Yes, she has. It has been a most unfortunate situation. We've all been very upset."

"Can you tell me anything about it? I have to find her. It's important."

"They couldn't stay here, of course," Federika Hunter said. "Not after what happened."

"Exactly what did happen?"

"They went after each other like a couple of rutting goats," she said. "It was a public exhibition. I couldn't tolerate it and I insisted that they leave."

"Do you have any idea where they've gone?"

"None. They simply left together, that's all I know. What exactly is your interest in all this?"

"I'm partners with Mrs. Cameron in a horse, a nice three-year-old filly named Mad Margaret," I said. "We boarded her here for a month or so—she had sore shins—then shipped her back to my trainer at Hollywood Park, Charlie Pickard. It's a business matter."

Federika Hunter smiled, but there was little warmth in it. "I don't think you're telling me everything, Mr. Anderson," she said. "Are you the man she left her husband for?"

"We were seeing each other, yes," I admitted. "I care about her and I'm worried. This isn't normal behavior."

"The woman is a slut," Federika Hunter said. "She began with Freeman the day she showed up here. It's been scandalous."

"What about Freeman?" I asked. "Who is he?"

"Someone my husband hired out of the blue," she said. "I was against it, of course, but Jed never listens to me. The man is dangerous and unbalanced. When this business started here, I insisted that they leave at once."

"You insisted? Why? Apart from the scandalous part, what difference could it make to you, Mrs. Hunter?"

"I have my reasons," she said. "May I give you some advice, young man?"

"Sure."

"Have nothing to do with her, with either of them. They are dangerous."

"Dangerous?"

"Extremely. And now you must excuse me, I have to get back to my garden."

She hadn't rung a bell or made any other sign, but suddenly I was aware that the Indian woman had returned. She hovered silently in the doorway like a huge, dark bird of prey, her ancient face half-hidden in the shadow. I rose to go. "Mrs. Hunter," I said, "what is your husband's connection to all this? I mean, might he know where they've gone?"

"I doubt it," Federika Hunter said. "He's always had this blind spot about young Freeman, but now, at last, I think he realizes what sort of person he is. He will have nothing further to do with him, if I have any say in the matter." She stood up and picked up her garden shears. "Eartha will show you out."

I followed the old woman back through the house to the front door. She moved even more swiftly than before and I didn't catch up to her until she had opened the front door for me. "Excuse me," I said, "but do you have any idea where Freeman and Mrs. Cameron might have gone? I have to find them, Eartha. It's very important."

The old woman looked at me sorrowfully, as if I had touched some ancient grief in her soul. "Do you believe in the spirit?" she asked.

"I'm a magician," I replied. "I believe in the unknown."

"Then you believe in evil as well," she said. "Here is evil."

"Here? Sovereign Acres?"

"The land has always been cursed," she said. "It was cursed before the white man came. Nothing has grown in this valley."

"Cursed? By what?"

But the old woman did not answer me. She waited until I had stepped out into the bright sunshine of early afternoon, then quietly closed the door in my face.

I showed up at Jay's box at Hollywood Park a few minutes after the fifth race that day to find Angles in a fury. Apparently some animal he had wagered on should have won easily but had received a questionable ride from his jockey, a journeyman rider named Ken Otay. "It was a revelation, a masterpiece of incompetence," Arnie Wolfenden informed me as I joined my friends. "First he had to steady out of the gate, then he got fanned on the first turn, then he somehow got the horse over to the rail where he got boxed in. When he did get clear at the quarter pole, he took him inside again, got shut off, had to take up and come around. Even so he only lost by a couple of lengths. I think that for once Angles has a legitimate beef."

"You should have been here," Angles said. "You've never seen nothin' like it."

"I'll bet I have," I said. "I've seen some, Angles, believe me."

"You know what we should do?" Angles said. "We should take the top sixteen riders and line them up against a wall. Then we shoot one of them."

"How would that help, Angles?" I asked.

"It would get their attention, these little pricks."

Arnie sighed. "Have you ever seen a horse get shut off or check or go too wide or take up on his own?" he said. "No, of course not. Horses never get in trouble running by themselves without those little monkeys on their backs. We should just load the horses in the starting gate by themselves; then, just as the gate opens, we play a recording of a lion roaring in back of them. That gets them all to running. When they near the turn, you have a loudspeaker there and more roar-

189

ing. That gets them to make the turn. One last roar at the head of the stretch gets them to finish the race. The winner will be the fastest horse. It's a way of eliminating these little Shakespearean actors from the scene."

"Where have you been?" Jay asked me, as I opened my *Form* to take a look at the rest of the card.

I told him about my trip to Sovereign Acres. "It seems that the lady has run off with one of the employees," I said. "I don't know where she is."

"And naturally you're concerned about her."

"Well, yes, I am. There's something a little peculiar going on here that I haven't figured out, Jay."

"Are you involved with her?"

"No comment," I said. "She owns part of my horse. Let's leave it at that."

"Women are different from us," Arnie observed. "They came to this planet from some other galaxy. Trying to figure them out is much like endeavoring to handicap cheap three-year-old maiden races. Past performances don't count, the workouts tell you nothing, and the results are unpredictable. Celibacy is the only safeguard against them."

Charlie Pickard had one of Abel Green's claimers, a seven-year-old gelding named Bouncing Willie, entered in the next race, so I went down to the paddock to have a look at him. He was one of the long shots in the field, but I had a sneaking suspicion that he might be live. Charlie liked to set up horses for certain specific races, particularly because his owner liked to cash tickets, and no one was better than Charlie at putting one over from time to time at good prices. I had learned to sniff them out when he was firing, but it never hurt, I reasoned, to seek confirmation of my estimate from the trainer himself.

Unfortunately, Abel Green was standing next to him, watching May Potter lead his saddled horse around the ring, so I couldn't ask him anything. "This horse has some speed," I heard Charlie say to his jockey, Dub Singer, a newly arrived hotshot rider from the Midwest, "but don't go usin' him up early. Try to sit behind the other speed in here and he'll have somethin' left in the drive."

I didn't need to hear anymore. It was clear to me that Bouncing Willie, then at odds of twelve to one, might be a good thing, so I waved good-bye to Charlie and headed back toward the grandstand. May Potter fell into step beside me. "I'm gonna bet on this horse," she said. "He's feelin' pretty good these days."

"Me, too."

"I rub him, you know," she said. "He's ready to run."

"I figured. Come on, we'll bet him together. Where are you sitting?"

"Oh, I gotta get back down there," she answered, with a quick smile. "I'm his groom. I sure hope we don't lose him."

"Oh, yeah, of course. How's Maggie doing?"

"Great, just great," she said. "She's real hard to gallop, Polo says, on account of she's so full of run. She just pulls him out of the saddle every morning. That lady that's your partner? Mrs. Cameron?"

"Yes?"

"She came by this morning to see her."

"Really?"

"Yeah. She didn't look too good, kind of drawn and real nervous and all. She only stayed a few minutes."

We joined a betting line and shuffled slowly toward the window together. "Mrs. Cameron didn't tell you where she was staying, did she? Or whether she might be back some other morning?" I asked.

"No, she didn't," May said. "She said she'd like to come to the next workout, that's all." May hesitated, as if wondering whether to pursue the subject, then glanced shyly back at me. "She had a fella with her," she continued. "He stayed kind of away from us, like he didn't want us to notice him."

"Tall, blond, with a mustache?"

May nodded. "Yeah, that's him. I think I know him."

"Win Freeman?"

"Yeah." May's expression hardened. "I know him from Florida. He ain't good news, mister."

"I guess I know that."

May didn't seem to want to pursue the subject, so we shuffled steadily ahead toward the window in silence for a minute or two. I noted that the odds on Bouncing Willie had dropped to eight to one. Abel Green was obviously betting solidly on his animal and I figured the horse would be no better than five to one by post time, especially since the board watchers would pick up the action on him and begin to bet themselves. May wagered twenty dollars on him to win and I risked fifty.

"See you," May said, throwing me a casual wave as she headed back downstairs. "Don't spend your money all at once."

I watched her go, mostly because I'm susceptible to attractive women and May Potter was looking especially well herself these days. She had on a tight pair of faded blue jeans that fitted very snugly over her hips and buttocks and she moved with the fluid grace of an athlete.

When I got back to our box, I told my friends about Bouncing Willie, but Jay decided to pass; the numbers simply didn't add up on the horse. Angles thought Willie had no chance either, but Arnie rose out of his seat and made a window in time to risk a hundred dollars on him. He got back to the box just as Willie sneaked through a hole on the rail at the head of the lane and came bouncing home, true to his name, by two lengths. He paid $10.80 to win. "Numbers don't mean shit," was Angles's view of the event. "I should have figured the angle."

On my way out of the track, I stopped at a public telephone and called Linda's newly rented cottage, but got no answer. Then I called Jamie Horton at home.

"Yes, Mr. Anderson, I've heard from her," she told me. "She called my office this afternoon. She doesn't sound well, but she said she would be coming in tomorrow. Have you tried her at home?"

"Yes, just now. There was no answer."

"I'd try her again later," the lawyer suggested. "I think she was going to see a doctor."

"What exactly is wrong with her?"

"I don't know, Mr. Anderson. She said she'd been having trouble sleeping. Perhaps stress."

"Did she say anything about a man named Win Freeman?"

"No. Who is he?"

"Someone she's become involved with."

"I wouldn't know anything about that."

"I'm not out for gossip, Jamie," I said. "I'm very worried about her. There's something very strange going on here. I thought you ought to know about it, as her lawyer."

"Thank you, Mr. Anderson, I'll bear it in mind," she said, before hanging up on me. Jamie Horton was clearly one person I was never going to be able to charm into my camp.

chapter 13

BUMPED HARD

I slept fitfully that night, my dreams full of the beautiful, lost face of Linda Cameron, and got up late, around ten o'clock. I knew that I needed desperately to get back to work, if only to forget her, so I called Hal's office and made an appointment to drop in on him around noon. I thought I would try to find myself another cruise or a gig somewhere in one of Nevada's casinos, anything to put some money in my pocket and distance myself from my involvement with this woman. Perhaps Alden Berry had been right about her all along, I told myself, perhaps she *was* emotionally disturbed. How could she have made love to me so openly, so passionately, with such commitment, and then thrown herself heedlessly into the arms of an almost total stranger? It was not normal behavior. I was hurt by it and anxious now to remove myself from it. Work had always been the best cure for disaster; I could lose myself in magic and also find myself again. I was determined not to allow Linda Cameron to shatter my world and I told myself, as I sat in my kitchenette sipping a second cup of coffee, that I was lucky to have found out about her so early in the game. I could retreat from the relationship without too many wounds to heal. I would survive, because I prided myself on having always been able to do just that. By the time I got back from wherever Hal could find me work, I'd be whole again and my filly would be ready to run again and all would be for the best in this best of all possible worlds.

My telephone rang and Jamie Horton's voice sounded alarmed in my ear. "Mr. Anderson, is Mrs. Cameron with you?"

"No."

"Do you have any idea where she is? I've tried her home, but there's no answer," the lawyer said. "She had an appointment with me at ten, but she hasn't even called. I thought you might know something. It's important."

"I haven't a clue."

"I'm worried about her. Do you have any suggestions?"

"No, I don't."

"I see. Well, if you do hear from her, please tell her to call me. I really can't do much for her if I don't see her or at least speak to her."

"I understand. I'll go by her place and leave her a note."

"Thank you. That would be most helpful."

I said good-bye to my number one fan and checked my watch. It was now a few minutes after eleven o'clock; I had time to drop Linda a note on my way in to see Hal, so I finished the last of my coffee and went into the bathroom to shower and shave.

It was eleven-forty when I parked on the street in front of Linda's cottage and walked up the slight rise to her front door. The building was dark, but I had a strong feeling that it was not empty. I walked around the side to test the back door leading out into the patio, but it was locked. I peered into the living room through a crack in the venetian blinds, but saw only an empty room, with mail piled onto the coffee table and a woman's sweater draped over the arm of the sofa. The bedroom curtains were closed and I couldn't see into the room. When I came back around the house I was confronted by a startled elderly Japanese gentleman holding an empty flower pot and a hoe. "Hello," I said, "I'm Mr. Anderson, a friend of Mrs. Cameron's. We haven't seen or heard from her for several days and we're worried about her. Are you the landlord?"

The old man nodded. "She heah yesterday," he said. "I see her with young man."

"Yes, but I'm still worried about her. She missed a very important appointment this morning with her attorney," I explained. "I'm afraid something may have happened to her. Would you mind having a look inside with me?"

The old man hesitated, then put down his pot and hoe and walked up to the front door. He rang the bell, then knocked, but no one answered. After another moment's hesitation and a suspicious glance back at me, he dug into his pocket and produced a great mass of keys through which he sorted like a miner sifting through sand for a gold nugget. Finally he emerged with one, inserted it into the lock, and let himself in.

I followed. The cottage was dark inside, with every blind closed and the shades pulled down. The old man stood irresolutely just inside the front door, but I pushed past him into the bedroom. It was even darker in there, but I found a switch on the wall to my right and snapped it on. A small overhead light fixture dimly illuminated the room and I looked around. The queen-size bed was unmade and women's clothes lay scattered about the floor and over an easy chair against the far wall. An open closet door revealed more garments, mostly women's, on a row of wooden hangers. A large Japanese print of a garden in flower hung lopsidedly on one wall and rows of paperback books took up most of three shelves in a bookcase below it. At first glance, it looked like a room that had been left unmade by a couple hurriedly going off to work or the day's events, except for the way the picture hung on the wall. And then I noticed a woman's handbag on the floor at the foot of the bed. It was open and contained makeup, Kleenex, bits of this and that, a coin purse, and a wallet. I took a handkerchief out of my pocket, fished out the wallet and opened it. It contained a hundred and twenty dollars and Linda's driving license. I dropped it back into the bag and stood up. The old Japanese gentleman was standing in the doorway. "Something's wrong," I said. "She wouldn't go out without her purse."

The bathroom door was closed. I walked across the room and opened it. Win Freeman was sitting on the toilet with his pants around his ankles. His body rested against the wall, his head flung back. Most of his face seemed to have been blown away and blood lay spattered against the walls and over the floor. Behind me I heard the old Japanese gentleman gasp in horror. I backed away, closing the door behind me again. I felt nauseous, but fought it off. "I'll call the police," I said.

I wanted desperately to get out of that room, so I went into the kitchen, where I found a telephone resting on the counter separating the cooking area from the eating alcove. Instead of dialing 911, I called the West Side station and asked for Jude Morgan. Luckily, he was there. "What are you up to, my man?" he asked cheerfully, when I identified myself. "You got a horse for me?"

"No, it's more in your line of work," I answered. "I have a body for you." And I gave him a few pertinent details and the address.

"What is it about you, man?" the detective asked. "Wherever you go, bad things happen. Don't move anything, hear? We'll be right on over."

"Well, my man, that's quite a story," Jude Morgan said, after I had finished telling him all I knew about events. "Now I want you to tell me what *you* think."

"What I think?"

"That's right. What do you think is going on here?"

"At the simplest possible level, I'd say that Cameron had Win Freeman killed and has arranged to have his wife kidnapped," I said, "but it seems depressingly simple. Anyway, it can't be the whole story."

"Pretty serious charges," Jude Morgan said. "The guy's got his hands full with this grand jury investigation of his business practices and the indictments against him, wouldn't you say? Why would he saddle himself with another murder and kidnapping charges to boot?"

"He's obviously a very possessive and jealous man," I answered. "He's so suspicious of his wife that he either had her followed that morning when we set out for Sovereign Acres or he immediately sent an investigator out to retrace our route, when he heard that we had disappeared along the way for a couple of hours. Then he sends a hood to talk to me, who threatens to break my fingers, after instructing his lawyer to bear down on me as well. I'd say he's capable of anything, wouldn't you?"

Jude didn't answer me right away. He leaned back in his chair and stared beyond me at the far wall, where a large bulletin board displayed official notices and personal messages of all kinds. We were sitting in a glassed-in cubicle at the end of a large room in the West Side station. It was fairly noisy, with the bustle of police officers moving past us on various missions, conversations on every side, telephones ringing, the clatter of typewriters, but at least we were isolated, a tiny island in the mainstream. It was Jude's personal territory, his small corner from which he operated in his endless, fruitless struggle with human chicanery. He seemed at home in it, comfortable, at ease and unperturbed by the follies around him. He radiated competence devoid of hope, indifferent to compassion, because in his world it was a luxury he couldn't permit himself. He was looking forward only to his retirement, which he planned to spend mostly at the racetrack. I understood him and I liked him.

"Cameron would have had to arrange all this from a jail cell," he said at last, "or at the last minute. He wasn't bailed out until yesterday afternoon. Freeman was shot this morning . . ."

"You're sure?"

"Absolutely," the detective said. "He wasn't even stiff."

"Delicately put."

Jude ignored the sarcasm. "What about the woman?" he asked.

"I told you all I know about her."

"She couldn't have done it?"

I shook my head. "No, Jude, I'm sure of that."

"But you said she was not all there. Or had a history like that."

"That's what Cameron's lawyer, Alden Berry, told me, but she's no psychotic, Jude," I said. "I'd stake my life on that."

"Oh, my man, you wouldn't do that, believe me," the detective said. "Some of the nicest people can kill you and will. The way she and this dude went after each other, that's not normal, would you say? Especially so soon after she got involved with you. Say, Shifty, what's your secret, man? You get all the good-looking women after you."

"I'm a man of devastating charm," I said, "or haven't you noticed? So Cameron put up the two million dollars?"

"No, his lawyer appealed and got the bail reduced to one-point-two."

"Still a sizable sum, but I'm sure he'd have raised the two million as well."

"Fella named Hunter put most of it up."

"Jed Hunter."

"Yeah. Cameron used to work for him or with him," the detective said. "Seems like they're pretty close."

"Sometimes I wonder about Hunter. Was he really such a good judge?"

"The best, they say. Could have had any kind of career on the bench he wanted, maybe even the Supreme Court. That's what they say."

"He loves racing."

"Yeah, that's done in many a good man," Jude said. "My daddy, for one. The bookies broke him, but he sure loved it."

"What now, Jude?"

"You ever hear the phrase 'pursue a line of investigation'? You ever hear that?"

"Somewhere, maybe on TV."

"Well, that's what we're about to do."

"You going to check out Cameron?"

"We can't. It's out of our jurisdiction, my man. But we'll be in touch with San Diego on it."

"And this guy Don Houps?"

"We'll try to locate him. Now you stay away from the press, if you can. And keep in touch. You ain't going anywhere?"

"I had an appointment this morning with my

agent," I said. "I was going to try and get some work. I might have to go out of town."

"Well, just stay in touch." He got up and shook my hand. "You want to go out the back here? There might be press out front."

"Yes, good idea. Thanks."

"And if you get a horse for me, you be sure to call, hear?" he said, as I moved away from him.

There were reporters and a TV camera crew waiting out front, but I managed to ease my car out of the lot through an alley that ran behind the station and escape without being interviewed. When I got home, I called Happy Hal's office. He had gone out to lunch, but would be back at three. I left a message with his secretary that I was involved in an emergency situation but would call him as soon as I could. Then I went back to my car and drove to Hollywood Park.

"Did you hear this one about the two hookers hitching a ride out of Houston?" Angles Beltrami asked, as the horses came out on the track for the fifth race.

"Oh, don't tell that one again," Arnie pleaded. "It ain't that funny."

"You got no sense of humor," Angles said. He smiled at me. "You ain't heard it, have you, Shifty?"

"No, I haven't."

Arnie stood up. "This would be an opportune time to relieve myself," he said. "The presence of great wit never fails to inspire me." He left the premises.

"Arnie, buy me a twenty-dollar exacta box," Jay called after him. "The four horse and the eight. Got it?"

"You're down," Arnie answered, moving slowly and majestically away up the aisle.

"So listen, Shifty, there's these two hookers, see," Angles said. "They're trying to thumb a ride and there's this bullfrog by the side of the road. And the frog says, 'Pick me up, pick me up.' So the first hooker leans down and picks him up. And the frog says, 'Kiss me, kiss me, and I'll turn into a Texas oilman.' "

"Have you heard this one, Jay?" I asked.

"Twice," Jay answered.

"It doesn't sound that promising."

"It isn't."

"Come on, you guys," Angles said. "Shifty, this is a good one, believe me. Let me finish."

"Okay," I said, "finish."

"So instead of kissing him, the hooker opens her bag and pops the frog into it and closes it. 'What did you do that for?' her friend asks. 'Why don't you kiss him? What have you got to lose?' So the first hooker says, 'What do I need one of those creeps for? I got me a talking frog.' "

I laughed. "I have to admit the story is not without a certain offbeat charm," I said.

"I told you," Angles said, grinning.

"It's one of your better ones, Angles," Jay said. "At least it isn't racist or totally disgusting."

Angles checked his program. "Shit, I could get shut out," he said, suddenly bolting from the box.

"You're late," Jay said, focusing his binoculars on the horses heading toward the starting gate. "Where have you been?"

"Watch the news tonight and you'll find out," I said. "Have you seen my trainer?"

"He had a horse in the first," Jay said, "but he hasn't been around since."

"I'll go check the Turf Club," I said. "He sometimes hangs around Abel Green, if they're planning to claim something."

I didn't care about the fifth race anyway, a sprint for medium-priced three-year-old claimers, but I figured Charlie might be looking to add to the stable of mediocrities he trained for Abel Green and he'd be with his owner. I went up the escalator and found the owner's box empty, then I watched the race on a TV monitor at the bar before heading back to Jay's box. It turned out to be a fairly exciting contest, with Jay's two horses locked into a desperate duel down the stretch with the favorite, a classic Dummy-God animal sent off at even money by an incautious public. One of Jay's choices got his head in front at the wire, but the favorite finished second by half a length, thus demolishing my friend's exacta box. "Hey, how about that?" I heard a familiar woman's voice call out, as the winner crossed the finish line. "I got me a winner!"

I turned around to find myself looking at May Potter, but a May Potter I had never seen before. She was dressed in a tight red miniskirt with a white blouse, a single strand of pearls around her neck, and her hair was pulled back into a ponytail. She was wearing lipstick, eyeshadow, and mascara and I suddenly realized she was beautiful. "May, how are you?" I said. "You had the winner?"

"You bet," she said. "Polo told me he was workin' real good, so I bet twenty on him. Whoeee! He's gonna pay better than ten dollars!"

"Nice hit," I said. "Can I buy you a drink?"

"Well, I'm with—you know Mr. Green, don't you?"

"Yeah, sure. How are you, Anderson?" Abel Green said, coming up behind her. "I told Charlie we should have claimed this colt."

"He's got a bad-lookin' ankle, Mr. Green," May said. "He could break down anytime."

"Honey, my name is Abel," the owner said. "I told you."

"Oh, sure. I plumb forgot," May said. "Anyway, Charlie don't want no cripples and you don't neither, Mr. Green. Abel."

"Where is Charlie?" I asked. "I've been looking for him."

"He was here," Green said. "We ran that piece of shit in the first. Finished his usual fifth. Charlie left after the race."

"Your filly's workin' tomorrow morning," May said to me. "You comin' out?"

"I guess so."

"She's doin' great."

"Wait here, honey," Green said, patting May on the shoulder. "I got to see a man about a horse." And he walked across the room to talk to a bloodstock agent I had once met through Charlie.

"Why doesn't he buy some decent horses and let Charlie turn him into a winner?" I asked.

"I guess 'cause he's real cheap," May said, smiling. "A lot of rich folks I know are just like him. That's how they got the money in the first place, I guess."

"Are you and Abel dating?" I asked.

"Well, he asked me out here today," she said. "It ain't often I get to the Turf Club."

"You look wonderful. A little different from the early mornings."

"I guess. Say, is Mr. Green married?"

"Oh, yes," I said cheerfully, "and has been for a long time."

"That figures," she said. "He wants me to go to Vegas with him."

"Well, that figures, too."

"I ain't gonna go," she said. "Say, remember I told you Mrs. Cameron come out to see the filly the other day? She had a fella with her?"

"Win Freeman."

"That's him. He's a bad dude."

"You know him?"

"Sure, from Florida. Him and me, we worked up

at Fogarty's place in Ocala. He was the foreman there when I come on.''

"What did he do, May? I mean, what made him a bad dude?"

She fingered the long, thin scar on her cheek. "He done this to me."

"How?"

"We was goin' together," she said. "We was datin' pretty regular. Not livin' together, nothin' like that, but the next thing to it, I guess. So one night we got into a bad fight. Thing is, I don't even remember what it was about. But I was scared of him by that time. I mean, he could be terrific and real sweet and all like that, but he could also be real cold, like ice. And he like to kill a couple of guys in a bar one night. I mean, he was like trained, you know? He could kill you with his bare hands. And when he got mad, it was like he was capable of anythin'. He'd as soon kill you as look at you. I'm tellin' you, mister, he scared the shit out of me. So I was gonna break up with him anyway. He wasn't much good as a lovin' man, to tell you the truth. He—he liked to hurt you, you know what I mean?"

"I think so. Did he recognize you the other morning?"

"He would have, if he'd seen me," she said. "Only, when I saw him, I run off and hid in one of the stalls. He's scary, I'm tellin' you."

"How did he cut you?"

"With a knife," she said. "He always carried this big switchblade. We was drinkin' in this bar in Ocala and some big dude come on to me and Win got real mad. He hit this dude about ten times, like to kill him he did, and I'm screamin' at him to stop, but it was like he was in this kind of cold fury he'd get into and there wasn't no way to deal with him. I kept screamin' at him all the way back to his place and then two nights later we got into it again. And he took this knife and he cut

205

me and all the time I was screamin' and hollerin' and tryin' to get away from him, but he was so strong and all. He said there wasn't anyone was gonna mess with him and no woman was gonna tell him what to do. He just wasn't himself when he got like that. Well, I called the police and they arrested him and he done six months for cuttin' me up like that. I moved away. I didn't want to be there when he come back. So that's when I come to California."

"When was all this, May?"

"Oh, three, four years ago. Yeah, more like four years ago, I guess. I mean, Win was some strange dude. Real educated and all and spoke real quiet like, very much like a gent—I guess he went to good schools and all—but he was like some big cat. You never knew what he was thinkin', and if you crossed him, he'd kill you, if he could."

"Win Freeman's dead," I said.

"What? You kiddin' me?"

"No, May, I'm not. I found his body this morning myself," I explained. "I went to see Mrs. Cameron and we found Freeman in the bathroom. Somebody shot him."

"You think she done it?"

"No, I don't."

"I guess it had to come to that," she said, "on account of he was so violent. Somebody figured to do him in. I wonder who it was."

"The police are wondering, too."

Abel Green rejoined us. "Hello there," he said, putting a proprietary hand on May's knee. "Can I buy you a drink, Anderson?"

"No, thanks," I said. "I'll see you, May."

I took another look at them as I left. Abel Green still had his hand on her knee and was leaning in over the bar to place an order. May was looking at me, smiling a little wanly. She pointed to Abel Green's hand on her leg and grimaced, as if to tell me not to worry, that she couldn't be held responsible for the man's behavior. I smiled back and waved. I wondered if she liked magic.

chapter 14

CLOSING

ON THE OUTSIDE

"Happy to see you again, Mr. Anderson," Luke Davis said, coming out of his tack room to shake my hand. "Charlie said you was comin'. Lookin' to buy a nice yearlin', are you? That's good. Come on, let me take you over. We got about thirty of our good ones over here in the east pasture."

I climbed into Luke's pickup and he drove us to a field about a mile or so east of his stable. It was up against the slope of a mountain whose jagged crags loomed over us as we walked toward the horses, most of whom were grazing in a corner under the shade of a small grove of oak and pepper trees. The day was bright and clear and a cool wind blew off the hills, rustling the leaves of trees and making the tall, rich grass shimmer at its passing. "Perfect weather, ain't it?" Luke said, as we neared the animals and they became restless at our approach. "In summer it gets hot as hell in this valley, but this time of year most every day is just like this."

"It's a little paradise," I agreed. "I guess you have to worry about the water, especially with this drought going on."

"Sure do," Luke said. "The lake, which is our reservoir, is down about four feet, which is a hell of a lot for this time of year. We didn't get the runoff we usually do from the winter snowpack. But we still got ground water, you know. Up there, at the end of the village by that old water tower when you drive in, there's an underground supply. It was on the old Harris Ranch, which the Judge bought up when he was puttin' Sovereign together back in the sixties and early seventies. Without that water he couldn't have done it, you know. There was some kind of trouble about it at the time, I heard, but it all got straightened out. That's when the Judge started puttin' this whole thing together." He put out a hand and stopped me. "Hold it right here. We get any closer, the whole bunch of 'em'll take off and we'll wind up havin' to chase 'em in the truck. I can pick out the ones I want you to look at from here."

We had approached to within fifty or sixty feet of the horses, most of whom continued grazing as we stood there looking at them. A few of the more skittish members of the herd moved nervously at the edges, tossing their pretty heads, snorting and keeping an eye on us. If they bolted, they would probably take the others with them, so we crouched down and rested on our haunches as Luke talked softly, picking out first one animal, then another for me to eye. To me they all looked pretty much alike, except for any spectacular differences in their markings and colors, but to Luke each yearling was an identifiable individual, as recog-

209

nizable to his expert eye as if he were a teacher looking at a crowd of children in a playground. "That chestnut over there, he's a nice little colt, well-balanced, nice straight legs, a good head on him, and he's quick and smart," he'd say. "Now see that big bay back there, to the right of the roan, he's got that big broad back all them Ack Acks have, which means stamina and durability. And now look over here, the gray filly with the silver patch on her shoulder, she's real quick and got a beautiful head on her, a real good eye. You don't want no dumb animal in your shedrow, 'cause they're the ones that get hurt and all and you can't teach 'em nothin'. Now this here colt, the bay over there with the white foreleg, he's by Moscow Ballet, should be a nice sprinter, got them big back thighs and a rump on him like a quarter horse, his mommy was a quick one, too . . ." On and on it went, with all the pedigrees and physical characteristics tripping off the end of his tongue as if he had learned them by heart. It was a dazzling performance and I told him so. He blushed. "Hell, I been lookin' at horses all of my life," he said. "I ought to be able to tell one from another. That's what I'm paid to do, ain't it?

"I'd go for that big bay, if I was you," Luke said, as we started back toward the truck. "He figures to go long and that's what you want for a racehorse. Most of 'em will go short for you, but the big purses is what the routers get to shoot at. This colt is one of the last ones by Ack Ack, who died last year, and you know what kind of a horse he was. You can get a full pedigree from Sherry back in the office. When you get ready to make an offer, you can talk to the Judge. I'd guess you could get this one now for maybe fifty or sixty, but that ain't up to me, of course. He's worth it. The filly you could get for less, I'm sure. She'd be a good one, too." And he ran down the rest of the candidates for me, going over each good point again as we walked. By the time we climbed back into the pickup, I had a list of eight horses to consider.

"Is Hunter around?" I asked, as Luke eased the truck back onto the narrow road.

"Ain't seen him for a couple of days," Luke said, "but Sherry in the office will know where he is."

"You heard about Win Freeman, I assume."

"Godamighty, yes. Ain't that somethin'? The Judge, he was so upset it was like he lost a son or some-thin'."

"That's strange, isn't it? I mean, he's the one who fired him, chased him off the property, didn't he?"

"Yeah, he sure was," Luke said, "but that was on account of what Win was doin' with the Cameron lady. Say, did they ever find her?"

"Not yet."

"I wonder who'd want to shoot old Win. Hell, he was a little strange sometimes, but a good ole boy just the same. Hell of a worker. And he just about wor-shipped the ground the Judge walked on. Them two was real close, I tell you. There's somethin' real funny about that whole deal, but it ain't none of my business. I guess the Judge just kind of went crazy when he heard. And Miz Freddie, hell, ain't nobody seen her for a week now. We think she's at the house, but she don't come out. Hell of a thing, ain't it? Who'd want to shoot old Win Freeman?"

Luke dropped me off in front of the administra-tion building and shook my hand. "Take the Ack Ack colt," he said, as we parted. "You can't go wrong with that one."

"Thanks, Luke, you've been a big help."

"My pleasure. Say, how's the filly doin'?"

"Very well. One more week and she's ready to run."

"Real fine." He smiled. "In the old days, when I was a gamblin' man, I'd have bet my eyeballs on her.

But I was so unlucky, she'd have propped in the gate. Don't tell me when she's runnin'. You're better off." He spun the truck around and drove away back toward his little feud in Barn 48.

"Hi," Sherry chirped, as I walked into her office, "how you doin', Mr. Anderson?"

"Just fine, Sherry," I said. "Is the Judge around?"

"No, but he'll be calling in this afternoon. Shall I tell him you want to get in touch with him?"

"If you want to, no rush," I said. "Meanwhile, I'd like to get a printout on a couple of your yearlings. There's an Ack Ack colt out of Water Maiden and another one by Moscow Ballet out of Lost Gold. Oh, and a filly. I think her sire was Pirate's Bounty and the mare is Laughing Girl."

"Sure thing," Sherry said, ever the perky soubrette. "You want to sit down? This'll take a few minutes. Want some coffee?"

"Thanks. Black, a little sugar."

"I won't be a minute." She hurried away into an inner room.

I sat down in a comfortable sofa against the far wall and leaned my head against it. I could have used another couple of hours' sleep, but then I had had to get up early in order to make Mad Margaret's workout. And then there had been the two-hour drive down to Sovereign, after the phone call from Charlie's tack room. I could not afford, of course, to buy another horse, but I needed a legitimate excuse to visit Sovereign again. I was convinced that the key to Linda's whereabouts, as well as Win's murder, had to be found somewhere in the vicinity of Judge Hunter's operation. It was all I had to go on and it probably wasn't enough, but I felt responsible for Linda's safety. Everything had started to come apart for her after those two hours with me in a cheap motel room. I felt an obligation to help, if I could. I shut my eyes and waited.

*   *   *

I had arrived at Charlie's shedrow just as Mad Margaret was being saddled prior to her scheduled workout. The filly knew she was going to run and was on the muscle, her ears cocked forward and her eyes alert, every inch of her a picture of barely contained power and grace. May was on her knees unwrapping her protective front bandages, while Eddie was making sure her saddle was properly in place, the cinch tight enough to prevent slippage but not constricting. "How's she doing?" I asked, as I came up beside her. "She looks terrific."

May looked up at me with a broad grin. "She's ready," she said. "This filly's a runnin' fool."

"Doin' real good," Eddie said, with a nod.

Charlie, holding a Styrofoam cup of coffee in one hand and a cigarette in the other, appeared in his tack room door. "You're up early," he said. "By the way, I called Luke for you. He's expecting you this morning. What are you up to, Shifty? You ain't really gonna buy another horse, are you?"

"I'm thinking about it," I lied. "Thought I'd go down and see what they've got down there. Maybe I can pinhook an animal or two."

"You don't know what you're lookin' at," Charlie said. "Don't buy nothin' till you talk to me. I'll go down and look at 'em for you."

"I'd appreciate that, Charlie."

Tim Lang, the jockey who was going to ride Maggie, showed up just as May finished removing her front wraps. Charlie put down his coffee, stamped out his cigarette, and leaned over to feel the filly's shins. He grunted with satisfaction. "Cool and tight," was his verdict. "I think we got that problem licked." He stood up and looked at Lang. "Hello, Tim, you look like shit. What have you been doin'?"

The jockey did look pale and his eyes were dark,

but he smiled wanly. "It was my birthday yesterday, Charlie," he said. "We did a little celebrating."

"You gonna be all right? I don't want you fallin' off this horse."

"I'm fine, don't worry about me," the jockey said. "I'm here to ride, ain't I?"

"How old are you?" I asked.

"Thirty," Lang said. "They threw me a party."

"Thirty," Charlie snorted derisively. "Hell, you're a baby." He put a hand on the rider's shoulder. "Now listen, Tim, this filly's a real racehorse. She wants to run and she's headstrong. I don't want you usin' her up in a workout, you got that? We're still a couple of weeks away from a race. I want you to breeze her five-eighths nice and easy."

The jockey nodded solemnly and Eddie now gave him a leg up into the saddle. Polo Rodriguez on the stable pony, an old Appaloosa named Toby, came up beside her and they began slowly to head for the gap. I fell into step beside Charlie and we walked briskly toward the guinea stand. "Come on, May," I called out, "don't you want to see her work?"

"Charlie'll fire me," she said, holding a rake in her hand.

"Not today," Charlie said. "Maybe tomorrow."

May practically flung the rake away and came running up beside us. "Thanks," she said. "I'm dyin' to see her go."

We found a good spot along the rail just as Mad Margaret appeared on the track below us. Tim Lang was standing up in the stirrups, keeping a tight hold on the filly, her neck bowed against the pressure of the bit, while Polo on Toby lumbered along beside her. To my amazement, I felt myself close to tears. The idea that this magnificent creature, this miracle of nature, actually belonged to me was almost more than I could handle. She looked in the early-morning light like something only one of the ancient Greek artists could have created, a pure expression of beauty and grace and competitive fire. I wiped my eyes and raised my binoculars to follow her progress around the track. Beside me, I heard May's rapid breathing and realized that she was as excited as I was. I glanced at Charlie. The trainer had a stopwatch in his left hand and was gazing after her impassively, with his cap pulled low over his eyes. I'd never seen him so grim and I understood that he, too, had a stake in this; Mad Margaret was his one potential big horse and there's nothing like an important animal to focus a horseman's concentration.

As they angled over toward the inner rail, Polo took Toby out of there and Tim Lang, now crouching low in the saddle, moved his hands up along the filly's neck, releasing some of the latent power within her. Mad Margaret took off, still under a good hold, but lengthening her stride as they passed the five-eighths pole. She seemed to be flying, eating up the ground with that big reach of hers, her head bowed low, responding to every movement of the rider on her back. I could tell that Lang was not asking her for speed, but even so she seemed to be giving it to him, easily switching leads as she moved around the turn and into the stretch. "Look at her go," May said. "She's eatin' 'em up!"

"Goddamn fool jock," Charlie swore under his breath. "This is his idea of an easy half." He clicked the stopwatch as Maggie passed the finish line and Lang again rose up in the irons in his effort to slow her down. After about another eighth of a mile, he was able to do so, then swung her out into the middle of the track to let her gallop back. "Shit," Charlie muttered.

"What did you catch her in, Charlie?" I asked.

"Fifty-seven and three," the trainer said angrily.

•

"That's this jock's idea of an easy five-eighths. I wanted her to go in a minute and change."

We arrived back at the barn as Lang was dismounting and Charlie wasted no time launching into him. "What the hell's the matter with you?" he snapped. "I told you to breeze her, for Christ's sake!"

"Charlie, I couldn't hold her," the rider protested. "She wanted to run so bad and she's hard as hell to rate. Anyway, she was goin' so easy. What did she run it in?"

"I had her in fifty-seven and three, the clockers a tick faster," the trainer said.

"I couldn't barely pull her up even," Lang continued. "She's a runnin' fool, Charlie."

"If you don't learn how to rate her, I'll put somebody on her who can," the trainer said.

"You don't want to strangle her, Charlie," Lang said. "This is a free-runnin' filly. You got to let her run or she'll pull you out of the saddle. I'm tellin' you, it took nothin' out of her. Look at her, Charlie."

We all looked at the horse. May had the saddle off her by now and the horse had her nose buried in a water bucket, noisily drinking her fill. She looked to me exactly as she had before her workout. Her coat gleamed with health and I walked over to pat her on the neck. May grinned at me. "She just wants to run so bad," she said, in a low voice. "Tim's right. It took nothin' out of her."

After Tim Lang had left to fulfill another riding commitment, I joined Charlie at the rail outside his tack room and we watched May walk the filly around in front of us. She'd cool out for at least forty minutes, then get fed and tucked away again for the rest of the day. "Maybe Lang is right," I said. "Maybe you got to let her run, Charlie."

"Don't listen to no jocks on serious stuff," the trainer said. "They all wear size-three hats." He turned his head to look at me. "What are you really going down south for, Shifty? You think your lady's down there?"

I nodded. "I don't know, Charlie," I said. "I'm a naturally nosy guy."

"Yeah, well, watch yourself. I'd stick to magic, if I was you."

"I feel partly responsible," I tried to explain. "I mean, if she hadn't met me, she might have been okay."

"You know what I think?" the trainer said. "I think the whole thing was ready to come apart. You just happened to come along at the right time. You know how landslides start? One small rock gets loose and then the whole thing comes crashin' down. It would have happened sooner or later, with or without you."

"I don't know why, Charlie, but I don't find that analogy especially comforting."

"You keep usin' these ten-dollar words around here," Charlie said, "they'll pull your credentials. This is a racetrack, not some goddamn literary saloon."

One thing about hanging around with horse trainers, they can always make you feel better about your own life.

The drive into Julian from Ramona took about forty minutes. It was still too early in the year for tourists in the middle of the week and the two-lane winding road up into the hills was lightly traveled. I took my time because the scenery was worth it. The old mining town sat isolated on its mountainside surrounded by orchard groves and pine forests. I had put the top down and the sweet smell of newly formed apple blossoms wafted over me as I rose above the valley floor. It was still only midafternoon and the widow had agreed to talk to me over a cup of tea at five o'clock. "A magazine story, you say?" she had asked me over the phone.

"About Sovereign Acres? Don't know as you'll want to hear what I have to tell you. About the horses? I don't know much about horses, but come on up. I'll give you a cup of tea. What magazine?"

"The *California Thoroughbred*," I had told her. "It's a monthly devoted pretty much to the California horse-breeding and racing industry."

"Never heard of it," she had said, "but come on by anyway. Don't know as I have much to tell you, not about horses anyway."

Her name was Elizabeth Noren and I had been put on to her by Wally Jones, the man I had talked to in the W. J. Richards realty office in Ramona. When I had told him that I had just visited Sovereign Acres and was looking to buy land in that valley, Wally Jones had simply looked at me incredulously. "There's nothing for sale in the valley," he had informed me. "Hunter bought up the whole valley, just about."

"What do you mean, just about?" I had asked.

"Well, there's one big parcel, about four hundred acres, up at the north end, but it isn't worth a dime," Wally Jones had said. "No water. When Judge Hunter put Sovereign together, he had all the water rights in the area. I guess you know about the reservoir. Well, there's ground water, too, but only at the southeast end, where the old Harris Ranch was. Once Hunter took over that place after the fire, he had all the water in the valley. Everybody else sold out to him. Everybody except old Liz Noren. She still owns that land up at the north end, where her family had a big ranch in the old days. The Norens and the Harrises were close. Her family bought water from the Harris Ranch. The Harrises used to sell the water to their neighbors at a decent price, so the story goes. Once the Judge got to building Sovereign, however, they wouldn't sell any water and that's how Hunter got hold of most of that land in there. It's worthless without the water. He bought it up real cheap, that's the way I heard it. But say, you want to talk to old Liz Noren. She's got a lot of miles on her, but she's still got all her marbles, I hear. She's always refused to sell her land, said she never would, not to Hunter anyway. If you could talk Hunter into selling you water, maybe you could buy Liz's place. There's an old ranch building on the property you could fix up and you could get the land cheap. Why don't you call her directly? She lives up in Julian. I guess her kids are real mad at her, on account of she won't sell out. They'd like to get what they can out of the property, but she's a stubborn old woman. Just don't let her know you intend to try and get water rights out of Judge Hunter. She doesn't want any part of him, I hear."

"You want to call her for me?" I had asked him.

He had smiled and shaken his head. He was a large, plump man of about forty-five, with curly blond hair, pink cheeks, and a benign look of good-humored innocence, but his small blue eyes were alert and shrewd. "Nope," he'd said, "we'd just be wasting time. I wouldn't tell her you want to talk about buying her out. She probably won't see you. She'd suspect you're working for Hunter. He's tried a number of times to buy her out, using different people. He got me into it once, but Liz won't talk to real-estate agents. Good luck is all I can say."

Like most small towns, Julian consists essentially of an aptly named Main Street from which the older residential areas fan out for two or three blocks on either side. It has the look and feel of an old Western hub, with an abandoned gold mine and a museum to visit and a single year-around hotel with what the guidebooks like to call "an attractive country atmosphere." Its shops and eating places are clearly geared to the tourist trade, peddling local honeys, arts and crafts, and fresh apple pies made from the local produce. In the fall and briefly in the spring, during an annual wildflower festival, the town is filled with visitors; but I had managed to arrive in between festivities, so I had no trouble parking just off Main and I spent the next hour and a half just walking around like any old tourist, taking in the sights and lapping up local atmosphere.

I arrived in front of the Noren house at five minutes after five o'clock. It was an old, ramshackle wooden structure with a front porch running the full length of the building, about a block and a half off Main behind the hotel. It looked deserted, with an untended front yard overgrown with weeds and paint flaking off the dark gray walls. Several ancient pine trees loomed over the roof, as if shielding the house from the outside world. I walked up a narrow flagstoned path, up the steps to the porch, and rang the bell.

Almost at once the front door swung open, revealing a tall, very wrinkled old woman dressed in blue jeans and a checked Western shirt. She wore no makeup and her iron gray hair was cut short and brushed straight back; her dark eyes were large and very bright, like those of a nocturnal predator. "Mr. Anderson?" she said. "You're late."

"Only five minutes," I answered. "I was brought up to believe it was rude to arrive exactly on time."

"You were brought up badly. Come in."

She led the way down a dimly lit long corridor whose walls were lined with large framed canvases depicting Western scenes, mostly landscapes, and finally into a small back parlor crowded with undistinguished but ancient furniture, including a large wooden rocking chair. "Tea?" she asked.

"That would be fine," I said. "Plain, with one sugar."

"I'll be right back. Sit down." And she moved swiftly away toward the kitchen.

I lowered myself into a small uncomfortable padded settee and looked around. The light was dim in here, too, mostly because the only daylight filtered into the room through drawn curtains and the only other illumination came from a heavily shaded floor lamp in one corner. The walls were mostly covered with what I guessed were family portraits of austere-looking men and women dressed in dark suits and long dresses staring somberly into the camera from in front of lonely-looking cabins set in the middle of prairies or from backgrounds of rocky mountain slopes. The faces spoke of hard times and a dedication to struggle that bordered on madness. "Great photographs," I commented as Liz Noren returned carrying a small silver tea tray.

"I took some of those," she said. "That's what it looked like when we first settled in the valley. I was about fourteen and that was my first camera. I took a lot of pictures in those days."

"Were you the first to settle in there?"

"Us and the Harrises. The families all came in about the same time, the late eighteen-eighties." She set the tray on a low table and sat down in the rocker. "My family homesteaded the land and the Harrises found the water. Those pictures were taken in 1915. We settled up at the north end, where we'd get the runoff, but there were always years when the water situation was desperate. Luckily, the Harrises were good neighbors and always shared their water in the bad times. One sugar, you said?" She poured me a cup of dark, smoky-looking tea that tasted of sagebrush, then glanced sharply up at me. "You aren't here to buy my land, are you, Mr. Anderson? It's not for sale."

I smiled. "I have no interest in buying anything," I said. "I'm here to do a piece about Sovereign Acres. I've spent a couple of days out there and I've interviewed the Hunters about their whole operation, but I wanted some early history. No one could tell me much, Mrs. Noren. The Hunters didn't want to talk about it. Then somebody there, I forget who, mentioned you, said you knew more about the history of the valley than anyone. That's why I called you. If you don't want to talk about it, that's okay, too, but I thought it might be interesting."

"Oh, it's interesting, all right," she said, fixing those large, luminous eyes on me. "Jed Hunter stole that land."

"How did he do that?"

"Well, he bought property in the valley and, like everyone else, he was dependent on the Harrises for water. We all knew he was a judge down in San Diego and he had horses, but we thought he'd bought his place as a kind of weekend retreat, maybe with the idea he'd retire there eventually. We didn't know anything about his real plans. He and his wife, Freddie, were very popular in the valley. They threw these great barbecues and parties and they really livened things up. So for a couple of years everything seemed just great. Well, it was during that time that Frank Harris was killed."

"How did that happen?"

"It was a hunting accident, they said. Jed and Frank and a friend of Jed's named Cameron went up into the hills after quail very early one morning. The story was that they were moving up the slope of a hill and Frank put his gun down to climb over a big boulder or something and the gun went off and damn near blew his head off. It was a shotgun and it just tore him up real bad. He was gone by the time anybody could get to him."

"You don't think it was an accident, right?"

"We all thought it was at the time, but now I don't think it was. Jed Hunter and Frank's wife, Brownie, were keeping company, as the saying goes. I didn't see it right away, none of us did, but it became very clear after Frank died. Jed was over at the Harris place a lot, supposedly helping out and comforting the widow. Well, he did a lot of comforting. Freddie got real upset about it and that was when some of us began to figure out that Jed had been seeing an awful lot of the Harrises even when Frank was alive. I mean, he was over there a lot and a couple of times the Hunters and the Harrises would go off on trips together, to Europe and other places. They were all real close. I figure the affair started long before Frank was killed. It was a damned convenient accident."

"How could they have gotten together without Frank finding out about it?"

"I don't know why I'm telling you all this," she said. "You can't use any of this stuff."

"I can use some of it," I said. "Anyway, it's pretty interesting."

"Frank also worked in San Diego," Liz Noren continued. "He was the president of a chain of hardware stores all over the state, so he had to travel quite a bit. That left Brownie alone, of course, and Jed took advantage of it. He was a good-looking man and had a way about him. I'm sure he'd had a lot of women in his life. He even made a pass at me once and I thought about it. Freddie used to hint about Jed and his ways and she could get pretty bitter."

"She could have divorced him."

"He was very committed to her, always came back to her," Liz Noren said. "Anyway, the story was that she was the one with the money. Jed had his judge's salary, which was adequate, but not for the plans he had. He'd always wanted this big ranch and to raise the finest Thoroughbreds on it. That was his big dream."

"What about Brownie Harris? I assume she fell in love with Hunter."

"Oh, completely. She was totally mesmerized by

William Murray

Jed, no doubt about it. She was nice-looking, but kind of a mousy little thing. Jed must have seemed like a god to her, especially after Frank, who was a nice guy but kind of stodgy, a businessman type, you know. Did you meet Eartha, the Indian woman who works for the Hunters?"

"Yes, I did."

"Say, how come you're not taking notes, Mr. Anderson? You are a reporter, aren't you?"

"Well, I can't use most of this, as you pointed out," I answered, aware that I'd been more than a little careless. "Just the general background, some of it, and that I can remember, you know. I can't afford to be sued and neither can the magazine."

"Too bad," Liz Noren said. "Too bad, because this is a story that needs to be told and someday it's going to be told and Jed Hunter will pay for his sins."

"You mentioned Eartha. What about her?"

"She used to work for the Harrises. She's an Indian, one of the local tribes, and she always said the Harris property was cursed, because it had once been the site of an Indian village and there was a burial ground nearby. I think Jed worked on her and somehow got her to persuade Brownie to sell out to him or give him the water rights."

"How?"

"I'm not sure, but Brownie wasn't a very strong woman. She was alone, you see, and in love with Jed. Eartha's whole family worked for him. He could put pressure on her."

"So she persuaded Brownie to sell?"

"Brownie was going to, but one of Frank's friends, his banker, I think, told her not to, that she had the only good land in the valley and she'd be crazy to do so. She had the kids, you see. They were just babies, but they had to be protected, especially with Frank gone."

"The Indian woman even told me the land was cursed," I said. "So what happened?"

"Maybe the Indian woman was right," Liz Noren said, "because about three years after Frank's death the Harris Ranch burned down."

"How did that happen?"

"Nobody ever knew for sure," Liz Noren said. "The theory was the usual—a faulty electrical connection or a heater. The Harrises had old-fashioned wall heaters in the bedrooms. But no finding as to the cause was ever made, or at least released to the press."

"What do you think happened, Mrs. Noren?"

"Well, Brownie made a deal with Jed," Liz Noren said. "More tea?"

"No, thanks."

"She signed some kind of a contract with Jed, turning over the administration of her property to him. That was when we found out what Jed was really up to. He began to expand and develop his place and he refused to sell off any of the Harris water. We all got together and went to see Brownie, about twelve of us, all the neighbors, but her hands were legally tied. She was very upset, because Jed hadn't told her what his plans were. But she promised to talk to him and get him to change his mind. It was a time of drought, just like this one, and without the water nobody could survive in there."

"And Hunter wouldn't sell you any water at all?"

"Not to us, not to anyone. That's when he began buying up all the land and founded Sovereign. We were the only ones who wouldn't sell out to him and we sued him, but it didn't do any good. We had no legal right to the water."

"What did Brownie do?"

"There wasn't much she could do. She and Jed had a big falling out over it, but in about a month or so they were back together. He's a very forceful man and she was very weak.''

"And then she died in the fire. How convenient.''

"Exactly, Mr. Anderson. How much of this do you think you can use? Not much, right?''

"Well, I can talk about the fire and the water rights. It's interesting background. Do you think the fire was an accident?''

The old woman shrugged. "We'll never know now, I don't suppose,'' she said. "Certainly Jed had a good reason to want her dead. But I can't say he was a murderer. Even Frank's death could have been an accident.''

"What reason did Jed have to want Brownie dead, if he had the water rights?''

"She wanted to marry him and he wouldn't leave Freddie. Anyway, when she died he got hold of the property.''

"She left it to him?''

"She'd made him the guardian of her children,'' Liz Noren said. "He loved those kids. He was always over there playing with them. He and Freddie had never had children, so he kind of adopted them as his own. Fact is, I think they were his, not Frank's. Frank and Brownie had never had kids either. He was ten or twelve years older and she was in her thirties when they all met. You couldn't tell just from looking at the kids, because they were just babies when the fire happened. They were born a few months after Frank was killed.''

"So when they all died in the fire, Hunter inherited the ranch?''

"There was something funny about that, too,'' the old woman said. "Nobody ever saw the will. There was an investigation into the cause of the fire and Jed Hunter came out of it holding the deed to the place in his name. And after he got hold of the property, that's when the last holdouts had to sell to him. Except us.

I'll never sell to him, never. And someday some real investigative reporter will write the story the way it ought to be written."

"How old were the kids, Mrs. Noren?"

"I think maybe not quite three," she said. "They sure were beautiful children, both towheads."

"Two boys?"

"No, a boy and a girl. Didn't look much alike at first glance, in fact, and they had very different personalities. The girl was kind of quiet and sweet, but the boy, I remember, was very aggressive and loud, a typical male. God how Jed Hunter loved that boy! That's what makes me think he couldn't have set that fire."

"They must have been born close to each other."

"No, no, didn't I tell you? They were twins."

chapter 15
COMING ON

"I can tell you're a magician," Jude Morgan said. "You can make something out of nothing."

"You call this nothing?" I asked.

"It's a terrific story, my man," the detective said, "but where's the proof? Where are the facts to back it up? You got to remember, I'm a cop. I can't make a move unless I got some hard facts to move on."

"Hey, Jude, I'm not asking you to arrest people and issue statements to the press," I said. "I'm just telling you what I think is going on. You *could* at least look into what I'm saying."

"All right then," he said, leaning back in his seat and folding those big arms of his across his chest, "give it to me one more time, Shifty. Tell me what you think this is all about."

"It's about an obsession and it's about blood and money and corruption."

Jude grimaced. "Come on, man, give me a break. Specifics, facts, that's what I need."

We were sitting in a twenty-four-hour coffee shop on Santa Monica, a few blocks from the station. It was eight o'clock and Jude had agreed to have breakfast with me after I had told him I had some useful information for him, but evidently I had so far disappointed him. I could understand his frustration, because I realized he was right; all I had to tell him was a highly dramatic tale of ruthless ambition, illicit lovemaking, betrayal, and murder, but I might as well have culled it from a pop novel by Harold Robbins or Judith Krantz for all the impression I was making on him. He was stuck with a killing he couldn't solve, one of dozens he'd been working on, and I was asking him to be imaginative, to envision the logical bloody outcome of a whole family saga of double-dealing and violence. He was right, I was a magician, but he was turning out to be a deaf and dumb audience.

"Let me take you back a few years," I said. "Maybe it'll seem more plausible to you then."

Jude groaned and signaled the waitress for more coffee. "Keep it simple, so my dull cop brain can take it in," he said. "Don't invent anything, my man."

"I'm trying not to, Jude," I assured him. "All I'm trying to do is get you interested enough so maybe you'll look into some of the things I'm telling you about."

"Like that woman's story about the water and her ranch? Forget it. It's ancient history, Shifty, and doesn't have much to do with solving the case I'm working on, which is the murder of this guy Freeman and the possible kidnapping of his girlfriend." The waitress arrived to refill our coffee cups and dropped the breakfast check on the table. "Thanks, honey."

"And I'm trying to get you to see that it's all connected, Jude," I said. "Where is Linda Cameron? Don't you want to know?"

"Well, she ain't with her husband, that much we do know."

"And how about Hunter? Has anybody gone to Sovereign Acres to look for her?"

"Why would she be there? Man, you sure got some wild ideas about stuff."

"Shut up, drink your coffee, and listen, okay?"

"Okay," he said, raising his cup to his mouth. "Shoot."

"I told you the story about Judge Hunter and the ranch, but I didn't tell you all of it. I just wanted to make sure first that you got the general picture. Jed Hunter is obsessed and ruthless, do we agree about that?"

Jude nodded. "For the sake of getting on with this, yes. Go on."

"No, it's fact. Look, Jude, he buys land in a valley where he wants to build his dream horse kingdom, okay? He befriends everyone, cons them into thinking he's just one of the neighbors. He begins to have a love affair with the beautiful, weak-willed wife of the man who controls the water supply. He gets the wife pregnant. Before the husband finds out about it, he dies in a convenient hunting accident. Who's the only witness besides Hunter? Why, a younger business associate named Michael Cameron, with whom the Judge has begun to do business, building shopping malls here and there. But there's no reason for the outside world to suspect that Frank Harris may have been murdered, is there? No, of course not. Jed Hunter comforts the widow. He also tries to buy the ranch from her and almost succeeds, but Frank's friend at the bank counsels her not to sell out. She does make a deal with her lover, however; she's going to let him administer her estate for her, also because by this time her children have been born and Jed is the father. How could she not trust him? The twins, by the way, are good-looking, healthy kids and the Judge seems genuinely fond of them, acts as a surrogate father to them. Meanwhile, he allots all the water to himself and begins to squeeze his neighbors out. He buys up every piece of property he can get his hands on. Some of the neighbors sell out and move away, but not all of them. Some, including the Norens, get together and make an end run around Jed Hunter to the widow herself. She's upset by what's going on and intervenes with Hunter on their behalf. She insists on selling them enough of her water so the Norens and their remaining neighbors won't have to sell out to Hunter. And within a year Brownie Harris perishes in a terrible fire that burns her ranch to the ground.''

"Stop right there," the detective said. "You're a great storyteller, but the piece has got a big hole in it."

"Really? Where?"

"The kids. Are you going to tell me, my man, that this guy would kill his own children, burn them to death along with their mother? Is that what you're asking me to believe?"

"What if the kids didn't die, Jude?" I asked. "What if only Brownie Harris died in that fire?"

The detective stared at me in undisguised wonder. "No shit," he said. "How do you figure that?"

"As far as I can tell, no thorough investigation was ever carried out," I said. "The ranch burned to the ground. The charred human remains were gathered together and buried in a common grave. There's a nice headstone right there on the property, in a little private cemetery where there's a handful of other graves, local people who died in the past century, since the valley was first settled. I've seen it. The names of the children, by the way, were Frank, Jr. and Lisa. It says so right there, on Brownie's tombstone."

Jude's jaw sagged slightly open. To cover his surprise, he raised his coffee cup and drank noisily from it. "Go on," he mumbled.

"Don't forget, Jude, this guy was a local superior-court magistrate with an impeccable reputation," I continued. "Who's going to investigate or ask a lot of questions? The Norens, but who's listening to them? Not even Liz Noren suspected Jed Hunter of killing his own children. Not even she could stomach that one. What she didn't know, what nobody knew, was that the kids didn't die in that fire. Jed wanted the Harris Ranch, wanted it enough to kill his mistress for it, so he could realize his big dream and get control of the whole valley."

"She left the ranch to him in her will?"

"There wasn't any will," I said. "I checked that out, too. I went into San Diego and I looked up every newspaper story I could find about the fire. There were two, in the *San Diego Union* and the *Tribune*. Both accounts mentioned that the widow died intestate and that a search was being made for surviving relatives. There were supposed to be some cousins of Frank's back in Ohio somewhere. But before anybody can surface to lay claim to the property, guess who turns out to be holding the deed to it?"

"Jed Hunter."

"Right. Say, Jude, you're getting good at this."

"And you, my man, have gone crazy with the heat."

"Maybe."

"How could he have gotten hold of it? How could that transfer of property have been made?"

"I made one more stop in San Diego, Jude," I said. "I went to City Hall and dropped in at the County Recorder's office. There was a very nice middle-aged lady in there who told me exactly what I had to do. It's called a chain of title, a procedure the computer has greatly simplified. I was in there about an hour and I traced the whole history of the valley, which used to be called the Valley of the Shadows in Indian times. Very poetic, don't you think?"

Jude stared glumly at me over the rim of his coffee cup and waited for me to proceed. "I don't need the whole history, Shifty," he said.

"I know, I know—facts." I took another sip of my own brew and fed him the fruit of my investigation, a small and bitter little plum for him to nibble on. "I went all the way back to the Treaty of Guadalupe Hidalgo, which is the document by which the United States screwed Mexico out of most of California."

"Shifty, man, I haven't got time for this," the detective began. "Either you—"

"Okay, okay, just thought I'd mention it," I said. "It's a fact and you wanted facts. Okay, the problem in the Valley of the Shadows has always been water, which is why not even the Indian tribes in the area could settle it. That problem was solved in a modest way when they found the underground source at the southeast end, on the Harris Ranch. It all checked out just as Liz Noren told it to me. And there, duly recorded, I found the passage of property from Harris to Hunter." I stopped and waited for Jude to say something appreciative, but he didn't rise to the bait.

"What do you want, a medal?" he said. "Look, Shifty, we know Hunter somehow got hold of the Harris property. What we don't know is how."

"I think I do know," I said. "The name of the County Recorder at the time the property changed hands was a guy named Albert Bergman."

It didn't register right away with Jude. "So?" he asked. "Who's he?"

"Linda Cameron's adoptive father," I said. "Her name was Bergman before she married Michael Cameron."

Jude put down his coffee cup and stared at me. "Are you telling me that Jed Hunter arranged to have Bergman adopt her?"

"Maybe. I don't know," I said. "What happened was, he put the children out for adoption. Probably he hid them somewhere first. He paid Bergman off to transfer the title of the land to him and Bergman left town. To further cover his tracks, Hunter split the children up. He provided for them by setting up small trust funds out of a bank in Chicago and intended to keep an eye on them as they grew up, separately and quite unaware of each other, in different parts of the country. His plan eventually must have been to bring them back into his orbit and into his life when they got older. At least that was his plan with the boy, whose name became Win Freeman and who was raised in Florida and on the East Coast. The girl he cared less about, but enough to set up a trust fund for her as well."

"Wait a minute, wait a minute, man," Jude said. "Why did he have to go to all this trouble and risk? Why couldn't he just have adopted the kids himself?"

"Brownie Harris died intestate," I reminded him. "They would have inherited the property. Also, there was Freddie."

"His wife? What about her?"

"A strong woman, Jude, who controlled the purse strings," I said. "She wasn't about to concern herself with Brownie's orphaned twins. Then, too, she may not have known."

"Known what?"

"That the kids didn't die in the fire," I said. "Jed may not have told her. Why would he have? She was mad enough when she did find out."

"When was that?"

"When Win Freeman came to work at Sovereign," I explained. "She was told or, more likely, she figured it out for herself before confronting Jed and she was furious. She hated Win. She wanted him fired. Everybody at Sovereign knew that, but they couldn't figure out why."

"And what happened to the girl?"

"Well, that's a little murky," I admitted. "Either Jed arranged to have the Bergmans adopt her and paid them to do it and to take care of her or Bergman found out where the child was and adopted her on his own."

"Why would he do that?"

"He thought Hunter had cheated him, hadn't paid him enough. He was always complaining about having been swindled and that someday he'd get even with him. My guess is that Hunter arranged the adoption, but didn't keep a close tab on what was happening out there in Louisville. He's a macho male and his big interest was always in the boy. When Linda ran away from the Bergmans, Albert didn't tell Hunter where she'd gone and Hunter didn't care enough or wasn't worried enough about her to find out where she was. When she showed up again as Michael Cameron's wife, it took him completely by surprise. Remember, Cameron never clued Linda in to any of his business dealings and during most of their marriage they lived in Houston. Cameron's relationship with Hunter was strictly business, especially after Frank Harris's death and Cameron's prudent withdrawal from the local scene. You like this story, Jude?"

"It's great, but I can't use any of it."

"You could have somebody look up Albert Bergman in Louisville," I suggested. "He shouldn't be too hard to find. Maybe he'd talk to somebody now, if he's as bitter as Linda said he was."

"Maybe he would," Jude agreed. "Maybe I'll put out a few feelers. But my main problem, Shifty, my man, is who killed this guy Freeman and where is—"

He suddenly interrupted himself and stared at me. "Hey, are you telling me that Win Freeman and Linda Cameron were getting it on and they were brother and sister?"

I nodded. "They didn't know," I said. "They obviously felt a tremendous attraction for each other—they were twins, remember—and they mistook it for love, or at least Linda did. Like her mother, she's a very weak woman, easily influenced, Jude, and deeply troubled. I know she must have been overwhelmed by what she felt for Win. But he wasn't weak, far from it."

"What do you mean?"

"He was a very forceful, tough, ambitious man, just like his father," I said. "That's why Jed loved him. He also had a record back in Florida. He was violent and ruthless about women and about getting his own way. When he went after Linda, he probably couldn't help himself either. He wanted her and he took her. But it ruined everything for him."

"With the Judge."

"Right. It gave Freddie the muscle she needed to get rid of him. She may have threatened to spill the whole story, if Jed didn't get rid of them both. She put enough pressure on him to force him to act. And so Win and Linda fled to her little cottage in West L.A., where somebody dropped in on them and killed him."

"Hunter?"

I shrugged. "Hey, that's your department. Don't you have any clues? Do I have to figure everything out for you?"

"The only clues we have are your goddamn fingerprints over everything," the detective said. "You are one messy fuck-up in that department."

"Well, we do know the motive wasn't robbery, don't we?" I observed, a little unkindly. "So now we would have to ask ourselves who would have a motive to want Win Freeman dead?"

"And that's why you asked me if anybody had gone to Sovereign to look for the woman. You don't really think she's there, do you?"

"No," I admitted, "I don't. If only because Freddie wouldn't stand for it. But you might also look into Win Freeman's background a little bit."

"You want to explain that to me, Shifty? I must be a little dense today, my man."

"Well, he isn't the only corpse on your hands, is he?"

"Who else in this case?"

"There's the Fazzini boys, Jude. Don't forget about them."

"You think it's all connected, do you?"

"Sure. Don't you? It cost a fortune to build that place," I said. "Eight or nine years ago, when the Judge began to build it up on a grand scale, the horse business was booming and he'd have had no trouble financing it. Then, about four years ago, the bottom fell out of the breeding industry. But Hunter went right on putting his dream facility together, at a time when other people were going broke and even today there are horse farms for sale cheap all over, in Kentucky, California, everywhere. The Judge isn't that rich. Where'd the money come from, Jude?"

I didn't hear from Jude again for over two weeks. I had no idea whether he had paid any attention to my tale and what must have seemed to him my outlandish speculations. Meanwhile, I tried to put my own life in order and to forget about Linda. I went out to the track early in the morning as often as possible and watched our filly work twice more, both times with Tim Lang on her back. She had settled down some and become easier to handle, so that Lang was able to breeze her both times and gallop her out, bringing her back to the barn looking as if she were fresh and fit enough to go back out and do it all over again. As we entered the dog days of July, with the Hollywood Park meet drawing to a close, Charlie Pickard scanned the condition book for a race. "I wanted to wait till Del Mar," he explained, "but she's trainin' so good I may have to run her short once here. She's liable to kick the barn down if I don't." And two days after that, he entered her in a six-furlong sprint for nonwinners of a race other than maiden or claiming. It would be a perfect prep, Charlie assured me, for a little overnight stakes race at Del Mar on the last day in July. "We'll win this one, too," the trainer said, "but it don't matter whether we do or not. We're pointing for the sixty-thousand-dollar pot two weeks later."

It gave me a good excuse to call Jude, who, it turned out, had been about to call me. "She can't lose, huh?" he asked, after I had told him what we were up to with Mad Margaret.

"They can all lose, Jude," I answered. "You know that."

"Yeah, my daddy always told me."

"But she's doing great," I said. "She ought to blow them away. Then, two weeks later, she'll try stakes horses for the first time. That'll be something you won't want to miss."

"Exciting, huh?"

"I'm damn near pissing in my pants just thinking about it," I said. "What's new at your end?"

"Funny you should ask," he said. "I was about to call you."

"What's up? Any sign of Linda?"

"No, but we ran a check on Win Freeman. You were right."

"About what?"

"He had a record, all right," the detective said. "He had a temper and got into fights in bars. He was a black-belt karate guy, so he didn't lose any of them. He also worked as an enforcer for a while for a syndicate based in Miami, loan sharks. He was also good with a knife, carried one strapped to his shin. I guess you'd say he wasn't as nice a kid as he looked."

"I know a girl he cut," I said. "She works for Charlie."

"No shit. Well, you were right about him. Now, about your man Albert Bergman, he's gone."

"Gone? Where to?"

"Not where to, but permanent. He died in an automobile accident about a month ago."

"Where?"

"In Louisville. Actually, outside of town. Driving up the highway along the river, veered off the road. Drunk as a skunk, they say."

"You believe that?"

"That he's dead? Sure."

"No, that it was an accident."

"What am I supposed to believe, Shifty? I only got the facts, my man, as reported to me out of Louisville, Kentucky. What do you want? Dreams? Speculations? Theories? Ain't got time for them, my man."

"So now what?"

There was a silence at the other end of the line, then a long, drawn-out sigh. "Ah, well, man, we just keep plodding ahead, don't we? And maybe someday, if we get lucky, we'll find out something really useful. That's how it usually works."

The next morning I picked up my copy of the *Los Angeles Times* and read that seventeen of the thirty-one charges against Michael Cameron had been dropped for lack of sufficient evidence. Among them was the murder indictment regarding the Fazzini brothers. The district attorney's office was compelled to admit that there simply wasn't enough to go on and that perhaps the state had been a little hasty to charge Mr. Cameron of so heinous a crime. He would be tried, however, on the various counts of fraud regarding city building contracts and the case would be in the court system by early fall. Oh, yes—Mr. Cameron's bail had been greatly reduced, to a mere fifty thousand dollars, in fact, and his lawyer, Mr. Alden Berry of La Jolla, California, predicted he would be acquitted of all charges. His client was innocent, Mr. Berry informed the press, as would be made clear once all the facts were known.

Facts. It was touching to realize how totally so many people seemed to rely solely on the facts. I knew, as I sat there that morning sipping my coffee and dunking my toast, that Michael Cameron was a swindler, a sadist, and a swine. I knew that Judge Jed Hunter was a great rascal and a hypocrite, so concentrated on his own lusts and dreams that he had undoubtedly looted, burned, and killed in pursuit of them. And I knew that Linda was a victim, not only of these men and their associates, but of her own sick, twisted, knife-wielding twin brother. But the facts rendered me helpless and disarmed the instruments of justice, either because they were too few in number or tended to contradict themselves or, as is often the case, obscured the larger view. Facts are facts, as solid as concrete blocks or as the stone pillars sustaining an edifice, but the view can often be obscured by them, as surely as the grand configuration of an entire forest can be hidden by its trees.

chapter 16

GOING AWAY

"How can we bet this filly?" Angles inquired, as indignantly as if I were personally responsible for the fact that she would almost certainly go off at odds of close to even money. "How can we make any money bettin' on odds-on favorites?"

"I have to confess, Angles, that the success or failure of your betting action was not uppermost in our thoughts," I admitted. "It's a thirty-thousand-dollar purse, that's what we're interested in. That and getting a nice prep under her belt for the stakes race two weeks from now."

"And besides, Angles, this is an exacta race," Arnie pointed out. "Find the second horse at a decent price and you can make some money."

"Unfortunately, the second horse will almost certainly be D. L. Gantry's filly," Jay observed. "She will be the second choice. That does not seem likely to pay off at decent odds.''

"That's what I'm sayin','' Angles said. "There's no way to cash a good ticket in the race.''

"Figure an angle,'' Arnie urged him. "You can do it, if anybody can.''

"Some propositions there ain't an angle,'' Beltrami replied. "The only possible break is that Gantry's filly drew the rail. If she don't break good, maybe one of the long shots in here could split them.'' He stared at me reproachfully. "Geez, Shifty, you could have told Charlie to bring her up to the stakes race on workouts alone, couldn't you? Think of the payoff down the line.''

"Maggie's too good to fool around with, Angles,'' I explained. "You don't fool around with a good horse, you know that.''

Angles nodded glumly and I felt a twinge of sympathy for him, but only a passing one. I was too elated at the prospect of my filly's triumphant comeback. She had drawn the five hole in the seven-horse field and looked primed to win. Listed at two to one in the morning line, the odds established by the track handicapper, she had been selected by the newspaper experts and the tout sheets as the best bet of the day, the horse most likely to win on the card, and would almost certainly go off at a much lower price, perhaps less than even money, once the bettors began to establish the true odds on the race by risking their capital at the pari-mutuel windows. I didn't care, mainly because I wasn't planning to bet on her; all I wanted Maggie to do was run her race and win the purse.

Mad Margaret was entered in the seventh, so I had nearly three hours to kill. I was too excited to pay any attention to the earlier races, so I left the box and wandered restlessly about the grandstand. Everywhere I went people came up to me to ask about the filly and to wish me luck, until I couldn't stand it anymore and fled into the Turf Club. I thought I'd have a quiet, solitary lunch and linger over my coffee until it became time for me to go to the paddock. I had a jacket and a tie on for the occasion, so I had no trouble blending into the more elegant Turf Club scene and I got myself a table in a corner of the dining room, out of the way of the main traffic but with a nearby TV monitor on which to watch the outcome of the races. Unfortunately, by the time my light lunch of a tunafish sandwich and salad actually arrived, I was too nervous to eat.

I don't know of any feeling quite like that of having your own horse entered in an actual race. Nothing in my long experience as a horseplayer had prepared me for the feeling. My heart seemed to be out of control, pounding away at a noisy and alarming rate, and my head was dizzy, as if I stood at the edge of a precipice poised to leap into space, with nothing between me and disaster but a tiny parachute. I could have faced the biggest audience in the world and easily performed Houdini's favorite stunt of freeing himself from chains inside a locked trunk dropped into a pool, but I couldn't just sit still now and wait for the minutes to count down to post time. I watched the races succeed each other on the monitor without registering or caring who won or lost; then, when I couldn't stand it anymore, I abruptly stood up, dropped a twenty-dollar bill on the table to pay for my ten-dollar lunch, and departed to seek solace in movement, like the Flying Dutchman of legend, condemned to wander endlessly until rescued by the unselfish love of a female. Only Maggie's heart and talent and strong legs could now bring me peace.

I strolled aimlessly about, grinning and nodding and chatting without being aware either of what I was saying or to whom, until I turned a corner of the main bar and found myself looking at a large round table presided over by some familiar faces. Judge Jed Hunter and his wife, Freddie, sat smilingly playing host to a group of friends and colleagues from the racing world, among whom I spotted D. L. Gantry, resplendent in a pale blue cashmere sports coat, and Alden Berry, a sleek little mink in a blue business suit. The sight stopped me in my tracks, as if I had been hit by a bucket of ice water hurled into my face. For the first time since I'd awakened at dawn that morning I was not thinking about Mad Margaret and the race. I felt myself go cold inside and then become wonderfully concentrated, like a wandering mystic suddenly granted a revelation that put all of life into a blindingly clear perspective.

I should have realized the Hunters would be there. Sovereign had two horses entered in the feature race, a Group I handicap on the turf course for four-year-olds and up, and one of them figured to win it. It made sense that they would be on hand for the event, one of the more important ones on the local racing calendar. I knew instantly that I couldn't let the opportunity pass, if only because I have this odd but deeply rooted belief that no bad deed should ever pass unnoticed or go unpunished. "A man must live," a toadying court poet had once said to Voltaire. "I don't see the necessity," the philosopher had replied. I don't always live up to such high standards of conduct, but it's not because I don't want to.

I forced myself to break into a broad smile and walked over to their table. "Hello," I said. "Just wanted to wish you folks good luck today all around."

"We'll need it in our race," Gantry answered, smiling. "I hear your filly's in good form."

"The best," I said. "Too bad my partner won't be here to enjoy it."

"Ah, yes, Mr. Anderson," Jed Hunter said, in that

black booming baritone that had dazzled courtrooms, "we can take some credit for that." He turned to his table companions. "Mad Margaret, Mr. Anderson's fine filly in the seventh, boarded with us for a while. She's a nice animal."

"Yes, I was hoping Linda could be here," I said. "She would have enjoyed it."

"It's tragic, just tragic," Jed Hunter said, fixing his one powerful eye on me, as if he expected his gaze to turn me to stone. "I wonder what could possibly have happened to her."

"Let me show you," I said, reaching into my pocket to produce a Susan B. Anthony silver dollar and a small blank sheet of paper. "I think you'll find this amusing."

"Oh, good!" one of the women at the table exclaimed. "I simply adore magic!"

"I don't think this is really the time—" Alden Berry began to say, only to be immediately silenced by my new fan.

She was a tall, imperious-looking brunette of about fifty with the leathery brown skin of someone who had spent much of her life outdoors, probably on horseback. "Honestly, Alden, don't be such a drip," she said. "It's all in fun, isn't it? And all we're doing is sitting around waiting for our wretched horse to run."

"Thank you," I said. "I'll try to make it interesting." I held up the coin. "Here we have a silver dollar with the portrait of a woman engraved on it. It doesn't look like Linda, but let's call her Linda, shall we? Now watch." I folded the coin up inside the paper and laid the packet on the table in front of my fan. "Now put your hand over it," I instructed her. "Is Linda still there?"

"Oh, yes, I can feel her," the woman said.

"Good. Don't take your hand away now." The woman pressed down hard on the packet. I shut my eyes. "All right," I said, "first we have Linda where we think we want her, then we don't." I clapped my hands twice. "Linda meets Win and Linda vanishes," I said. "Is she still there?"

The woman picked up the paper and unfolded it, only to find it empty. "Marvelous!" she said. "How did you do that?"

"It's easy to make things and people disappear," I said. "The hard part is finding them again. Want to try?"

"Really," Alden Berry said, "this is in very poor taste."

"Oh, do you think so? I'm so sorry," I said, producing a pack of cards out of my pocket.

"That's enough," Hunter said. "I think we've seen enough."

"I haven't," Freddie said. "I'd like to see more." She smiled brightly at me. "Can you really find her?"

"I'm not sure I can," I said. "I was going to let you try. Do you want to?"

"Absolutely," Freddie said.

"Mr. Berry, how about you?" I asked, turning with a smile toward the lawyer.

"No," he snapped and stood up. "I've had enough of this."

"Sit down, Alden," Freddie said. "I'll try. Will that be all right, Mr. Anderson?"

"Anyone can play," I said, "but it takes skill." I took the pack and fanned it face up on the table. "You're all familiar with Three-Card Monte, I'm sure. Although it's become a gambling game played on street corners all over the world, it's basically an ancient and honorable move. It's played with three cards and the maneuver is deceptively simple. Here, let's pick our cards." I selected the queen of hearts and the two black kings, then held them out for all to see. "The trick will be to find the queen," I continued.

"Obviously, our queen of hearts is Linda and our two kings—well, let's just call them the black kings."

I glanced up at the Judge and smiled. He was sitting up very straight in his chair, his large hands flat on the table in front of him. He did not smile back, but kept his powerful single eye fixed on me. The table had become tense and I was afraid that either Hunter or Berry would put a stop to my routine, but I hadn't counted on Freddie. She seemed excited, vengefully stimulated by the action. "Go on, Mr. Anderson," she said. "I'm eager to try."

I turned the cards face down and shuffled them, then displayed them again. "You see," I said, "there's Linda between her two kings. Now watch." I placed her face down on the table between the kings, then I picked up the king of spades and showed him to Freddie and dropped him on top of Linda. "Appropriate, don't you think?" Then I picked up both cards in one hand while holding the king of clubs in the other and performed the basic maneuver, which includes what magicians call a blind, a move of the hands so fast and effortless that it always escapes detection. "Where's Linda?" I asked Freddie.

She pointed to a card and I turned up the king of clubs. "Does the king know?" I asked. "If so, he isn't telling." I performed the maneuver again and this time Freddie came up with the king of spades. "Well, does he know? One of them must, don't you think? Here, let's take him out of the picture for a moment, since he isn't here anyway." I displayed the king of spades and discarded him, leaving me with only two cards, presumably the queen of hearts and the king of clubs. "Now let's see if we can find Linda." I moved the two remaining cards around, then again asked Freddie to find the queen. She came up with the king of clubs. "Well now, let's see who's really under here," I said and turned over the other card. It was the king of spades. "Amazing," I said. "Linda seems to have vanished permanently from the scene." I looked up at Freddie and smiled. "Funny," I said, "I thought you might find her."

"That is simply marvelous," the tall brunette said. "Wasn't that marvelous?"

No one answered. "Well, I'd better get down to my horse," Gantry said, pushing his chair back and standing up. "The horses for the sixth race are out on the track. Thanks for lunch, Judge, Mrs. Hunter." He waved good-bye and walked away.

Judge Hunter hardly moved. He sat in place like a statue, but I had the feeling he might explode if somebody struck a spark anywhere near him. Freddie rose to her feet and smiled brilliantly at me. "That was quite extraordinary," she said. "It must take a lot of practice."

I gathered up my cards and dropped the pack back into my pocket. "It does," I answered, "it really does. Of course, it's a lot harder making real people disappear and, I suppose, it's equally hard to rematerialize them. But I do think it's important to try, don't you?" I turned my back on the company and walked away.

"What can he mean?" I heard the tall brunette say. "What an odd thing to say. But wasn't it extraordinary? Absolutely magical, wasn't it?"

The boys came down to the paddock for the seventh and joined me on the patch of grass facing the saddling stalls. The horses filed into the ring from the track, with Mad Margaret fifth in line and being led by May Potter, who was in her working clothes of blue jeans, boots, and a blue cowboy shirt but who looked radiant. Her cheeks were flushed and I noticed that she had also added a touch of lipstick and mascara to enhance her natural good looks. She grinned when she saw me and gave me a little wave of fingers to say hello. "Hey, Shifty, you didn't tell us about the other filly," Angles said. "You give that a little of the old beef and cream treatment?"

"Shut up, Angles," Arnie said. "You're lowering the tone of the proceedings."

"Yeah, this is an allowance race," Jay said. "Try not to act like a cheap claimer for once in your life, Angles."

"Hey, hey," Angles said, shielding himself behind his upraised palms, "I was making a joke. Geez, what's the fuckin' problem?"

The filly looked so splendid in the post parade that even Charlie was forced to admit, although grudgingly, that she might have a chance. "All you got to do, Tim, is get her out of the gate," he told our jockey. "If somebody else wants to go early, let him. She'll tell you when she wants to run. You got that?"

The jockey nodded and grinned at us. "Piece of cake," he said. "There ain't nothin' in here that can run with her."

Oddly enough, the crowd didn't seem to share our confidence. As the horses jogged or galloped toward the starting gate, I looked at the tote board and was astonished to see that Mad Margaret was only a lukewarm favorite, at two to one, with Gantry's filly, a royally bred brown offspring by Alydar out of a stakes-winning mare, established as the second choice, at five to two. "Oh, my," Jay said, as he settled into his seat and reached for his Form, "this is a little too good to be true. This Gantry filly is a money-burning morning glory who'll spit it out if she's hurried early enough. There's a chance to make money here."

We waited until three minutes before post time, when the odds on Maggie had dropped to eight to five and Gantry's filly had risen to three to one. "You know what?" Jay said, rising from his seat. "I'm going to make a major play here. Gantry's always shooting his mouth off and this time it's a blessing. He's been telling everybody this horse is a late bloomer who's going to win some big races down the line. That's why the suckers are betting on her. At eight to five or even at three to two, Shifty's horse is an overlay.''

We followed Jay out of the box to the betting windows and dipped heavily into our cash reserves. I bet four hundred to win on my horse, while the boys emptied out their wallets. As the horses reached the starting gate, the odds on Maggie sank to three to two, then to seven to five. "Still an overlay," Jay murmured, as we all raised our glasses to focus on the start. My hands were shaking and my heart was threatening to pound itself to pieces, but the minute the gate opened and the horses burst into the clear I became wonderfully calm and concentrated, like a pilot on a bombing run, with time suspended and nothing but the target to hone in on.

Gantry's filly went to the front and for a moment I thought she might unhook to open up two or three lengths, but then I saw that Maggie had her by the throat, laying just off the pace by half a length with Tim Lang sitting chilly on her like a tiny multicolored doll.

The two of them opened up five lengths on the field and as they hit the turn the announcer informed the public that the contest had become a two-horse race. He was wrong. At the head of the stretch, Tim Lang tapped Maggie once with his whip. The filly quickly switched leads and seemed to go into overdrive, flattening out like a big cat in pursuit of a gazelle, each stride eating up the hard Hollywood earth. She swept past Gantry's filly to open up two lengths at the eighth pole, then stretched it to three and four and finally five as she crossed the finish line, with her rider merely sitting there and allowing her to do it all on her own. The timer clicked off a minute and nine seconds flat for the distance, close to a track record and a brilliant performance for a young filly running in only the third race of her career.

I don't remember much else about the occasion, at least not in sequence. I know that as Mad Margaret began her run, I hunched forward in my seat. "Yes, yes, yes!" I heard myself say as she came flying down the lane, a vision of power and beauty in action. When she hit the wire, I went up in the air as if fired out of a cannon, my program flying in one direction, my glasses in another.

In the winner's circle, I stood between Charlie and Jay, my arms around both of them and grinning like an idiot as the track photographer immortalized the scene. The calmest of us all was Mad Margaret, who stood quietly by, looking as if she had just returned from a stroll in the park. As May started to lead her away, I patted the filly's neck, then grabbed May and gave her a hug. She responded by putting her arms around me and kissing me briefly but hard on the mouth. It startled me for a moment until I saw her eyes full of tears and realized that she loved this animal at least as much as I did. "Wasn't that great?" she said. "Ain't she the best? Oh, Shifty, thanks for givin' her to me."

"Thank Charlie," I said. "He's the one."

The trainer permitted himself a tiny smile as he watched Maggie being led away, his eyes focused on her legs and the way she moved as she headed away from us up toward the clubhouse turn. "She's lookin' good," he said, as we headed back toward the stands and the official sign came on, showing that our filly had just paid off at $4.80 for every winning two-dollar ticket. "Say, Shifty, don't you know not to fall in love with your horse?"

"Screw that, Charlie," I told him. "What's all this about, if it isn't love?"

"Anything can happen, you know that."

"Sure, we could all drop dead tomorrow," I said. "But you know what, Charlie? I'm going to get killed right here or at some other racetrack. I can't think of a better way to go than holding a winning ticket on something as beautiful as that filly. Talk to me about anything but love, Charlie. It's the only chance a man has to justify his presence on this planet."

"How you talk, Shifty," Charlie said, smiling and giving me a light tap on the shoulder. "Sometimes I think you mean all that bullshit you spout."

chapter 17

FOUL CLAIM

Five days after Mad Margaret's winning race, Linda Cameron was found on the beach at Santa Monica. She was sitting on the sand, dressed only in a light raincoat, and staring out to sea. Nobody paid any attention to her at first, but at dusk, long after most of the other visitors had gone home, she continued to sit there, gazing vacantly before her. The lifeguard in the nearby tower had spotted her earlier, but had not imagined she could be in any sort of distress. Now, however, as it came time for him to go home, he began to wonder about her. It wasn't what she was doing that aroused his curiosity; it was what she wasn't doing, the absolute stillness in which she seemed to exist, as if she had become a fixed object in a painted landscape. He climbed down from his tower, walked over to her, and leaned down to look into her eyes. "Are you all right, miss?" he asked. "Are you okay?"

She didn't answer. She seemed to be unaware of him, as if she could look straight through him at the distant horizon, where the sea was turning to gold beneath the rays of the setting sun. The lifeguard reached out and touched her shoulder. "Miss? Miss?" He shook her gently, but she did not respond. She was lost inside herself; her eyes seemed to be seeing nothing. "Miss," the lifeguard said, taking her elbow now and trying to raise her to her feet, "it's time to go home now. It'll be dark soon and you don't want to stay here by yourself after dark. It's dangerous. Please, miss."

But he couldn't get her to move; she hung off his arm like a dead weight. As he tried to raise her to her feet, her coat fell open and he saw that she was naked underneath it, so he let her go and she slumped back into the sand. The lifeguard returned to his tower and called the Santa Monica police.

Two young officers in a patrol car came, saw the condition she was in, and summoned an ambulance. They bundled Linda into it and took her to Santa Monica Hospital, a couple of miles from where she had been found. She was admitted to the emergency ward and an attempt began to establish her identity. At about seven o'clock, Michael Cameron and a woman appeared at the hospital and he identified his wife. At his insistence, she was transferred to a private room at St. John's, a fancier medical facility a few blocks away, and entrusted to the care of several specialists, who set about trying to determine not only what physical condition she was in but what had happened to her. Michael Cameron informed the police that he had paid a ransom of four hundred thousand dollars for the release of his wife and he produced an apparently genuine note from her kidnappers to prove it. The money, he said, had been left in a locker at the Greyhound bus station in Santa Monica and been picked up the night before. He had not informed the police because he had been afraid to anger the kidnappers and so to jeopardize the possibility of his wife's release. He was able to prove that he had actually raised the money to seek her freedom.

I heard about it that night on the local six-o'clock news and I immediately telephoned Jamie Horton, who promised that she would concern herself in the matter. Then I called Jude Morgan, who was not at the station. I left a message for him to call me back, which he did as soon as it was relayed to him from the station switchboard. "The lady is pretty much out of it," he informed me. "She won't or can't talk."

"What happened to her?"

"We haven't got a full report yet," the detective said, "but she's been beaten, drugged, and almost certainly raped. We don't know who did this. If she comes around in a day or two, we'll get more information. Not much else I can tell you right now, my man."

"Are you going to let Cameron take care of her?" I said. "He's probably partly responsible, at least."

"We don't know that, Shifty."

"She'd left him," I said. "She'd hired a lawyer to draw up a separation agreement. Giving her back to Cameron is crazy."

"We'll just have to see what she says about it," the detective said. "We have to hope she'll come out of this."

I went by the hospital the next morning and inquired about her, but I couldn't get in to see her. A strong-looking, beefy blonde in a charcoal gray business suit came down to the lobby by the nurses' station to confront me. "Mrs. Cameron is in intensive care," she said. "She can't see anyone. Who are you?"

I told her my name and watched her eyes harden

into open hostility. "And you must be the infamous Richardene," I said. "How did you get away from the dog?"

"If you don't leave at once," she said, "I'll call the police."

"I'm surprised the police aren't questioning you," I answered. "Where were you when Linda was being held against her will?"

"Get out," she said. "Get out now or I'll have you arrested."

I went to a pay phone down the hall and called Jamie Horton. "There's not much point in trying to see her," she told me. "She can't talk to anyone. I spoke to one of the doctors, a neurologist, and he said that she's so traumatized by what's happened to her that she can't speak."

"What did happen to her?"

"She has been thoroughly brutalized," Jamie Horton said. "She has been repeatedly raped, beaten, and drugged. The doctors don't even know if she'll come out of this catatonic state she's in. Until she does, there isn't anything I can do to help her."

I called Jude Morgan and he confirmed Jamie Horton's account. "We've questioned Cameron as well as the Leider woman—"

"Richardene?"

"Yeah, that her name? They can both account for every minute of the time Mrs. Cameron's been gone. So until she can talk to us, we have nothing to go on."

"What about Don Houps?"

"We have a warrant out for him, but haven't found him yet. Oh, and that lawyer of Cameron's, what's his name?"

"Berry, Alden Berry."

"That's the guy. Anyway, he claimed to be representing Mrs. Cameron's interests as well. Says she had changed her mind about divorcing Cameron and was getting ready to go back to him."

"That's a lie. You don't believe that, do you? She was living with Win Freeman till he was killed."

"All too true, my man, but Berry claims she called Cameron the night before and begged to be taken back," Jude said. "She said she was afraid of Freeman, terrified, in fact, and wanted to go home. Cameron was going to pick her up the next day."

"It's crazy," I said. "She may have been afraid of Freeman, but the rest of it doesn't sound right at all. You do see that, don't you?"

"We're just sitting here, my man, twiddling our thumbs until something breaks," he said. "Meanwhile, let's just keep cool. If Mrs. Cameron comes around, we'll get some answers. Say, that was one hell of a race your filly ran the other day."

"Did you get down on her?"

"You must be kidding," Jude said. "If there's one basic rule my daddy taught me about horses, it's that no animal is worth risking a dollar on at less than two to one."

"She was an overlay at the price," I said. "And besides, your daddy died broke."

"Good point, Shifty, my man," he said, with a low, dark laugh. "I'll bear that in mind next time she runs."

I decided to skip getaway day at Hollywood Park, no hardship, and go down to Del Mar a couple of days early. For the past four years Jay and I had rented the same condominium for the seven weeks of the racing season, a two-bedroom apartment on the hillside overlooking the fairgrounds and with a terrace from which we could see part of the stable area and had a good view of the far turn. The rest of the year, the place was occupied by students at the University of California campus in La Jolla, which meant that the premises remained in a more or less permanent state of disrepair. Most of the dishes and glasses were cracked and chipped, the furniture looked battered and stained, and the walls looked as if they had been used for some form of target practice. The landlord didn't care. He was a retired stockbroker who had bought several such properties simply as real-estate investments and his only concern was to keep them rented year-around so he could meet his mortgage payments. We paid him twenty-five hundred dollars for the season, a very reasonable sum for such a handy location, and we pretty much camped out in it. The beds, at least, were comfortable and I alleviated the prevailing squalor by tacking up a couple of my magic and racing posters. Jay and I hadn't missed a Del Mar meet in eleven years and for us it represented the high point of our racing year. Much to Happy Hal Mancuso's disgust, I never accepted a job during the time, from the last week in July to the second week in September, that the horses ran at Del Mar. And this year promised to be special, if only because I knew that Charlie was now pointing Mad Margaret for a stakes race, the Fleet Treat, to be run at seven furlongs for a sixty-thousand-dollar pot during the first week of the meet.

I tried to put the whole question of Linda Cameron out of my head, but I found that I couldn't. My nights were haunted by her pale face and I kept remembering the lovemaking we had shared during our brief time together. Three days after my arrival, I called Jamie Horton again to find out what was going on. Her news was fairly shattering. "She doesn't remember anything specific," the lawyer told me, "nothing about what happened to her. She has talked about Freeman, but only hesitantly and with fear, not as if she'd been involved with him in any way. She has no idea what's happened to her."

"Nothing about the murder or the kidnapping?"

"Nothing. At least, not as of forty-eight hours ago. I spoke to the neurologist in charge of her case. He said it was not uncommon for the conscious mind to blot out horrendous traumatic experiences such as the one she's obviously been through."

"You said 'as of forty-eight hours ago.' You haven't been in touch with her since?"

"No. I'm not representing Mrs. Cameron now."

"Why not?"

"She's evidently agreed to a reconciliation attempt with her husband. She's been released from the hospital and gone home."

"Home? To Rancho Santa Fe?"

"Yes, I believe so."

"That's crazy. Did you speak to her directly?"

"Yes, I did. She seemed quite lucid, if subdued. She was absolutely determined to give it a try."

"But that's terrible," I said. "Isn't there anything you can do?"

"I can't go against my client's wishes, Mr. Anderson."

"But she's not herself, Jamie. Surely you know that."

"Unfortunately, I don't know anything of the kind," the lawyer said, "and, in any case, my hands are tied in this matter."

I called Alden Berry, ostensibly to inquire about the joint ownership of Mad Margaret. He not only didn't seem at all surprised to hear from me, but acted on the phone as if he had been trying to contact me and was glad that I had called. "I imagine that you could get considerably more now for Mr. Cameron's share of the horse," he said, "seeing as how she has run so impressively."

"I don't know," I answered. "I haven't thought about it."

"I suggest you do think about it."

"It was my understanding that Mrs. Cameron was to be part-owner of Mad Margaret," I said. "Why don't you have her get in touch with me?"

"Obviously that's out of the question at the moment," Berry said. "Surely you're aware of the ordeal Mrs. Cameron has been subjected to. She's in no condition to make any decisions for herself. When you find a purchaser for the Camerons' share, please contact me directly. We'll accept a hundred thousand dollars for our forty-five percent."

"I'm not going to look for a buyer for you or negotiate a price," I said, "not unless I hear directly from Mrs. Cameron herself."

"That's very shortsighted of you," Berry said. "You're a difficult man, Anderson."

"No, I'm not," I said. "I just don't like to be threatened and to be told my fingers are going to be broken. Where is Don Houps, anyway? You know the police are looking for him, don't you? Though I don't imagine he had the ingenuity or skill to blow Win Freeman's face off while he was sitting on the toilet. Just keep him away from me, all right?"

"What are we to do with you, Anderson?" Berry said, with a sigh. He reminded me of a history teacher I had once had in the sixth grade who despaired of my preference for acts of sleight-of-hand over the outcome of the Peloponnesian War.

"Well, I don't know," I said. "You see, I really don't think this is all just going to blow away and disappear for you. At some point Linda might even begin to remember some details of what happened to her, in which case I imagine relationships at home could become a little strained. I wouldn't want anything else to happen to Linda, Alden. I've made it pretty clear to the L.A. police that I consider Cameron a leading contender for scumsucker of the month."

"Anything else, Anderson?" the lawyer asked, unruffled by my verbal assault.

"Not right now," I said, "but I'll think of something."

"I wouldn't bother. You're really a pretty sad figure, you know; I'd stick to what you do rather well, all that business with cards and coins. Be entertaining, Anderson. Don't make a nuisance of yourself."

I tried to lose myself in the early days of the Del Mar meet and almost succeeded. I got up very early every morning and went into the stable area to mingle with the horsemen. I hung around with May, helping her in a minor way with Mad Margaret. I'd follow the filly out to the track to watch her gallop, then come back and walk her for an hour before May took over again and tucked her away for the day. Most of the time Maggie behaved with me like a big, friendly dog, curving her beautiful neck and head around me as I petted her and fed her her ration of chopped-up carrots. But whenever it was time to go to the track, she'd become like a caged tiger, all repressed power and grace, and I'd have to turn her over to May or Eddie to get her ready for Polo. Three days before her race, Charlie let her run a little under Tim Lang and she blew out in thirty-five seconds flat under a tight hold, then came back still so full of run that she seemed to be bouncing inside herself as she made her way back to the barn.

I love the backside at Del Mar. It's shabby-looking and dusty and smells of manure and hay. At dawn the premises are usually still shrouded in fog and the horses moving out onto the track at that hour seem surreal, spectral figures in a painted landscape as imagined by Whistler. Often they would disappear from view and only the sounds of their hooves striking the soft dirt testified to their presence until suddenly they

261

would loom back into view, sweeping past along the rail or galloping out in the middle of the course, manifestations of creation, miracles of evolution. I would take a post up in the guinea stand and watch them for an hour or more, then retreat at the break to the cafeteria for a half hour of chatter, gossip, jokes, and horse talk at the tables with the horsemen. By nine or nine-thirty, it would be pretty much all over and I'd go back to our apartment, change into swimming gear, and head out to the beach for a couple of hours of sun and surf before it would be time to go home, shower, and change for an afternoon of racing, first post time at two P.M. There are worse ways to live.

One morning, as I was heading to my car, May came out of Charlie's tack room holding a container of coffee in one hand and said, "Where you goin'?"

"The beach. Want to come?"

"Sure. But my car's broke down. Can you wait a minute and give me a ride?"

"Of course."

"I'm right over there," she said, pointing to the second story of the dormitory building nearest to Charlie's shedrow. She ran up the outside stairs to her room and emerged a couple of minutes later in a ragged-looking pair of cut-off jeans, a pink halter top, and thongs and carrying a small string bag. "Let's go," she said, smiling with delight.

We drove back to my place and I ushered her inside, expecting to find Jay at his usual post, sitting at the dining-room table and hunched over his statistics. But the apartment was empty and a note taped on the bathroom mirror revealed that he had finished early and gone for a run on the beach. "I'll see you either on the beach or at the races," it continued.

"Want some more coffee?" I asked May. "There's some on the stove. I'll go change."

"Sure. Thanks."

She headed for the kitchen and I went into the bedroom. I had finished shaving and had just put on my trunks when I heard the door open behind me. May was standing in the doorway, holding a cup of coffee and looking at me with a strange little smile on her face. "Hi," she said. "How you doin'?"

"I'm doing okay. What's up?"

"I don't know," she said. "Let's find out."

She closed the door behind her, put her cup down on the bureau, and took off her halter top. I pulled her quickly into my arms and we descended onto the bed tearing at each other's clothes. It was lovemaking without finesse or foreplay, into the gate and out, bang bang bang, right down the straightaway in about twenty-one seconds flat. "Wow," I said, as I rolled away from her, "we just broke a world record."

"It's okay," she said. "I been wantin' you, Shifty. You don't never say nothin' or come on to me or anythin'. What's a gal to do?"

"I guess I was a little nervous about you," I said. "I mean, you work for Charlie."

"So? I don't fuck Charlie. Don't you like me?"

"I like you a lot, May. I was going to ask you out."

"Shit, if I had to wait for you to make a move, mister, I'd die of old age."

I reached out for her, but she laughed and backed away from me. "Come on, let's hit the beach," she said. "We can pick this up again tonight, hear?"

"I hear you, all right."

She bounced to her feet and began to wriggle back into the orange bikini bottom she had been wearing under her jeans. She had a lean, tight body, not an ounce of fat on it, with small, knobby breasts, and it was fun to watch her move, but she'd had enough of that. "Come on," she said, "get your ass up, Shifty. Surf's up, ain't that what they say out here?"

*   *   *

Two days before the running of the Fleet Treat, I came back to the barn from my half-hour break in the cafeteria to find a stocky, informally dressed young woman waiting for me outside Mad Margaret's stall. She had frizzy dark hair and an intense, worried expression on her face and she was holding a small tape recorder in one hand. She stood up as I came toward her, smiled tentatively, and introduced herself as a reporter for the *Racing Times*. "Mr. Anderson?" she said. "Hi. I'm Donna Connors. You own Mad Margaret, don't you? Well, I'd like to interview you. I hear you're a magician. I thought it would make a nice little color story. I don't think there's ever been a magician owner before."

"Lots of magician trainers," I said. "They're the ones whose horses loom up at the head of the stretch and disappear by the eighth pole."

She laughed. "That's funny," she said. "Can we talk?"

"Sure." I introduced her to Maggie, who immediately thrust her beautiful head into my arms. Donna Connors petted her on the neck, then turned on the tape recorder. I told her how I had acquired the filly and then something about my profession as a close-up artist. To establish my credentials, I did Ring on a Stick for her, which left her amazed and charmed. "And I think we're going to win tomorrow," I added, "even though we drew the rail. This is a classy, competitive filly and we don't need the lead."

"Well, you'll have to beat that Sovereign horse," Donna Connors said. "What's her name?"

"Valkyrie. Yeah, she'll be tough."

"She's undefeated and no one's come within three lengths of her in four starts."

"She's never run against anything, either," I said. "This will be a horse race, I guarantee you."

"By the way, I meant to ask you, are you the sole

owner? I see she runs under a partnership name. Is this the Cameron who's under indictment up in L.A.?"

"Yes, it is. We don't talk to each other, Donna," I explained. "I sold him and his wife a minority share in the horse about three months ago, when I needed the money. I didn't know what a rotten sonofabitch he was."

"I guess I won't quote you on that," she said, with a smile.

"Quote me all you want." I looked at her and a great light suddenly seemed to shine all around me, as if an angel had landed on my head. "Is your tape recorder still on?" I asked.

She nodded. "Want me to turn it off?"

"No, I'd like all this on the record," I said. "Did you know that Linda Cameron is Jed Hunter's daughter?"

"What? No."

"Well, she is. Her real maiden name should be Harris. Her mother met Jed Hunter when they were neighbors in the Valley of the Shadows—"

"Where?"

"What's now mostly Sovereign Acres."

"Oh, I see."

"No, you don't, Donna. But this is a terrific story. You see, Linda had a twin brother. When they were about three, they were supposed to have died in the fire that burned down the Harris Ranch in the valley and killed their mother. But they didn't die. They were raised separately and didn't meet until recently, when Linda went to Sovereign to see our filly. Her brother's name was Win Freeman."

"Freeman? You mean the guy who was shot to death up in L.A. a couple of weeks ago?"

"That's the one. He worked as a hired gun for Jed Hunter. He didn't know he was Hunter's son either, but Hunter knew. The Judge had lost track of Linda

265

and he was surprised to find her married to his old business associate, Mike Cameron. When Linda and Win got together, Mrs. Hunter was more than a little upset. She forced her husband to throw Linda and Win off the property. Then somebody went and shot Win dead and kidnapped Linda, held her for ransom. But you know that part of it.''

"You don't expect me to print this?''

"Why not?''

"You mean, I can quote you?''

"Sure.''

"You aren't afraid they'll sue you or something?''

"It's the 'or something' that worries me,'' I said. "Let them sue. I'd insist that they exhume Brownie Harris's grave, where her kids are also supposed to be buried. They'll find only the mother's bones, I guarantee it.''

"But why? I mean, why did all this happen the way you say it did?''

"It has to do with building Sovereign and it has to do with the original water rights, which the Harrises owned. Mr. Harris had a hunting accident. You know who was with him at the time?''

"Jed Hunter?''

"And Michael Cameron, who then left town and went to live and work in the East, later on in Texas. Interesting?''

"That's an understatement. Can you prove any of this?''

"No, but I know it's true. Well, I suppose I can prove some of it. There's a woman named Elizabeth Noren, who lives in Julian. She can corroborate the early history. She's the one who told it to me.''

"Can I call her?''

"Why not? I have her telephone number, if you want it.''

Donna Connors turned off her tape recorder and

stared at me. "Boy," she said, "I don't know what this has to do with a horse race, but it's a hell of a story. I guess you could say it's about Sovereign and all that."

"Yeah, you could. I suggest you call Liz Noren and write the story quickly, because there's an ongoing investigation and eventually all of this will out."

"I'll get right on it," she said. "And where can we reach you, if we have to?"

I gave her my phone number and told her I'd call her to give her Elizabeth Noren's number in Julian as soon as I got home from the track. "What I think is going to happen, Donna, is that we're going to learn eventually that all these events are connected," I said. "You might ask yourself, for instance, where Jed Hunter got the money to build Sovereign, at a time when the bottom fell out of the breeding industry. And you might want to ask yourself what he pledged in order to build it. In other words, what about the Fazzini brothers? You've heard of them?"

"Vaguely," she admitted, again snapping on her tape recorder. "Who were they?"

"Builders and contractors," I explained. "They worked with Hunter and also with Cameron and they're both dead. Interesting?"

"Fascinating," she said, staring at me wide-eyed, as if I had materialized a genie out of the ground at our feet. "I sure hope I can write this story. Are you sure you want me to quote you?"

"What's the best way of getting rid of a bad smell?" I said, smiling with more confidence than I actually felt. "You open windows and you let in the light and air. That's all I'm doing, Donna—cleaning out the room where the rot is."

chapter 18

BLACK TYPE

The afternoon before the running of the Fleet Treat Stakes, Donna Connors's story broke on the front page of the *Racing Times* under the headline, "Horse Owner Claims Sovereign Involved in Scandal." The article quoted me at length and included every major charge I had leveled at Jed Hunter and Michael Cameron. "Anderson even asserts that Cameron's wife, Linda, is Hunter's illegitimate daughter and the sister of Win Freeman, who was murdered three weeks ago in Los Angeles by the unknown person or persons who kidnapped Mrs. Cameron and held her for ransom," Connors wrote. "What makes his allegation even more sensational is the fact that the Camerons own a minority share of Mad Margaret, the Pickard-trained filly expected to give Sovereign's Valkyrie a run for her money in the Fleet Treat today. If there is any truth to Anderson's allegations, they will undoubtedly lead to an investigation of Sovereign and will broaden the case

268

against Michael Cameron, who is scheduled to stand
trial this fall in Los Angeles on charges of corruption
and fraud in several public real-estate projects. Neither
Jed Hunter nor the Camerons were available to comment, but Alden Berry, the lawyer who represents both
accused parties, has issued a strongly worded denial
and has declared that legal action will be taken against
Anderson."

I had picked up the paper on my way out of the
track that afternoon and I found Jay waiting for me
when I got home. He was incredulous. "Have you gone
crazy?" he asked, as I came through the door. "These
people will crucify you."

"Every word of what I said is true, Jay," I told him,
as I fished a beer out of the icebox and sank into the
sofa. "I hadn't planned to do it, but as this lady was
interviewing me I suddenly saw a great opportunity to
shine a bright little light into some dark corners."

"Shit, man, if even part of what you said is true,
these people will kill you."

"It's funny, Jay, I've been thinking about that," I
said. "And, as I was talking to this reporter, it occurred
to me I'd be a lot safer if I could get what I know out
into the open."

"How do you figure that?"

"Well, if anything happens to me now, the cops
will know just where to look, won't they?"

"Still, I wouldn't want to be in your shoes. You'd
better cover your ass." Jay sighed, leaned back in his
seat at the dining room table, where he had been bus-
ily assembling his statistics, folded his arms, and stared
at me. "Did you mean everything you said in that
story? Did she quote you right?"

"Every word," I answered. "And I'll tell you what
else I think. I think Hunter and Cameron had Freeman killed and engineered the kidnapping of Linda."

"Her own father? You think he okayed what happened to her? You think he agreed to have her beaten up and raped?''

"If he was capable of killing his own girlfriend and then his son . . .''

Jay didn't answer for a while, but continued to stare at me. "Why?'' he asked at last. "Tell me why he'd do that, Shifty? It doesn't make sense.''

"He's a driven man,'' I said. "His big dream was building Sovereign, the finest breeding and racing operation in the state, maybe anywhere. He did what he had to do to get the land, to secure the water rights, all that. Then he ran out of money, Jay, so he went to the Fazzini brothers. Cameron was involved, too. He probably owns a share of Sovereign. He may have made the original contact with the Fazzinis. They were politically connected in L.A. and Cameron had done business with them. They built Sovereign Acres for Hunter, but they exacted a big price.''

"What price? Money, you mean?''

"I think Hunter gave them the deed to the land as security,'' I said. "He got it originally by bribing Albert Bergman in the San Diego county recorder's office. Bergman kept quiet for a while—he was paid off—but he got the idea he'd been screwed by Hunter and he got his hands on Linda, raised her as his daughter, intending eventually to use her to get to Hunter. That didn't work, mainly because Linda hated him and ran away from home, so he finally got in touch with Hunter directly. This was at the time everything was beginning to come unraveled for the Judge. The Fazzinis were refusing whatever Hunter offered them as a payoff and were threatening to evict him and grab Sovereign for themselves. I'd bet it was Hunter who put the D.A.'s office in Los Angeles onto the Fazzinis in order to put pressure on them. He knew they'd been involved in all sorts of sweetheart deals with the city. The fact that Cameron was also involved caused some trouble, but

Hunter promised to help him. A couple of months ago, the Judge had Bergman killed. It's listed as an accident, but I'll guarantee you it wasn't. Then he enlisted Cameron, promised to go on helping him with his legal problems, if Cameron would work with him as he had in the past. Cameron agreed, because he had no choice, really. After he was also indicted in the Rhineland investigation and then was considered a prime suspect in the Fazzini murders, he found himself locked into Hunter's big scheme. So they worked together. It was Hunter who had the Fazzinis killed, with or without Cameron's connivance, and his hit man was Win Freeman."

"What makes you think so?"

"He loved and trusted Freeman. He'd followed his whole career and engineered it. He eventually brought Freeman to Sovereign, treated him like a son. I don't think he told Win he was his father, but he didn't have to. The two men were very close. It angered Freddie, Hunter's wife, but she was forced to keep quiet and accept it. And Win Freeman turned out to be the perfect instrument for Hunter. He had a psychotic personality with a history of past violence. He killed both the Fazzinis. I think he also found the deed Hunter wanted back. He tore Giorgio Fazzini's house apart looking for it. My guess is he found it."

"Jesus, Shifty, what a story! How come you didn't tell this to that reporter, too?"

"Because this is the part that's hard to prove," I explained. "I'm laying it all out for you, Jay. This is what they'll find, if I can get enough of the story out into the open and get the cops to really investigate it."

"Man, you're wild, you know that?" Jay said. "You figure more angles than Angles."

"You haven't heard all of it. Want to hear the rest?" I asked. "Want to know why it all fell apart?"

"Hell, yes," Jay said. "Shoot. This is better than a movie."

"Well, it was bad enough for Freddie Hunter when Win showed up and her husband began acting like a father to him," I said, "but what she couldn't stomach was Win and Linda together. It was Freddie who forced Jed to get rid of them. Just who killed Win is still a question mark and then what happened to Linda to traumatize her. I don't think the latter was part of the plan at all. I suspect Cameron, because he's a violent man and hated his wife. Also, it was a way to stick it to Hunter, who clearly despised him and whom he also hated. Interesting, isn't it?"

Jay looked at me in amazement. "You know, Shifty, if I didn't know you well," he said, "I'd have to think you're a little nuts. How'd you get so involved?"

"The lady," I said. "I thought Linda and I really had something going. When I came back from the cruise and found she'd run off with Win Freeman, I began to try and figure it out."

"What happens to Linda now?"

"I don't know," I admitted. "She's soft-hearted, easily dominated. She was the perfect prey for these rapacious schemers. With Win she was helpless. She was swept away by him, because she felt this incredible atavistic attraction to him. Twins have this for each other. With Win she mistook it for love. She told me when she left me for him that she'd found her soulmate. As for him, I don't know. He probably felt it, too, because he must have known the Judge couldn't sit still for it, if only because Linda was Cameron's wife."

"Wow," Jay said. "You got guts, Shifty, I got to hand you that. If these characters are as ruthless and driven as you say they are, they'll come after you."

"They already have," I said. "Cameron's hired goon has made two passes at me. I have nothing to lose, Jay, by shooting off my mouth. It's like lancing a big boil. I want all that pus cleared out."

"Good luck," Jay said.

"In the meantime, let's talk about something important. How does my filly look to you tomorrow?" I asked.

"It's a two-horse race," Jay declared, "your filly and Valkyrie. I'd give your filly the edge, but you drew the inside. So the numbers say pass." The telephone rang and Jay answered. "Just a minute," he said. "I'll see if he's here." He put his hand over the mouthpiece and looked at me. "It's some guy from one of the local TV stations. Want to talk to him?"

"Not tonight," I said. "Tell him to call me tomorrow, after the race."

After Jay had hung up, I went upstairs, threw some clothes and my toilet kit into a canvas sack, and headed for the door. "Where are you going?" he asked.

"I'm going to hide out till tomorrow afternoon," I said. "If anybody else calls, you don't know anything."

"It's true," Jay said, as I left, "I really don't know anything."

The Del Mar backside at night is a mysterious world of shadows, dim lights, hushed voices, tinny radio music, all overlaid against the steady pulse of the horses alive in their stalls, stamping, coughing, stirring restlessly in sleep. A musty odor of straw and hay and manure rises from the earth into the soft, misty air, which brings with it, in occasional gusts, the sudden tang of the sea off the nearby Pacific. It is a time that has its own specific rhythm, a beat of life suspended, like the sound of a drum from behind distant hills, barely audible across a vast distance.

I parked the Toyota against the side of May's building and sat there in the darkness for a few minutes, basking in this atmosphere. A pale half-moon

lingered overhead, obliterating stars and casting a glow
over the roofs of the barns and against the walls of the
surrounding structures. The flow of traffic on the freeway to the east became a presence, like the steady wash-
ing of surf over sand. I sensed the breathing of all the
living creatures around me and I felt myself a part of
the scene, a private in a sleeping army on the verge of
an epic struggle to survive that would resume, in its
full, chaotic force, with the sun's first rays. As if to pre-
sage the event, a rooster suddenly crowed once, then
became silent again, the false herald of an untimely
dawn.

I got out of the car, tiptoed softly up the outside
stairs to the second landing, and tapped on May's
door. "What is it?" her voice called out.

"It's me, May. You asleep?"

"Not now," she said. The door opened and she
stood facing me. She was dressed in a white T-shirt that
came to her hips and her hair hung lopsidedly off her
face, as if she had buried herself under her pillows.
"Shifty? What are you doin'?"

"I don't know," I confessed. "I had to get out of
my place. I've been walking on the beach, killing
time."

"Speakin' of time, what is it?"

"About ten-thirty."

"You wanna come in?"

"Yes."

"I only got a cot in here. It ain't too comfortable."

"It's okay, it's fine."

She pulled me inside and shut the door behind us.
She took my hand and led me over to the bed. She
snapped on a small reading light mounted on a cardboard carton at the head of her cot and we sat down
together. "What's goin' on?" she asked.

"I'm too nervous to sleep," I said. "I'm sorry I
woke you up. I'm trying to stay clear of everybody till

after the race tomorrow. Did you read the *Racing Times?*"

"Sure did. Everybody's been talkin' about it back here. Charlie thinks you've gone crazy."

"Maybe I have. But it's all true, May, every word of it."

"I believe you." She put a hand up to my face. "You want to lie down?"

"I can go to a motel."

"No, it's all right, stay here. We'll make out okay." She got up. "Wait, I'll be right back." She slipped into a pair of thongs, took a frayed blue terrycloth robe off a hook on the wall, put it on, and scurried out, pulling the door shut behind her.

I looked around. Except for the bed, the room was unfurnished. A couple of large cushions in one corner served as a chair and several other cardboard cartons scattered about the floor contained her possessions while also serving as tables. Her clothes, mostly jeans and long-sleeved shirts, hung from a row of hooks screwed into the walls and two large canvas suitcases had been stacked in one corner to serve as a dressing table for a portable mirror and her makeup and toilet articles. A hand-sewn brown Indian rug lay next to the bed and on one wall she had tacked up a calendar and a poster of the Grand Canyon. It was a gypsy's room, but it was clean and it smelled of her, an aroma of soap and cheap scent and warm flesh.

The door popped open and she reentered, closing it behind her and then leaning back against it, smiling at me in the glow from the reading lamp. "You took me by surprise," she said. "I wasn't ready for you, Shifty."

"Hey, I didn't come here just to make love to you, May," I said. "Mainly, I just wanted to be with you."

"Well, sure," she said, "but now that you're here, what the hell—" She slipped off the robe and pulled

off her T-shirt as she hurried toward me. I reached out
for the lamp. "Leave it on, mister," she said, as she
descended on me, her long, lean body glowing in the
light. "I want to see what we're doin'."

A bell rang somewhere, the gates popped open,
and we were off. "I'm gonna ride you right down to
the nuts," she said. And she did.

I didn't go near the frontside the next day, but
hung around Charlie's shedrow until it was time to
walk Mad Margaret over to the receiving barn, after
the sixth race. I stayed with the filly all through the
saddling procedure, then walked with her into the paddock at twenty-two minutes before post time. Jay,
Arnie, and Angles were standing in a group on the
patch of grass under the electric odds board. In their
casual summer attire of ragged shorts, lurid sports
shirts, and scuffed sneakers or loafers, with racing
forms and programs protruding from their back pock-
ets, they looked blindingly out of place, even for Del
Mar, where the dress code is all but nonexistent. Most
of the other owners and their friends in the walking
ring had spruced up for the occasion, in homage to
the fact that this was, after all, a stakes race and called
for some show of respect to the sport's ancient tradi-
tions as a pastime for gentlefolk. Even I was wearing a
summer jacket, in my new role of owner and improver
of the breed. "Gentlemen," I said, as I approached my
group, "you aren't exactly dressed up for the occasion."

"What occasion?" Angles asked.

"Don't tell him," Arnie cautioned me. "I regret
to say I neglected to bring what's left of my nighttime
finery to Del Mar. Still, I wouldn't have missed this for
the world."

"How's she doing?" Jay asked, as he watched May
lead Mad Margaret around the ring.

"Great," I said. "Doesn't she look it?"

"Yeah, she looks terrific," Angles said. "Too bad you drew such a lousy post. With the Sovereign horse on the outside, you're gonna have to gun from down in there. It'll take too much out of her."

"That's what Jay feels," I said. "Right, Jay?"

"Yes, that's right," the handicapper agreed. "All I can do is wish you luck. It's you and the Sovereign horse, one-two."

The bettors were obviously in agreement. The board showed Valkyrie favored at eight to five, with Mad Margaret the second choice at five to two, exactly as the oddsmaker for the track had predicted in his morning line. None of the other six fillies in the race were being given much of a chance. I didn't care what the odds were, because we were running for a pot of sixty thousand dollars, about thirty-five thousand of it going to the winner, and I didn't have to wager to make a score. "You could cold-deck an exacta box, Jay," I said. "Triple your money, at least."

"Yeah, I could," the handicapper agreed, "but the one hole at seven furlongs here can be death, you know that. I'll just root for you, Shifty."

"Death, death," Angles said, nodding. "Secretariat could get buried in there along the rail. I'm passing. But hey, good luck, Shifty."

"I shall indulge in a small, sentimental wager," Arnie said, like a pope granting dispensations to a particularly noxious sinner. "What is racing devoid of pure sentiment? Merely the crass pursuit of a buck. Fifty on the nose in your honor, Shifty."

"Jesus, Arnie, you sound like a true phony," Angles observed. "Who do you think you are, King Shit?"

"Coarsely put, as is your wont," Arnie said, "but I forgive you, Angles. You know not what you say."

We stood there, huddled together in the sunlight, and watched the horses parade around us in single file.

I had to admit to myself that Valkyrie looked formidable. She was a big, black filly, built more like a colt, and she was clearly on the muscle, on her toes and tossing her beautiful head up and down, as if about to jump out of her skin. I looked at Maggie. She was much calmer, self-contained, her ears pricked and her eyes taking in the crowd of watchers around the ring. May smiled and waved a couple of fingers at me. "She can't lose," she had told me that morning. "She's a champ, Shifty. You'll see."

Charlie Pickard came out from under the shedrow and took up his post near the gap, where he positioned himself to give Tim Lang a leg up. Judge Jed Hunter, Alden Berry, and a large group of admirers, some of them the rich women with their blocked nasal passages who seemed always to be in the vicinity of the lawyer, now came out of the Turf Club entrance and headed for the paddock. "Hey, Shifty," somebody called out from the crowd, "tell it to the judge!" A few people laughed, but the sight of Jed Hunter quickly shut them up. He towered over his group, looking straight ahead of him as he approached, an impressive figure radiating power and certitude. He was impeccably attired in a dark gray business suit, his black eyepatch gleaming in the sun, the picture of a rich breeder and owner, heir to a long tradition of wealth and generations of great horses. He looked straight at me as he walked into the paddock but as if I did not exist, then shook hands with his trainer, J. R. Lamont, a chunky forty-year-old Kentuckian.

"I think I ought to walk over and wish him luck," I said, as Hunter leaned down to hear what his trainer was telling him.

"You crazy, Shifty?" Charlie asked. "Forget it."

"No, I think I ought to tell him."

"What?"

"What my friend Jude Morgan told me this morning when he called me at the barn," I explained. "I want him to have something to think about."

I forced myself to smile and walked across the grass toward Hunter and his entourage. Alden Berry was the first to notice me and he stepped forward to cut me off, but Hunter put a hand out to restrain him and fixed that one large, luminous eye on me, his face expressionless and his mouth set into a tight, thin line. "Just wanted to wish you luck, Judge," I said, as nonchalantly as I could manage it, hypocrisy not being my strong suit. "And I thought you might like to know I got an interesting phone call this morning. A friend of yours and Cameron's named Donald Houps seems to have popped up in Texas. I guess he'll be extradited and brought to L.A. for questioning."

"What are you talking about, Anderson?" Berry said, thrusting himself forward to confront me. "You must be crazy!"

"Be quiet, Alden," Hunter said. "There's no point in this sort of public confrontation." He smiled, but it was not a pretty sight; his face seemed about to shatter from the strain and I could see his large hands trembling. "You'll have to answer for this in court, Anderson."

"I look forward to it, Judge," I said. "I've always believed in justice. I wonder what they'll find when they dig up Brownie Harris's grave."

"Riders up!" the paddock judge called out and I turned back just in time to see Tim Lang being hoisted into the saddle. Mad Margaret suddenly seemed to wake up as she felt the rider on her back and became a concentrated mass of gleaming muscle, her neck bowed, as she led the line of horses out through the gap toward the racing surface.

If I never see another horse race, I could live the rest of my life on the memory of this one. When the gate opened, Valkyrie outbroke the field from the outside and had about half a length as the eight fillies got their running legs under them. Mad Margaret came out well enough, but from her inside post position Tim Lang had to hustle her so as not to be shut off. As the horses came thundering out of the chute, Valkyrie still had about half a length, with Maggie and two other fillies vying for the place. Wib Clayton, the jockey on Valkyrie, then took a slight hold on his horse, perhaps to make sure she wouldn't use herself up too early, but it was a mistake. It enabled Maggie to draw even with her; then, as they neared the turn, to pull away by nearly a length, with Lang sitting up there and just letting her run on her own courage. But Wib Clayton now clucked to his mount and she responded, so that, as the fillies started around the turn, Valkyrie had closed the gap to about a neck.

It was clear by this time that the race would be decided up front, as we had all suspected. Mad Margaret and Valkyrie had opened up a gap of two lengths on the third horse and it was widening as the two leaders began their private duel. At the head of the lane, Maggie still had a neck over Valkyrie, but the real running had not yet started and Valkyrie had not yet really been asked, whereas Maggie had had to sprint hard at the start.

I saw Wib Clayton's whip flash in the air as the drive began and his big, black filly responded with a surge that carried her past my horse and enabled her to put her own neck in front. Tim Lang seemed to have disappeared, he was so low on Maggie, only the top of his helmet visible as my filly threatened to be swallowed up by the powerful animal outside of her. But May had told me about Maggie. "She's a champ," she had said. And now the filly set about proving it.

Instead of being intimidated by her larger rival's move and folding up, as any lesser animal would have done, Mad Margaret fought back. Inch by inch, foot by foot, she closed the gap from the inside, her beautiful golden head focused on the finish line. By the eighth pole, she had drawn even and by the sixteenth pole she had her head in front. And there she stayed, as the fillies strained for the wire, each one a study in power and grace and pure heart.

If the sight of two great athletes in perfect condition running their hearts out for victory is not the sort of spectacle that moves you, then the sport of horse racing is not for you. Because this is what it is all about. We rose to our feet as one, screaming ourselves hoarse as Valkyrie and Mad Margaret battled down the stretch. Maggie was not tiring and never faltered, but Valkyrie still managed to close on her, finally drawing even. And there they stayed, nose to nose, stride for stride all the way to the wire, so that as they hit it together I knew it was now a question of whose head had been down and whose up as the photo-finish camera clicked. It was so close that I found myself rooting for a dead heat.

"You got it," Arnie said, beaming. "You got it, Shifty."

I looked at Charlie, who shrugged as he arose to head for the winner's circle. "Too close to call," he said. "A hell of a race, either way."

"I think it was the outside horse," Angles said. "The angle favors the outside."

"You and your angles," Arnie said. "Why don't you go sit on one?"

"Good luck, Shifty," Jay said. "It was a horse race."

It turned out to be the longest photo of the meet. "I think we got it," Tim Lang said, as he jumped off the filly's back, but nobody seemed comforted by this assurance. We stood out on the track in a tight, little knot, waiting for the verdict, while May walked Maggie around to keep her loose. Finally, the official sign blinked and the number one appeared on the tote board. Maggie had won, by what looked like a lip when I saw the photo later.

I don't remember much else about the next few minutes. May was crying as she led Mad Margaret into the circle for the winning picture and Jay, Angles, and Arnie were down there, too, pounding on me in appreciation and pleasure. The cameras clicked and a grinning middle-aged man in a dark blue suit handed me a silver bowl. Even Charlie looked almost moved and grudgingly consented to be included in the photograph, but I remember, too, that his gaze never wavered from the filly. Mad Margaret was drenched in sweat this time and looked around a little wild-eyed, as if startled by all the excitement she had caused. May kissed her and the filly bobbed her head up and down as if to acknowledge her extraordinary feat. My God, I thought, as I stood and looked at her finally being led away back toward her shedrow, how can anything in life top this one great moment? What could I ever do for this fine animal to repay her for her courage and talent and grace? Charlie saw this look on my face and smiled a little grimly at me. "Just hope she comes out of it all right," he said. "There ain't nothin' better, is there, Shifty? Just remember, she put her life on the line out there for you today."

chapter 19

DEAD HEAT

The celebration lasted until well past midnight. We all met an hour after the race at the bar in Bully's, a favorite hangout in downtown Del Mar, where Angles picked up Gina and Tanya, a couple of slightly worn divorced women in their mid-thirties, and added them to our party. I had incautiously announced that I was taking everybody to dinner and I had reserved a table at Le Bon Marché, a new French restaurant in Encinitas, a few miles up the coast, that Abel Green had touted me onto as the best new eatery in the area. By the time we arrived there, an hour late, we had lost our reservation and were forced to wait an additional hour at the bar.

Nobody minded because we were all flying high. I wasn't drinking, but I didn't have to. The euphoria of winning the race had made me higher than I'd ever been before. I bought rounds of champagne for our party, now swollen to a total of eight, and leaned happily against the bar, reliving that glorious stretch drive over and over in my head. Then, too, I had May beside me. She looked terrific in her miniskirt and red silk blouse and her eyes were as full of the sight of our filly making her run as mine were. We were hand in hand and impervious to everything else around us.

Charlie had one glass of wine with us and left before dinner, saying that he had to get up too early to linger on and warning May that he expected her at the barn the next morning on time, as usual. "I'll be there, Mister Charlie," May told him, laughing. "I don't need no sleep tonight."

Charlie looked dourly in my direction. "Shifty, you're corruptin' the help," he said. "Damn owners, if they don't screw you up one way, they'll screw you up another."

"Charlie, the sun is out all over this golden land," I said. "Let it shine and let the music play."

"Say, girls, you into threesies?" I heard Angles say, as Charlie left. "Jay here is gonna go handicap and Arnie ain't had a hard-on since his mother died."

"What a mouth you got on you," Gina said. "Anyway, you ain't man enough for the two of us."

"No?" Angles said. "Mr. Tireless, I'm known as."

"Tired ass would be more appropriate," Arnie observed amiably. "Sex, in any case, is a vastly overrated activity. The pleasures are fleeting and the consequences endless, to paraphrase Lord Chesterfield."

"That the guy who invented the cigarettes?" Tanya asked. "He must have been some kind of faggot."

"A creep," Gina added, then looked indignantly at Angles. "Get your hand off my ass or I'll sock you one!"

"Hey, no offense, baby," Angles said. "You got a great ass. I couldn't resist it."

"Yeah? Well, watch it, buster."

"Yeah," Tanya said, then giggled. "Even though you are kinda cute."

"Premature expectation," Arnie observed, "another of Angles's many faults."

It was the sort of dialogue it was easy to shut out. Jay ignored it. After Charlie left, he joined May and me and again and again we rehashed the race, while Angles and Arnie continued their barbarous verbal assault on the two women, whose last names we didn't even know.

By the time the maitre d', a tall, distinguished-looking Frenchman in a tuxedo, showed up to escort us to our table, Angles had embarked on a long, convoluted story about a major betting coup he had put over at Hollywood Park the previous year. "It was unbefuck-inlievable," he said, as we left the bar. "One of the greatest fuckin' days ever."

The maitre d' cast a disapproving glance in our direction, but led us to a corner table diagonally across the room. Angles herded Gina and Tanya before him and sat down between them, with Arnie on one side and Jay on the other. "We could make it a fuckin' foursome," Angles said, "though Arnie here ain't much for fuckin'. He'll probably just watch."

"You're so crude," Gina said, smiling.

"Yeah, you got a mouth on you like a sewer," Tanya added. "Anyway, I'm hungry. Let's eat."

Le Bon Marché was located in a corner of a shopping mall, but it clearly had pretensions to grandeur. The dining area was large and furnished with elegantly appointed tables set well apart from each other. Small candles gleamed in the dim light and soft music played in the background, mostly old Piaf and Trenet recordings. The walls were decorated with framed posters celebrating the various provinces of France and a large chandelier hovered over the scene, enhancing an obviously cultivated atmosphere of old-world charm. The staff spoke in hushed tones and conversations tended to be subdued. As I looked up to receive my printed menu from our waiter, I spotted Alden Berry three tables away from us. He and one of the women I had seen him with before were dining with another couple and he had his back to us, though I imagined he must have seen us. I decided to ignore him, because I wanted nothing to interrupt the pleasurable course of my evening. I sat close to May, our hands locked together under the table.

No sooner had we ordered than Angles resumed his foulmouthed detailed account of his betting triumph. "So listen to this, Gina," he said. "Tanya, listen to what I'm tellin' you. It was fuckin' amazing. I get a tip on this fuckin' horse in the fifth. Can't lose, this fuckin' tout tells me. Now usually guys will tell you any fuckin' thing just to get a kickback from you if they happen to pick a fuckin' winner. You understand me? Okay, so this fuckin' tout comes up to me while I'm standin' in the fuckin' betting line for the double and he fuckin' says to me . . ."

In the relative serenity of Le Bon Marché, with its aspirations to fine dining and refined discourse, Angles's voice sounded as clear as the call of a demented muezzin summoning the faithful to prayer. A pall of disapproval spread over the adjacent tables, but Angles was oblivious to the effect he was having on the rest of the room. His obscene account of his triumph proceeded at full decibel count, punctuated by the repeated use of his favorite expletive in every conceivable permutation. "Now listen to what this fuckin' bozo says to me after the race," he trumpeted, as he neared the climax of his tale. "I fuckin' grab him by the fuckin' throat and . . ."

It was at this point that a well-dressed middle-aged man, who was dining with his handsome wife at the next table, rose to his feet and approached us. "Excuse me," he said, interrupting Angles in full, foulmouthed flight, "but my wife and I are trying to have dinner and talk to each other. Not only are you being loud, but you seem to be incapable of speaking the English language without the repeated use of a four-letter word my wife and I find offensive. Now, would you please . . ."

Arnie stood up as the man continued to protest and signaled for the maitre d', who immediately hurried over, a look of concern on his face. *"Monsieur?"* he asked.

"I was asking these people here to please tone down their conversation," our visitor began to explain. "My wife and I can't help overhearing—"

"Listen," Arnie said to the maitre d', "we didn't ask to sit in the no fucking section."

In the ensuing uproar and confusion, with Angles and our neighbor involved in a vigorous shouting and pushing match, I quickly dropped two hundred-dollar bills on the table, grabbed May's hand, and tugged her out of the room, with Jay following in our wake. As we passed Alden Berry's party, I let go of May's hand long enough to linger for a moment at their table. "Alden, we have to stop meeting like this," I said. "People will talk. Sorry about the confusion. It's just a little victory celebration. I did want you to know, however, that you and the Judge made a bad mistake using a bumbler like Houps. He's going to make a terrific witness. And you can tell Cameron I have a buyer for his share of the horse. I'll call you in a day or two."

The lawyer didn't answer, but merely looked at me coldly, then picked up his wine glass to take a sip. I noted with satisfaction that his hand trembled noticeably.

"Who's gonna buy her?" May asked, as we resumed our flight from the restaurant. "You got somebody?"

"Abel Green," I said, as we reached the bar. "Charlie told me he wanted in. It'll be the first good horse he's ever had."

"Wow," May exclaimed. "He's such a cheapskate."

My last glimpse of our aborted dinner party was of Angles toppling backward from a hard punch to the nose, the two women screaming, and Arnie backing cautiously away, holding a chair in front of him. Out in the street, Jay and I were laughing so hard that we had to pause in midflight. "Hey, you got some nutty friends," May said. "Who *are* those guys?"

"Hard knockers," Jay explained. "Too bad Arnie couldn't get hold of a ketchup bottle. He always said that if you hit them with one of those, they think they're bleeding to death."

Nobody knows how the fire at Sovereign Acres started, but it must have been sometime after midnight. It would have been difficult enough to extinguish under ordinary circumstances, but it took the fire engines from nearby Ramona a long time to get through the pass, due to a rockslide, and when they finally arrived on the scene the house was all but gone. I first heard about it from Charlie when I showed up at the barn the next morning. Luke Davis had called Charlie to tell him all about it. "They all think the fire was set," the trainer informed me. "It couldn't have burned that hard and fast if it hadn't been. And the sprinkler system either didn't work or somebody turned it off."

At first, everybody suspected the Indian woman. She had been seen outside the house just before the fire broke out, but she protested her innocence. She had been awakened in her ground-floor rear bedroom by the sound of gunshots, she said, and gone outside to look, then had hurried back in and run upstairs. She had knocked on the door of the master bedroom, but had received no answer. She had opened the door and found the room empty, then had hurried downstairs, this time to find the body of Freddie Hunter lying on the floor of the living room. She had been shot in the back of the head, the woman maintained, but there had as yet been no way to establish that fact. There would have to be an investigation of her remains, which now would have to be sifted from the charred ruins.

By the time Eartha had found Freddie Hunter, however, the house had been set ablaze and was burning fiercely. She had called out for the Judge, but had received no answer and she couldn't be sure that she had actually seen him. She said that she had tried to find him, but he had presumably gone back upstairs and been trapped by the flames, then roaring up the stairwell and the circular main staircase. The Judge's office door was open and Eartha guessed that he had been in there, working on his papers, when the fire broke out. Just before fleeing the premises, she thinks she may have glimpsed him, but she said she couldn't be certain of it. He appeared to be standing motionless on the landing directly below the dome, as if waiting for the fire to consume him. He was fully dressed, she said, and very pale, so that his face seemed to glow like a dim moon through the smoke of the ascending flames. But it was only a glimpse, she insisted, and she couldn't be sure. Almost overcome by the heat and smoke, she had then staggered outside and watched helplessly while the house burned.

There had been little for the firemen to do when they eventually showed up. The dome had caved in and the whole building was well on its way to becoming a charred ruin. Davis and the other hands on the premises had tried to help, but the heat from the conflagration had been so intense that no one had been able to get near the structure. They had all stood by helplessly while the firemen poured water onto the site; it had taken nearly three hours to put the blaze out.

As soon as Charlie finished telling me about it, I went into his tack room and called Jude Morgan. "Yeah, I already heard about it," the detective said. "It's interesting, Shifty. This was the day he was scheduled to testify here. The D.A.'s office subpoenaed him."

"For what?"

"They wanted to know about his dealings with Cameron and the Fazzinis," Jude said. "Seems like a lot of what you shot your mouth off about could be true."

"Houps has been talking, right? I figured he would."

"He's trying to plea-bargain. He says he doesn't know anything about the murders, but he claims Cameron came to him to take out Win Freeman and he refused. He thinks Linda killed Win."

"Do you believe that?"

"Well, if he was this bad dude, like you say he was, she might have, you know. Then maybe the whole kidnapping business was a setup."

"What about what happened to her after she was kidnapped? She couldn't fake that, could she?"

"It could have happened to her before, Shifty."

"You mean, Win beat the shit out of her and abused her and then she killed him?"

"That's what Houps says."

"Then she called Cameron and he got her out of there and set up the whole kidnapping scenario."

"Could be."

"Cameron would have a complete hold over her, so she'll never talk."

"She's in pretty bad shape, I hear."

"She isn't going to get better staying with Cameron."

"She isn't with him anymore."

"Where is she?"

"In a hospital in San Diego," Jude said. "She's had a total breakdown, can't talk or anything. She's pretty much out of it, Shifty, maybe for good."

"That bastard did it to her."

"Maybe, who knows?"

"Can't we do anything?" I asked, feeling impotent and angry.

"Like what, Shifty?"

"What about all that stuff I told you?"

"The early stuff involving the Judge and Sovereign and all that?"

"Yeah."

"Hell of a story, Shifty, but we'll probably never know now."

"Why not? Can't you investigate it?"

"Not likely to happen, my man," Jude said. "We got an overworked department here and mostly it's ancient history. Of course it might all come out at the trial and then maybe Houps can tell us a little more. He may have to, if he wants to beat a murder one charge."

"You think they'll nail Cameron?"

"Sounds like they have a good strong case, my man."

"And nobody's going to do anything about the Judge."

"He's dead," Jude said. "Nobody cares about history and the dead except writers and historians. You see my point?"

"Maybe Berry will sue me," I said. "That way somebody will have to look into my story."

"You're a betting man, Shifty," Jude said. "What's your morning line on that possibility?"

"Twenty to one against," I said glumly.

"Right. Take what you can get. Cameron will go to jail. Say, Shifty . . ."

"Yeah?"

"That was one hell of a race your filly ran. Thanks for the tip. When's she going to run again?"

"Not for a while," I said. "That took a lot out of her."

"Well, you be sure and let me know. Ain't nothin' I like better than cashing tickets."

It wasn't until five days later that I found out Mad Margaret wouldn't be able to run again for at least six months. Charlie had checked her out every morning since the day of the race and had become increasingly concerned over the presence of heat in her right flexor tendon, about halfway between her knee and hoof. At first he kept the news from me, but I sensed that something wasn't right. I could tell that May, whom I'd been seeing every night, was worried. Finally, I confronted Charlie and he told me. "I was gonna tell you, Shifty, but I was hoping it would clear up," he said. "If we don't back off of her, she could bow and might never run again." That big tendon, he explained, could hemorrhage and swell up, causing a horse to go lame, and then it could be as long as a year or eighteen months before the animal would be sound enough again to put into training. "And usually, after a bow," Charlie continued, "they ain't got but about five or six races left in 'em. You don't want to take chances with a nice filly like this one."

Charlie had been right about Maggie, of course. She had, indeed, put her life on the line for us. Valkyrie had pushed her to the limit and Maggie had given everything of herself to win. "You do what you have to do, Charlie," I said. "I don't want anything bad to happen to this horse."

Luckily, I was now in a financial position to be able to absorb the expense. I had over sixty thousand dollars in the bank and the interest I'd earn from that money would go partway toward absorbing the expenses, including vet bills, of Maggie's layoff. The only truly unhappy person involved was Abel Green, who had no sooner paid seventy-five thousand dollars for Cameron's share of the horse than he was informed she wouldn't be in competition for a while. "There's some kind of a black cloud hanging over me," he said to me in the Turf Club that afternoon. "Where I am it's raining all the time."

I tried to sympathize with Green, but basically I didn't care about him. I would rather the horse never run again than risk her welfare on the track. I was at the barn at dawn that morning when the van came to take Maggie away. She was being shipped north to a farm near Solvang, where she'd be turned out to rest and recuperate. If all went well, she'd be back in training at the end of the year and ready to compete again at Santa Anita in the winter. May stood next to me, holding my hand, as Maggie walked calmly up the ramp and disappeared from view. We waited until it drove away, rumbling ponderously past the barns and kicking up dust in the cool light of the early morning. May was crying. "Come on, let's get to work," Charlie said, though I could tell he was more distressed than any of us. "This ain't no country club, Shifty. You can hot-walk the gray." He picked up a rake and disappeared into a stall, where I could hear him set to work with a fury. I felt sorry for him. Mad Margaret was the first good horse he'd had in years and he deserved better. I had my magic to fall back on, but all Charlie had was these fragile beasts.

I talked it over with May later that afternoon. We were sitting on a blanket at the beach in Del Mar, watching the sun go down over the ocean in a great red ball. A flight of pelicans skimmed the waves and sandpipers scurried along the water's edge, probing for prey with their long, thin beaks. I was feeling gloomy about life in general, but May would have none of it. "What's the matter with you, Shifty?" she said, grabbing my hand and rising to her knees to confront me. "Don't you know life ain't easy? You gotta take the good with the bad, honey. Maggie'll be back and until then you got me."

I smiled and kissed her. The wind blew her hair around her eyes and she looked about thirteen years old. "I've always wanted to fall in love with a positive thinker," I said.

"Hey, don't make fun of me," she said. "I know I ain't educated and all and I don't know shit about a lot of stuff, but it could be worse. And don't worry about Charlie, he's got a couple of good two-year-olds comin' in next week."

At the racetrack, it's always tomorrow.

William Murray's
Shifty Lou Anderson

"There's no better writer than Murray working today."—*The New York Daily News*

TIP ON
A DEAD CRAB

Don't miss the very first of William Murray's acclaimed Shifty Lou Anderson mysteries!

"Besides horses and magic and card cheating, Murray offers up love and sex, murder and menace, friendship and betrayal...This is a true sweetheart of a book, prime Edgar material, made to be read and read again. Grab it."—*Washington Post Book World*

"Run, do not walk, to your favorite bookstore. Immediately purchase *Tip on a Dead Crab*...What a wonderfully readable novel about horse racing, magic and murder."—Larry King, *USA Today*

THE HARD
KNOCKER'S
LUCK

A beautiful woman, an assortment of Vegas hustlers, an international card shark, and an Italian film producer give Shifty a run for his money in William Murray's second Shifty Lou mystery.

"What really separates Murray's books from run-of-the-mill stuff like Dick Francis is the quality of the writing. For *Tip on a Dead Crab* and especially *The Hard Knocker's Luck,* Murray has developed a brisk, literate blend of Damon Runyon and Raymond Chandler."—*Los Angeles Herald-Examiner*

***Tip on a Dead Crab* and *The Hard Knocker's Luck* are both coming soon from Bantam Books!**

AN 422 7/92

William Murray is back with the further adventures of Shifty Lou Anderson, professional magician, racetrack degenerate.

THE KING OF THE NIGHTCAP
❑ 28426-6 $4.50/$5.50 in Canada

Distracted by a feisty girl jockey with great legs, then seduced by a gorgeous Mexican singer with a secret, Shifty finds himself embroiled in a deadly and desperate con involving high stakes and ruthless players—a game Shifty doesn't want to play.

"There's no better writer than Murray working today."
—*New York Daily News*
"Murray has the lighthearted touch of a contemporary Damon Runyon."—Digby Diehl, *Playboy*
"A wonderfully witty excursion through the world of horse racing as seen through the eyes of the incorrigible horse player."
—*The Detroit News*
"William Murray bumps Dick Francis at the three-quarter pole and prances into the winner's circle."—*The New York Times*

THE GETAWAY BLUES
❑ 29103-3 $4.99/$5.99 in Canada

The horseplaying prestidigitator becomes a wanted man when a friend loses her life. Can the best magician in the business conjure up the real murderer...or is he finally out of tricks?

"Murray's genially satiric asides on horses, opera, pretentious drama teachers and set of devoted gamblers are as tart and fresh as gelato."
—*San Francisco Chronicle*
"*The Getaway Blues* firmly establishes [William Murray] as the USA's Dick Francis, only funnier."
—Larry King, *USA Today*
"[Murray] comes up with a winner!"—*The Washington Post*

Available at your local bookstore or use this page to order.
Send to: Bantam Books, Dept. MC 35
2451 S. Wolf Road
Des Plaines, IL 60018
Please send me the items I have checked above. I am enclosing
$_____ (please add $2.50 to cover postage and handling). Send check or money order, no cash or C.O.D.'s, please.

Mr./Ms._____

Address_____

City/State_____Zip_____
Please allow four to six weeks for delivery.
Prices and availability subject to change without notice.   MC 35 7/92